A GIFT OF STARS

"Look up," Sara said, staring upward over his shoulder.

He was so happy at the moment that he didn't want to move. His head was still pressed against her pulse and his heart pounded almost in tandem with hers.

"No. Look up." She pushed against his shoulder.

It took all his strength to release her and roll away. As he did, she slipped away from him, rising to her feet and running away.

He lay flat on his back with eyes closed and arms spread at his sides. He listened to her running and wondered how she could race so haphazardly through the incredible dark. But she'd always followed her impulses.

He'd probably scared the wits out of her, going all heavy just because she thought they could take up their old childhood friendship. Only then did he allow his eyes to follow where she had directed.

He looked up at the sky. Suddenly, he felt as if he'd been slammed in his gut.

The sky was a dark velvet pit, liberally sprinkled with millions upon millions of stars. He felt as if she'd given him a gift—as if she'd given him the stars.

With Sara I'm going to lay my soul bare. I'm going to do whatever it takes to have her.

LOOK FOR THESE ARABESQUE ROMANCES

SILVER LOVE

Layle Giusto

Pinnacle Books
Kensington Publishing Corp.

http://www.arabesquebooks.com

PINNACLE BOOKS are published by

Kensington Publishing Corp.
850 Third Avenue
New York, NY 10022

Pinnacle and the P logo Reg. U.S. Pat. & TM Off.

First Printing: March, 1998
10 9 8 7 6 5 4 3 2 1

Printed in the United States of America

Prologue

Scarsdale, October 2002

Before Sara Turner-McMillan could dial the phone, she glanced at her hands, and stopped momentarily. She replaced the phone to stare at them. They were steady and sure. That comforted her. It was a sign that she'd made the right decision. It meant she was ready for what she was about to do. It had taken more than twenty-five years to reach this point.

She had already cried herself out, and now she was ready. She'd dreamed about this moment, she'd even had nightmares about it, and now she could finally begin.

As she reached for the receiver again, the phone rang. She picked it up impatiently.

"May I speak with Mrs. Sara McMillan?" a cool male voice asked.

His not calling her Turner-McMillan alerted Sara that it was one of Geoff's government connections.

"Yes. Speaking."

"Mrs. McMillan, this is Michael Todd, from the State Department. I have bad news." Her heart seemed to slam into her throat. "I'm sorry to say," the man went on, "that your husband Geoff McMillan's plane has been forced by terrorists to land. We'd like you to come to the White House.

Not Geoff, she thought. It couldn't be Geoff. *Nothing bad ever happens to Geoff.*

"Mrs. McMillan, are you still there?" she heard the man ask when she didn't respond. The phone slipped from her fingers and she realized that her hands were no longer steady.

Book One

Chapter One

Mid-April, 1977, Manila, Philippines (Olongapo Province)

The note on the rickety table beside the bed was the first thing Geoffrey McMillan saw when he opened his eyes that morning. It had caught up with him sometime yesterday, and he'd read it before sticking in into his pocket and going out to get stoned.

He could just barely make out the handwriting from where he was; it was a note from Sara.

He turned his head slowly, trying to avoid the pain that he knew lay in ambush as punishment for his excesses of last night. His efforts failed, however, for an excruciating throbbing hit him right between the eyes and he lowered himself slowly onto the pillows, waiting until it passed.

He'd realized that he was in an unfamiliar room. He also discovered there was a woman lying beside him. He looked around at the rickety furniture—a night table and a low bed, built on a platform. The walls needed painting. He could hear the vendors noisily setting up on the street.

Now he remembered coming to the woman's room, and some of what had gone on last night. His stomach lurched.

The room smelled sour. He smelled sour, too. When the woman had picked him up, he'd followed her to the room and tossed the envelope on the table.

Geoff rolled out of bed and reached for the letter. Inside was a small note with flowers. It was from Sara. She wrote, *I'm getting engaged and wish you'd come to the wedding.*

He wanted to smile. Imagine little Sara getting engaged. Of course, she wasn't little. She was actually a year older than he, but she'd always seemed younger, for some reason. Maybe it was simply that she'd always been more innocent.

He put the note to his nose and inhaled. A residual clean, wholesome scent seem to waft upward, but he figured that was surely just his imagination. It had followed him from Hong Kong. How could any such smell remain after all that traveling?

He stood up, searching for his clothes. The woman murmured something vague in Tagalong as she lifted her head.

"I'm going home," he answered and she turned over with a disinterested smile.

Once he'd said it he knew it was true. Suddenly, he did want to go home—not to his room, but to America. He'd been in Asia since his discharge, since Viet Nam. He had traveled in some beautiful countries, but in the mental state he'd been in the beauty had been wasted on him.

Now, all he wanted was to attend Sara's wedding.

He sat down heavily on a chair, intending to put on his boots. Instead, he put his head in his hands. God knew he was sick of traveling. He wanted his life back. He wanted to do all the things he'd dreamed. Life was nothing as he had once wanted.

He felt on the verge of a plunge into hell. He wanted to live, and Sara's letter had come, seemingly, like a lifeline.

Outside on the street, crowds of people moved hastily toward work. Despite the sea of Asian people, it still seemed no different than any other city he'd ever been in. Many of the people were in jeans, which were an expensive item here on these beautiful islands. Many of the older men wore business suits. Black music spilled out of a local honky-tonk. Many of the vendors were older women, and had stocked their goods to sell to American sailors.

He had to turn to figure out where he was, and then he started walking toward his own room. He was seriously hungover but determined to reach his destination. It was as if he'd finally gotten a goal, although he wasn't certain what it was. He knew he wanted to attend Sara's wedding, but surely it wasn't that which caused him to move this desperately. Surely that could wait till later.

As he walked toward home, he glanced at the sights around him. It was early and still relatively quiet. The loud, noisy bars were still closed and the women who solicited from the corners had gone home to bed. The place always reminded him of Forty-Second street in New York.

Every few hundred yards, he stopped and leaned against a post. Several times, he reread the note.

On one corner, a bunch of giggling children surrounded him but he could see how uncertain they were. They were going to ask for money but instead stared at his hair for a long time. Then they glanced at each other, before laughing and running on. They were growing used to black people's hair because there were African-Americans stationed at the United States Subic Base in the bay. There were also stories of Negritos, a native people that lived in the hills on other islands. What puzzled them was that his was braided, reaching past his shoulders, while the sailors at the base wore theirs close cut.

Once, he came to a small general store with old yellowed postcards displayed on a stand. He stopped to look at them. After some hesitation, he bought one, adding stationery and a ballpoint pen to his purchases.

He paused to jot down a hasty message on the card before he could change his mind, and he left it with the proprietor, to be sent out with the next post.

In his room he found a large bottle of whiskey. It surprised him. It had been a long time since he'd been in the habit of leaving a nearly full bottle of booze sitting around. Usually, he'd have finished it off, but there it sat, staring malevolently at him this morning.

He glanced at Sara's letter, placing it on the table in front of him. Then he took the whiskey, pouring it out the window onto the ground.

He sat on his bed, taking the paper and pen to compose a letter. It took him a long time to write the few words.

Later, he washed up and shaved. He looked in the mirror at his reflection. He'd lost a little weight but it looked okay. His deep tan skin, from a mix of his black father and white mother, looked slightly sallow but a lot better than he deserved. Considering his mixed parentage, his coloring was darker than many would expect, and he had always been glad. There wasn't much about Hugo that he wanted but he believed being more dark than light gave him less problems.

Lastly, he glanced at his hair and paused. It had been years since he'd had a haircut. It had started with an Afro and had kept on growing until now the long, thick braid, its texture a mix of both parents' hair, touched his shoulders.

He considered getting a pair of scissors but he'd gotten used to the long hair. It had been with him a long time, and he hesitated. Finally he decided against cutting it for now. *I'll wait and see how I feel later.*

After he'd cleaned himself up, he decided to go to one of the cheap hotels and eat breakfast. But before he left the room, he did something that surprised him. He started packing.

He hastily threw his small stash of personal belongings— a guitar, a few items of clothing plus some stock market books and papers, into a knapsack. He pulled up a floor-board and removed a wad of cash, which went into his sock. Then, although he did eat breakfast, he headed afterward for Manila International Airport. He couldn't wait any longer; he was going to see Sara.

Late April, Middletown, NY 1977

Twenty-five year old Sara Turner walked into the kitchen, balancing a load of papers and books. She was dressed in a simple cotton blouse and skirt.

"I'll be late tonight. I'm going to stop at the student center," she said to her mother, Edna.

"Are you going to work with that alcoholic group?" Edna said, moving her head out of the fridge to stare at her daughter.

"That's not all we do there," Sara answered patiently, knowing what her mother was going to say. "But, yes, I'm going to work with the addiction group this evening."

"Another meeting for those wayward girls. Why couldn't you be on the committee to visit the elderly or something like that?" Edna insisted.

"Because I feel as if I'm really needed there. Besides, we've had this conversation before. Alcoholism and drug use are two of the biggest problems in America. Many of the students here are exhibiting serious problems, and I want to help."

"Hippies!"

"Not necessarily," Sara said. "This isn't the sixties any-more."

"It's a weakness, that's what it is," Edna muttered.

"Oh, Lord," Sara said, leaning over to peck her mother on the cheek. "Anyway, stop worrying. Hippie-ism isn't contagious.'

"Humph, you're too smart, Miss. Getting like your sister." Edna watched her older daughter leave the kitchen. When Sara returned with more papers, Edna asked, "You taking that old car?"

"Yes," Sara answered, "I'm taking it to the mechanic's."

"How are you going to come home? And don't be late. You know I hate for you to come home late."

"Chuck's going to pick me up after the class and drop me off."

"You're lucky Chuck even talks to you. When are you going to give him an answer? He's been patient a long time. A man don't like to wait when he's asked a woman to marry him."

"It's only been a few months. Marriage is a serious step, and I want to make certain this is right for both of us."

"You need to stop stalling before you don't have any choice to make. Better remember that a good man is hard to find. Plenty of women out there would grab him up in a minute, wouldn't need months to think about it, either. That real estate business of his is doing very well, so don't be so choosey."

"Sure sounds like you're eager to get rid of me," Sara said, ribbing her mother.

"You know better than that. I've always enjoyed my children, despite their being two of the most aggravating females." They both laughed.

Sara left the kitchen to collect more books. When she returned, Edna was still in the spot where she'd left her.

"Our family's been blessed. Sometimes, life binds us with incompatible souls," Edna continued.

"Oh, Mom, please don't start. Dad would die if he heard you say that. What would the church sisters say about all your secret reincarnation thoughts?"

"Never mind what they'd say," the older woman retorted. "Besides, did I say anything about reincarnation? No, I didn't."

"Don't forget being married to a minister means you have to be like Caesar's wife—above reproach," Sara teased.

"I only say these things to my family. All I'm trying to say is that life can be hard when people who don't agree are yoked together. Even with your sister—who's always been a more difficult child than you ever were—we've been blessed."

Sara had stopped to listen and thought of her sister, Judith. There was more trouble with Judith than her mother knew, but Sara had no intention of mentioning this now. Soon enough she would have to talk to her mother for Judith. She had promised Judith that she would try to help, but she didn't relish the idea.

"Well, see you later," Sara said, and shifted the papers in her arms to free a hand.

She opened the door and came out the side door of the sprawling white frame house that her father had bought over fifteen years ago. He'd been a professional musician in his earlier years. They'd moved to Middletown from New York when he'd left the world of jazz music. He'd always wanted to be a minister, and with her mother's support he'd followed that dream.

Sometimes Sara wondered if the change had been difficult for them—the jazz world was a far cry from Middletown—but neither of her parents ever mentioned this. She smiled to herself. Guess they were totally acclimated by now. All they ever talked about was the church, or the need to enlarge the church building.

Walking around to the front of the sprawling, white frame house, she saw that the lever on the mailbox was flagged. First she dropped the papers into her car, then opened the box to retrieve the mail. When she saw the still familiar writing on the postcard she was surprised.

It was from Geoff and from The Philippines, of all places. It had been years since she'd heard anything from him.

Her heart thudded against her ribs. She stared off into her own inner space for a few moments, remembering Geoffrey Stone-McMillan. They'd been friends ever since she could remember. Well, perhaps, friends was a slight exaggeration. It wasn't easy being a friend to Geoff. Even as a child he'd been prickly, and getting close to him had been difficult. Although he was a year younger than she, he'd always managed to be aloof and superior.

None of that had ever mattered. In her little girl eyes, he'd always been wonderful. For as long as she could remember she'd followed him around, his adoring fan. By the time she was a teenager, she'd had a king-size crush on the brilliant, troublesome boy.

She shook her head and smiled ruefully. *Thank God I'm over that, now.*

Sara knew the card was in answer to a note that she'd recently sent him. She had long since stopped writing pen pal letters, although while Geoffrey had been in the Navy she'd written a few times. She couldn't remember the last time she'd received a letter from *him*. Yet, a few months ago she had sent him a short, chatty note.

She couldn't quite figure out why she'd done it, but some inner prompting sent the impulse and she had sat down one evening and hastily jotted a few words to him. And shock of shocks, he had answered, though it wasn't much of a note. All it said was, "Been thinking of you and everyone."

Quite by accident she glanced at one of the letters on the car seat, one addressed to her father, and noticed it was written in the same handwriting. That was certainly a real mystery. Why would Geoff write her father?

She went back into the house. "Guess what," she said to her mother, "There's a postcard from Geoff, and I think he wrote to Dad, too."

"Geoff who?" her mother said in a voice so strange that Sara glanced at the woman.

Her mother turned around with a facial expression that matched her voice.

"Geoff McMillan," Sara said. "What other Geoff do we know?"

Edna Turner seemed almost frightened as she reached backward for a chair and sat heavily. Then she reached out for the letters. First, she stared at the postcard for long seconds. Sara came to glance at it again, over her mother's shoulder.

"Only a few words," Sara remarked. "But for Geoff, I guess that's quite a bit."

"Yes, it is," her mother said, still in the strange voice. "But why? Why now? How could he know?"

"Know what? He's probably answering my note," Sara

said, coming from behind her mother and taking an apple from the fruit bowl on the kitchen table.

"You wrote him after all these years?" Her mother rounded on her suddenly, sounding accusatory.

"Yes," Sara said, stepping back suddenly. "What's wrong with that?"

"Oh, Sara." Her mother sounded sad. "You're too impulsive. It's going to cause you trouble some day. When did you send it?"

"A few months ago," Sara shrugged. "Why?"

Looking at the letter that Geoff had sent to her husband, Edna didn't answer. Her face screwed up in consternation. "He *has* written your father, too."

"Yes, isn't that weird?"

"Is it?" Edna looked up from perusing the letter to stare at her daughter.

Sara didn't know what to say to that, and was more bewildered by her mother's mood change than she wanted to admit. It wasn't that Edna wasn't prone to having an occasional strange mood—for she was. It was that the family had come to dread these moments. There were times when Edna seemed clairvoyant. Her mother's peculiar prescience was often too close to the truth, shaking her faith in a more rational, ordered world.

Edna looked long and hard at the letter addressed to her husband. For a few seconds, Sara felt as if Edna would break open the letter, but the older woman appeared to think better of it. Then, as if wanting to get rid of the envelope, Edna stood up and walked over to stick the missive between the colorful kitchen canisters where she usually kept her husband's mail. She wiped her hands afterward.

When Edna sat back down again, she clasped her hands tightly on the table in front of her.

"Why are you so bent out of shape about Geoff's writ- g?" Sara asked. "You've known him all his life." She used in her efforts to leave and stopped, totally distracted by her mother's behavior. "Daddy likes Geoff. Why don't you?"

"Did I say I didn't like him? Besides, your father and I don't have to agree on everything," Edna snapped. Then in a more conciliatory voice, she added, "You're going to be late for work."

Sara glanced at her watch. "Oops, you're right." She grabbed up her handbag and rushed out the door.

Sara heard her mother mutter something that sounded like, "A woman needs to be careful of what she sets her heart on."

Sara came back and spoke to her mother. "Now, what?"

But Edna shook her head and waved her away. Sara hadn't forgotten her question, but in truth she didn't truly want to hear Edna explain about Geoffrey. She shrugged and left. On the way to her car, she thought fleetingly of the way Edna had responded, but soon let it go. Her mother had been raised in the south and she frequently spoke like that, in her "voice of doom," as Daddy called it. She had a lot of old fuddy-duddy sayings that she would pull out at the least provocation.

Yet, her mother occasionally did have moments when she seemed to have some sort of otherworldly way of knowing. It used to cause her sister and her to laugh. Occasionally her father would voice some annoyance. He wasn't too sure that these strange beliefs jibed with his more orthodox religious tenets. As minister of a small local church, Martin Turner had to consider such things. Edna Turner claimed visions were divinely sent. But just as she and her sister had come to respect Edna's second sight, Martin had come to be wary of her mother's predictions, too.

She wondered why her mother was so upset about Geoff's letter. Her parents had always appeared to like Geoff.

Later that evening, Martin, Sara's father, read Geoff's letter with Edna looking on.

"It looks pretty simple to me," Martin remarked, shrugging. "He wants to enroll in a few summer classes."

"Why here?" Edna insisted.

"Why not here? He wants to discuss something with me," Martin looked back at the letter.

"What things could he want to discuss?" Edna demanded.

"Why are you asking me?" Martin questioned impatiently.

"So what are we going to do, Martin?" Edna asked.

"What any God-fearing family would do—we're going to welcome him. He's the child of an old friend. Anyway, I've always liked Geoff."

"Yes, but—"

"But what? If that boy's asking me for help, I'd be derelict in my duty to ignore him."

"He's got parents," Edna said.

"Hugo and Nora? They've probably forgotten he's still alive, with the two younger children they have now," Martin said with a sad shake of his head.

"He gives me a funny feeling. He always did. I always felt as if he'd cause Sara pain," Edna said.

"Pain? What kind of pain?" Martin shot back.

"It was as if they could read each other's minds, as if they knew each other from before."

"Before what?"

Edna was flustered and decided to take another tack, "I always had a bad premonition about that boy." She wrung her hands. "When he was young it was all right, but now he's a man ..." She stopped in frustration. "I don't know," she said. She felt deflated. "Maybe I just saw his mother in him. You know she registered him in the first grade when he was only three?"

"Yes, I know all about that."

"Then the two of them just ran off and left him with the servants. He never had any kind of home life because she never cared."

Martin stared at her and then at the letter. He shook his head sadly and dropped the letter on his desk. "Nora was a kid. What could you expect? Maybe it wasn't Nora you saw in him. Maybe it was Hugo."

Edna stopped. Although, Martin knew Hugo's faults, it was rare for him to say anything against his friend this way. A sudden chill ran through her, as if someone walked over her grave.

It was several weeks later when Geoff arrived at around five o'clock on a spring evening. The sun was low in the sky. He stopped at the top of the gently sloping hill and cut the engine of the motorcycle. He remembered that the house was close to the perimeter of the city, and the area was a combination of suburbia and city. The houses were simple enough but there was plenty of land space. Sara's house was only a few hundred feet away. He'd come slowly, to keep some of the sound down.

Suddenly, he felt out of place. He looked down at his cycle, wondering what they'd say about it. Funny, he'd been so determined to get here that he hadn't thought of that before. He ran his hand over his hair, fingering the long braid. His clothes were a little tattered. The jeans and navy T-shirt had seen a lot of wear. Fortunately, he'd had the presence of mind to stop and toss everything into a washing machine. At least they weren't as grungy as they could have been. He glanced down at the old, worn, black leather vest, and suddenly remembered that he'd gone through a black leather period, and smiled. Heck, his jeans were definitely an improvement over the leather outfit he'd worn the last time they'd seen him.

He rolled the cycle to her door and dismounted. Shouldering his backpack, he walked to the door. Before he could knock it opened, and an older woman stood there staring at him. It was a few moments before he recognized Edna, Sara's mother. It made him a bit edgy, wondering what her response to him would be. He remembered she'd never been too enthusiastic about him, although, curiously enough, he'd always sort of liked her.

you wearing that braid? He always wanted you to be so macho."

"I never asked him," Geoff responded.

"Some kind of new style, I guess? Don't know what you kids will do next, what with those platform shoes and pants showing people's belly buttons," Edna said, shaking her head.

There was the sound of a door opening from the back of the house. They all turned to listen.

"Shush," Martin said. The older man's eyes glinted with pleasure as he put a finger to his lips silencing them. "It's Sara. You go and surprise her," Martin said to Geoff.

Geoff was on his feet almost before Martin had finished. Suddenly, there was nothing he wanted more than to see his childhood friend. Before he left, he saw Edna look angrily at her husband.

When Geoff left the room, Edna rounded on Martin. "Why did you do that? You know I don't want them being as close as they used to be."

"Edna, stop. It's just Geoff. Maybe he looks a little shabby, but all the kids look like that. If he's a little confused what can you expect, with the childhood he's had? You'll give them ideas with all your superstitious nonsense."

"Superstitious nonsense? That's what you think. You think you know everything? Tell me, do they look like kids to you? Well, not to me. To me they look like a man and a woman."

"Edna, enough of this. You're right, Sara's not a child. She's a woman grown, and you can't protect her from life."

"Don't listen to me. You never do. But watch, this time you'll be sorry," Edna muttered.

As Geoff walked toward the sounds in the kitchen, he realized that he heard two voices. Sara wasn't alone. There was a man with her. This knowledge hastened his steps.

Before he even realized it, he had seen everything. Sara and a man were in a clinch in the darkened kitchen. The man held her possessively. It was this which had Geoff's total attention.

They were completely unaware of him at first, but something alerted them to his presence. Some change in the air, perhaps. He wondered if they'd heard the sound of his heart ready to break.

They jumped apart, embarrassed. For a second, he'd stood there, wondering if it *was* his heart that was going to break or if the top of his head would explode instead. In the split second between their jumping apart and his turning, he'd seen Sara.

She'd always been a pretty girl. But this couldn't be said of her any more. Now she was beautiful. She took his breath away. Her hair, which used to be a long, thick bush, black and crinkly, had been cut. It was barely an inch long now, and very curly. There were so many Afros on the street, yet hers seemed to be made for her. You could see her scalp.

She was about five-foot-four and sleek, wearing a loose T-shirt over khaki shorts that showed a shapely expanse of deep brown thighs. Her tiny wrists and ankles seemed to arch when she moved, in lovely, flowing patterns. Her slim, tapering hands were graceful and expressive. She was barefoot, and the small bones in her feet were like works of art. The whole of her beauty was somehow connected in a sort of absolute symmetry. Her lips were molded in what had to be one of the most pleasing of curves, and she smiled, showing bright, even, white teeth and dimples. Every movement was a poetic line. She was the stuff of which dreams were made. His heart ached. He grieved, feeling as if he'd come too late.

Now he realized for the first time that he'd come back to her wedding expecting Sara to be waiting for him. He left the kitchen quickly, before he did something so totally insane that they'd all know he'd lost his marbles. In that blinding moment he quickly left, intending to leave the house, not knowing what he would do or where he'd go. Without realizing it, he'd pinned too many hopes on Sara Turner.

She came running behind him, crying, "Geoff!"

When he turned to face her in the short hallway, she leaped across the expanse of space that separated them to throw herself at him. He caught her and her arms went around his neck. She kissed him. Suddenly, he came back to life.

When she moved away, talking animatedly, she said, "How long have you been here?"

"Not long. We've been waiting for you," he said.

"But I didn't know you'd come today."

Geoff glanced briefly over her shoulder at the man who'd been with her in the kitchen. The man, likely the fiancé—looked miffed, probably at the interruption.

Sara clasped Geoff around the waist and pulled him into the living room where her parents waited. Her enthusiasm was contagious. Sara had always had the ability to brighten any space she entered. They all talked together, and he felt as if he'd come home.

Suddenly he felt like a million dollars, and he started laughing. Everyone joined him, although he knew they didn't have a clue as to why he was so happy.

Sara looked happiest of all. She kissed him square on the mouth again.

She's still a tease, he thought, and wanted to laugh his head off. She was trying to treat him like a little brother, he realized. But then he thought better of it. Maybe she was as aware of him as he'd suddenly become of her. One couldn't always tell with women. They moved on different wavelengths sometimes.

The rest of the evening went more smoothly. They talked about things past. Even Edna loosened up.

He watched Sara's boyfriend like a hawk. He couldn't seem to stop. Actually, they watched each other. Their gazes met assessingly over Sara's head and fell away. *Good,*

Geoff thought. *Let there be no misunderstanding about it. There would never be any friendship between them.*

By now, the boyfriend had reclaimed her. Once the man stood behind Sara with his hands on her shoulders. Geoff looked at them, where the other man touched her. It made his gut clench and he wanted to grab her away. The insane notion was so powerful that he feared he'd act before thinking. Somehow, he restrained himself and tried to act unaffected.

Sara knew that Chuck was annoyed with her for the attention she lavished upon Geoff. But after seeing Geoff for the first time in several years, she simply didn't care.

Geoff was a part of her history—her very life—like a brother, or closer. Sometimes a person didn't love a brother as much as she loved Geoff. She couldn't stop smiling all evening.

And Geoff now looked cool and distant—totally unapproachable. However, when she had thrown her arms around his neck he'd looked positively unhinged, and that made her kiss him on the mouth. Then he'd looked relieved and even happy. That was so unlike Geoff that she had kissed him again.

When Chuck rose to leave, he stood waiting pointedly for her to accompany him to his car. She almost resented the implied request. Anxious not to miss anything said between her parents and Geoff, she was reluctant to leave them. It was only a call to good manners that made her think better of it. She probed around with her feet, looking for her shoes. Not finding them, she remembered leaving them in Chuck's car.

"Wait for me," she said, and reluctantly stood. She excused herself and Chuck took her hand as they left the room. Geoff's eyes followed their progress.

Outside, she walked silently at Chuck's side. She could barely talk with him because her thoughts remained with

Geoff in the house. Fragments of old childhood incidents teased the edges of her memory.

"Who is he?" Chuck said when they were halfway across the grass toward his car.

"Geoffrey?"

"Yeah, who else? Mr. King Tut, himself," Chuck answered impatiently.

"Don't call him that," she defended the distant, difficult boy she'd known all her life. "He's an old friend. I've known him as long as I can remember. Our fathers used to play in the same jazz band many years ago."

At Chuck's car, he touched her shoulder as if to kiss her, and instinctively she stepped back.

"The way he jumped every time I touched you, I thought he was an old boyfriend," Chuck said.

In her heart she knew Chuck was right. Geoffrey had been even tenser than she remembered, and for him that took some doing. But some perversity made her refuse to acknowledge the truth of Chuck's words.

"Your imagination," she said and started to saunter back to the house.

"Sara, let's get married now. No more waiting, nothing. We'll just tie the knot."

The urgency she sensed in his voice made her pause, but she chose to ignore it. Instead, she said teasingly, "Tie the knot, huh? Did I say I was going to marry you yet?"

"Come here," he said, chuckling.

"Oh, no," she answered.

"Just remember you two aren't children anymore. You and the old family friend in there."

"Really? I hadn't noticed." She was still in her euphoric mood. In her heart, she knew exactly what Chuck was saying. There had been a strange, frenetic intensity tonight. She'd been as affected as anybody.

"*He*'s sure no kid anymore. Keep an eye on him."

"Oh, for Pete's sake," she said, getting more impatient to return to the living room.

"Okay." Chuck seemed determined to keep her from

going inside. "I'm just saying be careful of him. He may not be the same person you remember."

She didn't answer because she'd felt the same way. Geoff had changed. At one time he'd always been aloof, even invincible. Tonight, he appeared more angry than anything else. And while Geoff's being angry was not unusual, he'd also seemed less aloof. His old aura of invincibility was clouded tonight.

"Chuck, please, she said, "I'm going in. See you tomorrow at church." She started walking slowly, although she wanted to run.

Wait for your sandals." Chuck had retrieved them and held them toward her.

She paused and looked back, but even that short walk seemed too long. Suddenly, all she wanted was to be back with Geoffrey.

"Leave them on the curb," she said.

"What's wrong with you?" Chuck said when she kept on toward the house. Suddenly, she sprinted up the stairs into the house.

Back inside, everyone had left the living room. She glanced around, looking for Geoff. The door to her father's den, where he did so much of his church business, was closed. Her mother was in the kitchen preparing to set dinner on the table, and she went to help.

"Where's Geoff?" she asked.

Her mother peered up at her for a moment before answering. "In the den with your father."

"Oh," she said.

Feeling jittery and lost, Sara reached to pick up one of the serving dishes, intending to take it into the dining room. Before she could lift the dish, she knocked a spoon off the top of the stove.

The sudden clatter of the utensil made her exclaim and jump back. Meat stock from the spoon splattered across the stove and floor.

"What's wrong with you tonight?" her mother hissed impatiently.

"Nothing." Sara realized that was the second time someone had asked her that question within the last few minutes. Hastily she wiped the side of the stove, then bent to
retrieve the spoon and clean the floor.

"Don't look like nothing to me," her mother muttered,
head still bent over the food she was preparing.

"Maybe I have spring fever," Sara said, straightening.
She added in a rush, "I'm just happy to see Geoff here."
That, she realized, was the truth.

Her mother watched a few moments before saying, "Fix
the salad."

Once they were seated at the dining table, she watched
Geoff. She kept glancing at his hair. It looked perfect with
his burnished bronze skin. It made him look like a pirate,
and only added to his beauty. He was more beautiful as a
man than he'd been as a boy. He'd grown into his rangy
height of six feet. Though he was slim, his shoulders were
broad, and he walked with an incredibly sexy awareness.

She was aware of him as if her very pores knew him.
Whenever she looked up , she caught him staring at her.
His eyes smoldered from across the table.

Suddenly, she remembered something out of her childhood—his mother saying that he was her "prettyboy." It
gave her a strange, uncomfortable feeling.

When they'd first come out of her father's office, he
had appeared relieved to see her. It was as if he'd thought
she wouldn't be there. It gave her a strange feeling, a
sensation of power. In their long friendship, Geoff had
always been the leader. Now suddenly that seemed to have
changed.

Geoff started to pick up his fork and looked slightly
disconcerted when her father bowed his head and began
to say grace. She wanted to laugh. Geoff's eyes rose swiftly
to hers and the trace of a smile dwelt momentarily on his
lips. Then he meekly bowed his head.

Lord, she wanted to laugh. Imagine Geoff praying.

Later, as the two men sat in the living room, she helped
her mother clean up. Her mother had barely said a word

most of the night. Although she was curious about Edna's silence, she wasn't as interested as she might have been at another time. Tonight, she was straining to hear what the men were saying in the other room. Lord, she hated the antiquated system of men's work versus women's work that ruled in her mother's house.

Finally, with the finishing of the dishes, she was able to join the men. Geoff's smoldering glance settled on her as soon as she did.

Her father said, "Geoff is going to take a few summer courses here at the college."

She heard her mother's sharp intake of breath. Edna had followed on her heels and heard Martin's announcement. "Undergraduate credits?" Edna said, "Aren't you past that?"

"I'm thinking of a second major," Geoff said to her mother, but his eyes were on her.

Her own response was, "Oh, that's great." She almost jumped up and clapped her hands.

"Can't figure why you'd want to go to our little school. You were past that by the time you were barely a teenager," Edna muttered. "In truth, I always thought it was a mistake for your mother to let you finish so early."

It was Martin who came to Geoff's rescue, saying, "If he was bright enough to finish the work, then there was no reason for the schools to keep him back. He deserved to graduate, whatever his age. Besides, the Reverend Doctor Martin Luther King entered Moorehouse College at fifteen, so what could be wrong with Geoff graduating early?"

Martin's words seemed to cut off anything more that Edna would have said, and Sara was glad to see the topic die.

Sara sat on the couch across from Geoff while her mother joined her there. Geoff seemed barely able to keep his eyes from her. Once again, that sense of sudden power flowed through her. She wondered if anyone else could see his interest and knew that her mother, of course, must know. The older woman rarely missed much, while her father had a natural innocence that never seemed to tarnish.

She felt like a teenager again, and she couldn't sit still. She kept crossing her legs, and every time she did her mother and Geoff looked up. Geoff appeared tight as a drum.

"Where are you staying?" she asked Geoff.

"At the Hudson Inn."

"Oh, no!" she said, and turned to her father. "Daddy, he should stay with us."

She'd spoken without thinking, but as soon as the words were out she realized she hadn't been fair. At twenty-five, she rarely called her father "Daddy" anymore. So why had she done so tonight? When the older man spoke, she realized that he was responding to the plea in her voice more than anything else.

"Sara's right," Martin directed to Geoff. "We won't hear of you staying anywhere but here."

"Well . . ." Geoff took a long time to answer. He glanced at her before finally saying, "Thank you. I appreciate your offer." The last words sounded stiff and cool.

She felt slightly deflated at Geoffrey's expression. He didn't exactly look as if he appreciated her father's invitation. Some of the glow dimmed and she realized that maybe she wasn't so powerful, after all. Geoffrey McMillan seemed like a man who still had quite a bit of power himself.

"Do you have enough money?" Martin said, reaching for his wallet.

She was embarrassed for her old friend. "Daddy, Geoffrey's not a kid," she blurted when Geoff looked uncomfortable.

"Nonsense," her father answered, not realizing that he'd embarrassed anyone. "Students always need money, no matter how old they are."

Finally, Geoff answered. "No, Sir, I don't need any cash."

"Your mother still showering you with expensive gifts?" Edna cut in. It sounded like an accusation to Sara.

"No," Geoff answered without any apparent rancor, "I earn my own."

"How's that?" Edna persisted.

He exhaled and said, "I invest in the stock market, options."

"That's like gambling, isn't it?" Edna challenged, and shot a quick glance at Martin.

"It is high risk," Geoff admitted.

To change the subject, Sara cut in, "What classes are you planning on?"

He glanced at her, appearing totally unaffected by her mother's grilling. "I was considering computers."

"Computers?" Edna questioned. "Isn't that the thing which some people say will put people out of work?"

Before Geoff could respond, Martin said, "Now, Edna, no one can predict that. God always works things out."

Not to be outdone, Edna spoke to Geoff, "Sara's interest is to help people *find* jobs."

Sara knew Edna had said that to show the differences between her and Geoff. There was a short pause after this. Sara was annoyed with her mother, and glad when her father said to Geoffrey, "Tell me about this computer thing."

That set the conversation off on another path, and it was several hours before everyone decided to turn in.

Later that night Geoff had stripped down to nothing and lay abed, trying to get comfortable. It seemed impossible. The house was quiet, but he was too keyed up. He couldn't believe what had happened tonight. He'd seen Sara and suddenly turned into a madman.

He was stunned by what he'd discovered about himself. It was by far the most insane he'd ever been. Had he expected to find Sara waiting for him because of a childhood promise?

It also hadn't been his intention to stay with the Turners. Why had he let Sara and Martin convince him? Exasperated, he answered his own question. Because he *did* want to stay with her, that's why.

More than anything, he'd wanted to remain in the same room with her. He had felt as if his heart was being ripped out of his chest when she'd left the room with Chuck.

Geoff paused, remembering how annoyed he'd felt when Martin had asked about money. He knew it wasn't Martin's fault. How could the older man understand? It had been years since he'd allowed anyone to give him anything. First it had been his father that he'd shunned, but soon it had spread. When he needed money, he made it himself or he starved. Starving had made him ingenious.

Finally, admitting he was too restless to sleep, he rolled over and sat up. What he really needed was a smoke. He stood and slipped into his jeans to walk onto the porch.

He knew Edna would be furious if he lit up near her house. He was a bit antsy because he couldn't figure where he'd drop the ashes. He'd forgotten Edna had always watched him like a hawk, as if expecting him to do something wrong. Probably because Edna and his mother, Nora, used to be at each other like cats.

Tomorrow, Edna would probably be out bright and early checking that he hadn't left any signs of his having stayed over. Ashes on her turf would probably have her hexing him or something.

On the porch, he decided to stroll along the sidewalks away from the house. He walked across the yard toward the street, intending to walk to the corner. He hoped the neighbors wouldn't be alarmed at his presence and call the police.

He didn't get far when he spied something on the sidewalk. It was a pair of sandals. He went closer, remembering Sara's bare feet. He hunkered down on his heels and paused before picking them up.

There was so much about her that he'd allowed himself to forget. Seeing her shoes dumped on the street reminded him of the wild girl Sara running through his youth. God, how he needed that love of life. She'd always been able to make him laugh, to make him hope.

He stayed there, musing. Suddenly, he realized that was the reason he'd come, expecting her to be there for him as if she'd had no life until his return despite her being engaged. Just like a man, he realized. In the past, she'd been like a touchstone in his life, always there at his brightest moments. He wanted desperately to return to life, and Sara exemplified that life to him.

All thought of smoking vanished and he picked up the worn leather sandals and started back to the house. He'd walked up the stairs and was almost at the door when he glanced up at her window. Although the rest of the house was dark, there was a small light in her room.

He stared at it for a long time, wondering what she was doing. He listened, holding his breath, hoping to hear something. Could he knock and give her the sandals?

Suddenly, as if by magic, he heard the whisper of faint footfalls. He sensed her nearness. It was as if she'd heard his heart beat. The hairs on his arms swayed.

Still barefoot, she stood in the light that spilled through the opened door.

She was just inside the doorway. Like a gentle doe, she appeared to sniff the air. Because he was standing perfectly still in a shadow outside, she hadn't seen him.

She moved through the opening as light as a fairy. Without causing a ripple of air to move, she went quickly across the front porch and tiptoed down the stairs. Every motion she made was of rare, wondrous grace. When she ran across the grass his heart started pounding, and he could barely breathe. She was gone before he could reveal his presence.

She was obviously looking for her shoes. Not seeing them, she came back and walked slowly up the stairs. As she neared him, he held them toward her. "Your sandals."

She wasn't startled, and he wondered if she'd known he was there all the time.

"What are you doing out here?" she asked. She didn't take the shoes.

"Looking for someplace to smoke."

"Nasty habit. You'd better not let Mother know."

"Okay, I won't tell her."

"But then, you always did have nasty habits."

Her words, shocked him for a moment until he realized she was joking. "That's because I was always a nasty little boy."

She looked at him from sideways and he thought, *What fools men are for beautiful women.* She sauntered a few feet and there was a gentle and incredibly sexy sway to her hips. He followed as if he had been chained to her.

"So what do you have to say for yourself?" she demanded, sounding playful.

He had to clear his throat before speaking. "About what?"

"Start with why you never answered any of my mail."

"Not true," he said.

"Postcards with two or three hastily scrawled words don't count." She leaned backward against the wooden railing. He was so taken with the vision of her that he didn't answer quickly enough for her. "Cat got your tongue?"

"Well," he stumbled, "I guess . . ."

"Never mind. I don't want to hear any of your corny excuses."

She slapped at him, catching him on his arm and ran down the steps into the field toward the back of the house. Lord, it was such a childlike thing for her to do. Then he remembered that she'd always been full of fun. Without another thought, he took out after her.

She disappeared so fast he thought she must be a wood sprite. As he turned at the back of the house he stopped. Away from the streetlights it was very dark. He listened as he made slower progress. He'd just come near a small storage cabin.

"Boo!" Sara said in an exaggerated whisper, and jumped at him.

He grabbed her, jerking her close to his body. She tried

to move away and he held tighter. He grew hard, and knew she felt him.

"Let go. I didn't say you could touch me," she said.

"You didn't say I couldn't, either."

They struggled briefly before going down, with her straddling him and fighting like a she-cat. It was a mistake, for the whole thing left him more aroused than he'd ever been in his life.

He wanted to hold her, but wouldn't. Not now. He'd be taking advantage of her. She obviously thought he could still play the role of her little brother, and he could never go back to that.

Then suddenly all his control broke. He couldn't help himself. He pulled her down and kissed her. At first she went all soft and pliable. Her mouth opened and his heart turned over. He wanted to roll the shorts down over her hips and have her right there, but he knew she was only experimenting. They'd been close, but nothing like this.

He rolled her under him and lay between her legs. He didn't want to move. He felt as if he was at the door of paradise. His hand inched up to her breast and she tried to push him away and sit up. He held her there but he moved his hand from her breasts.

It proved a Herculean effort to keep himself from touching her further. His breathing sped up with his determination. She stopped struggling and lay perfectly still. With his face against her throat he could feel her heartbeat. Neither of them stirred for a few moments.

"Look up," Sara said, staring upward over his shoulder.

He was so happy at that moment that he didn't want to move. His head was still pressed against her pulse and his heart pounded almost in tandem with hers.

"No. Look up." She pushed against his shoulder.

Geoff had broken out in a sweat, wanting her more than he'd ever wanted a woman. It took all his strength to release her and roll away. As he did, she slipped away from him, rising to her feet and running away.

He lay flat on his back with eyes closed and arms spread

at his sides. He listened to her running and wondered how she could race so haphazardly through the incredible dark. But she'd always followed her impulses.

He'd probably scared the wits out of her, going all heavy just because she thought they could take up their old childhood friendship. Only then did he allow his eyes to follow where she had directed.

He looked up at the sky. Suddenly, he felt as if he'd been slammed in his gut.

The sky was a dark velvet pit, liberally sprinkled with millions upon millions of stars. He felt as if she'd given him a gift—as if she'd given him the stars.

He was totally out of his element, thrown for a loop. He hadn't looked at the stars in years. He'd been living in red light districts in cities all over the world, where looking up wasn't exactly what you did. It was a dangerous move because it exposed too much of your throat.

He exhaled in resignation. *Forget your throat*, he told himself. *With Sara, I'm going to lay more than my throat bare. I'm going to lay my soul bare, if I have to. I'm going to do whatever it takes to have her.*

Chapter Three

Sara ran back to the house and hastily undressed for bed. She was a mass of swirling emotions. Her body ached. When Geoff had kissed and touched her, she'd wanted desperately to make love with him. It had been one of the most powerful emotions she'd ever felt. She'd been driven by a hunger that left a ravenous emptiness within her. She'd never felt that way before.

Indeed, she'd never believed such feelings even existed. She wasn't an innocent, but she'd never felt in the throes of any overwhelming desire when she'd made love with Chuck. With Geoff tonight, she'd been almost mindless before she realized that she couldn't submit to this thing as she'd wanted. In truth, it had been Geoff's hesitation that had given her time to think. If Geoff hadn't stopped when he did, she'd have gladly given herself to him. Even now she was on fire for him.

She heard mumbling in her parents' room, which was right next to hers. Most of it was inaudible.

Her mother's voice rose suddenly. "You can't make him the son you never had."

"Edna, leave it alone. Can't you even consider the possibility that you might be wrong about him?"

"No, I was right. He's a cauldron of emotions ready to boil over."

In that instant of hearing fragments of her parents' conversation, Sara remembered that as a child she had once heard them arguing about Geoffrey. Her mother had been angry because Geoff had been dragged to a party by his parents, Hugo and Nora. Edna had found Geoff reading by flashlight as he'd hunched in a corner. She remembered Martin telling her mother to mind her own business that night, too.

She was glad when their voices faded and she could hear nothing more. She turned over and tried to sleep.

Sara heard the telephone and glanced at her bedside clock. It was six o'clock in the morning. She hastened from her bed and hurried out into the hall. There was a telephone in the upstairs hallway, but she didn't want to wake her parents. She quickly went downstairs to use the extension in the ground floor hall.

Too late she remembered that Geoff was in the downstairs bedroom. She realized that all she had on was a white, lightweight cotton nightgown. Her robe was still laying across her bed. The guest room where Geoff stayed was on the first floor. She glanced down at herself, realizing that it wasn't quite the thing one greeted one's guests in, should she run into one in the hallway, but she doubted he'd wake before she was finished on the phone.

She was surprised to hear her sister Judith's voice. Judith, unlike her, never woke this early—not if she could help it.

"Is something wrong? You're never up this early," Sara said. She spoke in a near whisper in an attempt not to wake everyone. It was an old house but the acoustics were very good.

"I'm fine. I know it's an ungodly hour. But I needed to

speak with you, and I was hoping Mother wouldn't be up yet. Is she?"

"No, the coast is clear," Sara said, feeling concerned. "What's going on?"

"Did you get chance to talk with her about . . . you know? Me and Larry?"

"Not yet. I got sidetracked. But you know there's nothing I can say that will convince either of them."

"Yeah, I know, but they've just got to accept it. This is the seventies. Larry and I are living together, and that's all there is to it."

"Why can't you get married?" Sara said in a near whisper.

"Forget about marriage. I don't want to live with the same person all my life. Our parents are still operating as if we're in the dinosaur age."

"They love us, Judith, and they want the best for us."

"They love you, and they're praying for me. They still think people should be married before they sleep together."

"They're not that innocent. Don't forget Dad was a musician when they got married. They know about these things."

"Then it was entering the church that did it. They don't want to admit that life's different now. Maybe you can be the little Goody Two-Shoes that our parents want, but I can't."

A sudden image of Geoff came into Sara's mind. "I'll see what I can do. I promise."

"Good. If *you* talk to them, they may listen."

"Don't get your hopes up. They still think of me as their little girl, too," Sara said ruefully.

"That's your own fault. Why are you still there? You're older than me. The reason they give me such a hard time is because you're so amenable. But anyway, let's not get off on that."

"Why, thank you for small mercies, Sister Dear."

"Your talking to them is bound to help. You're so sweet

and open that people just naturally want to hear what you have to say.''

"Yeah, yeah. First I'm too amenable and then people are dying to hear everything that I have to say. Tell me anything to get *me* to beard Mom in her den.''

"It's true. Besides, you've always been the peacemaker between Mom and me. Nothing at all like me, or even Mom, for that matter. She's too much like me.''

"You said that backward. You're like your mother,'' Sara corrected.

"Please don't say that, it gives me the horrors. Well, guess as long as I don't have any otherworldly premonitions . . .''

The words made Sara think of Geoff again. "Guess who's here." Judith had already been told about the cryptic postcard.

"Geoff? He came already? Oh, no, I missed him!''

"He's still here.''

"Geoff's there? How'd Mom swallow that? Dad's idea, of course.''

"You know it. Why not come down next weekend? I'll even help you with your laundry." They both laughed at that.

"Oh, heck. I'm getting to hate that house. It's not Dad so much as Mother. If she doesn't make me feel like a ten year old, she manages to make me feel like the greatest sinner of all time.''

"Come on home. They'll both be so happy to see you that they'll be on their best behavior. You haven't been here in months.''

"I'm tired of having to lie to them. How about you? Are you going to spend your life in Mother's house, being the perfect daughter?''

"Let's stick to the subject. Are you coming? I know Geoff would get a kick out of seeing you again.''

"Oh, Lord, don't I wish I was there? But it's going to be a few weeks before I can take the time away. You should fall on your face and thank your guardian angel that I ain't there. You know he always preferred me. If I was there, he probably wouldn't be able to resist me, gorgeous as I am.''

When she hung up the phone Sara turned and there was Geoff standing in his doorway, wearing the same outfit he'd had on last night, jeans and a Navy T-shirt top. The top clung to him and looked supremely sexy. He was more muscular than she'd originally expected. In his clothes he looked trim, but not overly muscular. Staring at his body she thought of the kiss last night on the grass. It should have been a surprise, but hadn't been. She'd known from the moment she'd seen him that a whole new relationship was in store for them. What surprised her were the stirrings of desire that rose within her. That had never happened to her before, not with that intensity. She'd never felt for Chuck the heat that she'd experienced in that brief encounter last night.

Thinking of Chuck made her feel guilty. She pulled her thoughts away from last night reluctantly as she faced Geoff.

Geoff's eyes traveled down her body. She wondered if he could see through the fabric. She regretted not having donned the robe. There was nothing indecent about the gown, but she wondered how much it revealed. When his eyes came back to hers, his smile was slow and lazy. She refrained from any attempt to cover herself and faced him boldly.

"Good morning," he said.

"Shush," she answered, her eyes going upward to her parents' door on the second floor. Then she asked in a lowered voice, "What are you doing up? You've got a little more time before church."

"Church?" he queried, his eyebrows rising.

"Surely you don't think my mother will allow you to escape that on a Sunday morning?"

"I wouldn't dream of it," he answered, keeping his eyes on her face.

"You're a part of the Turner household, now."

"Then I'll need to repair my wardrobe a bit." He indicated his jeans, and she wanted to laugh. "I'll need an iron."

"Give them to me. I'll do it," she offered.

"No, I'll do it, but you can keep me company. Knowing how nosey you always were, you can use that time to ask all the questions you'd like."

"Nosey?" She protested. "I was never nosey. I simply had a natural healthy curiosity. Besides, you were always so secretive you made me think you had wonderful secrets."

"Why, I did have wonderful secrets." He smiled at her.

It took her breath away for a second before she remembered to respond. "Sure, I'll bet," she said.

"So, how about that iron, or do you want me to disgrace myself in front of Martin's parishioners?

Okay," she said, after a quick upward glance at her parents' room. Then, because she couldn't brazen it out any more, she said, "Just give me a moment." She ran upstairs to her room and donned the robe.

When she came back he was in his room, and she looked inside. There was an old poster of Angela Davis hanging on the wall. Judith had put it up there a while back when Angela was still a fugitive. However, the room had already become Geoff's, in a way. Now there were books and papers spread over the bed. Curious, she walked in to look.

"Are these your stock market papers?"

"Yes," he answered from the closet, where he was picking out a jacket and shirt.

"You said it was risky, yet you're making a living from it?"

"A living of sorts. I'm not getting rich, if that's what you're asking."

She tilted her head as she picked up one book to peruse. After a moment of flicking through the pages, she dropped it back on the bed. Much as she hated to admit it, she agreed with her mother. It did seem a peculiar way to earn money.

"Looks interesting, "she said, noncommittal. "Come on, I'll show you where the iron is."

On the first floor at the back of the house was a small alcove that served as a washroom. There they could talk more freely, for voices didn't carry as loudly as in other parts of the house.

She set up the ironing board and plugged in the iron. Geoff surprised her, for he had more clothing than she'd first imagined. He looked pretty competent with the task of getting himself ready, so she sat down to talk.

"So, first thing I want to know is why you never wrote me."

"I did write," he insisted.

"I told you I don't consider those pathetic missives writing. I guess you were too busy with all your activities. And why did you join the navy?"

"When I didn't enter my master's program and quit school, I knew I'd be drafted if I didn't do something."

"Your quitting school, now—that really surprised me. You always loved it. I was so impressed when you graduated at nineteen. And then to just walk out." She shook her head.

"I guess everyone was surprised." He spoke quietly.

"What did your mother say?" she asked, curious about Geoff's enigmatic mother.

"You know Nora. She figured I needed time to sow a few wild oats."

"Oh," Sara said.

She remembered Geoff's mother as a very beautiful woman. However, whenever Nora came to visit she had always seemed eager to be someplace else. Nora and Edna had never gotten along, and they were part of the reason for the break-up of the old jazz band. That, and her father's desire to go into the church.

Martin and Hugo had been friends since they were small children. They both came from Tennessee, and when her father was orphaned at five he'd been raised by Hugo's parents. Hugo, five years Martin's senior, had immediately taken to the younger child, and that was the beginning of their friendship, which survived Hugo's fighting in World War II and her father going to Korea.

They'd both been musicians and had started a moderately successful band. However, it was Hugo who'd actually been famous.

According to her mother, her father had quit the music world when Sara was seven years old. She became ill, and he'd prayed for a cure. When Sara was cured, he felt that his life was totally changed and he wanted to serve God as a minister. The first thing they did was move from Manhattan to Middletown.

However, music was still a big part of her father's life, and the church where he was pastor, although small, was known for its music, including an incredible choir.

Edna called Geoffrey's mother decadent, and even worse. But then Edna, as everyone knew, was inclined to judge people harshly.

"Why did you quit?" she couldn't help asking.

"Guess I was just at loose ends," he said slowly, as if trying to understand himself. "The master's didn't seem worth it, and the navy was there offering me food and shelter."

"I always expected you to burn your draft card or something like that."

He chuckled. "Yeah, I guess you're right about that. I did think of going to Canada for a while."

"Why didn't you?"

"It just seemed too much trouble."

"Was it awful? Viet Nam?" she asked.

He didn't answer for a while. Then he finally said, "Yes. Nam was bad. Worse than anything I'd ever imagined. It would have been better if I'd gone to Canada." He stopped for a moment. "Life is strange."

"How do you mean?"

He glanced at her and then back down at the ironing board. "Hard to explain."

She understood he didn't want to talk about the war any longer, and changed the subject. "Then you traveled after you were released?" He nodded and she went on. "Well, where did you go?"

"You do ask a lot of questions." He laughed before adding, "Mostly Asia, although I did get to Africa for a little while."

"That sounds so wonderful. I wish I could have been there."

"You would have loved it. I met some men there just like your dad." When she screwed up her eyebrows he said, "Old men who wanted a bride price for their daughters."

"Hey, watch what you say about my dad," she retorted in fun. Then after a small pause, added, "So, you're going back to school? For your master's?"

"Maybe," he muttered.

"Are you still going to be a mathematician?" He looked up and shrugged. "You can't do that."

"Why not?"

"It sounds too stodgy. You in black leather and riding your Harley? No way."

"Once I've shown them how to demolish the national debt, you'll learn some respect." He changed the subject with, "Who were you talking to? On the phone?"

"That was Judith."

"Good grief, little Judith. What's she up to?"

"She's not so little anymore. She's twenty and at Syracuse U. She's dying to see *you*, of course. She'll be coming down in a few weeks."

"Hey, that's great. I want to see her, too."

Somehow, that caused a slight twinge in her heart. She remembered Judith teasing that he'd prefer her. Once again, Sara was surprised by her own response.

However, what she really wanted to mention was the way he'd kissed her last night. She wanted to ask him why he'd done it, but something held her back.

"Well, I see you two are up already," a grim-faced Edna said from the doorway.

Later, Geoff managed to look quite respectable for church. He had a white shirt in fairly good condition and a black linen blazer that looked as if it had cost quite a bit at sometime. He even had a beautiful silk tie. With a pair of clean washed jeans and his boots shined he still looked like a pirate, but a gloriously beautiful one.

As for the hair, it was neatly smoothed down. She knew it would be disconcerting to the older members of her father's church when they saw the long braid down his back. Foolish as it seemed, she was proud of him. Who but Geoff could look so good in the outfit? All he needed was a gold earring.

Just before they left the house, Chuck called. "Sorry, I won't be there today. One of the houses that I manage had a fire last night, and I have to be available for the fire inspectors."

"Oh, I'm sorry," she said. "Anyone hurt?"

"No, just a little damage, that's all. Will you miss me?" he asked, changing the subject.

The intimacy in his voice disconcerted her. It always made her uncomfortable, which was the main reason why she hesitated to accept his proposal. He was a nice man, but somehow she often felt there was something missing in their relationship.

She had mentioned it to Chuck, but he didn't understand what she meant. Even their becoming lovers hadn't supplied that missing element.

"I have to go, Chuck. Everyone's waiting for me." She hung up gently.

Outside, Martin smiled when he saw Geoff. "Okay, let's go."

When her mother and father headed toward their car, she put her hand on Geoff's arm to detain him. With a wave to her parents, she said, "Geoff and I will take my car."

Edna watched them as they sat in her car. Geoff glanced

once at his motorcycle and Sara said, "No way. You've got
to be respectable for Dad's church."

He looked at her and laughed before speaking. "Anything you say, Ms. Sara."

They both laughed but there seemed something
strangely sincere about Geoff's answer. He sounded as if
he was making her a promise. She shook that thought away
as they followed behind her parents' car.

She didn't mention Viet Nam anymore, but spoke about
the local college in which he'd expressed interest. She
burned to question him about last night. They'd talked
this morning as if the incident had never occurred. This
was Geoff, the friend from her childhood. They'd been
about as close as children could be. Okay, so that was long
ago. Still, she had a right to know. Yet, the coward in her
rambled on about college credits and second majors.

Once at the church, she realized that without Chuck
she was better able to focus on Geoff. That thought made
her feel disloyal. She showed Geoff around Martin's small
church and introduced him to the parishioners. She
remained with him except for time spent assisting the
mission sisters in setting up for the service.

The service went well. Her father was not the kind of
great, fiery preacher many preferred, but he was sincere,
and his listeners always seemed to sense this. Even Geoff's
attention was totally on the sermon. Unfortunately, hers
was not.

The more she thought about last night, the more she
wanted to know what it meant. She wasn't a woman good
at subterfuge or hiding her feelings.

After the sermon, Sara, overriding her mother's objec-
tions, left the church and returned home. Geoff went with
her. They were silent on the drive back. Now that they
were alone again, she still found herself unable to speak.
It wasn't until they'd arrived at the house that she found
the courage to talk.

"Why did you kiss me like that last night?" she asked.

"You mean like a man, and not just your childhood friend?"

"Okay, that's one way of putting it. Why?"

"Why did you send me a letter saying you were getting engaged and asking me to come?"

A sense of dread went through her. He suddenly sounded like Edna.

"Why not? You're an old family friend. I wanted you to attend the wedding."

"You're not going to marry that guy, Sara."

"Are you nuts? Of course I am."

"No, you won't. I know many things about you. I know you're a clean and wholesome spirit. I know about your honesty. You don't love him, and you won't marry someone you don't love. And what about me?"

"You? What do you mean?" she said, realizing she'd been holding her breath all while he spoke.

"I know what your response to me means. I felt your heart racing. You wouldn't feel that way about me if you loved Chuck. You want me as much as I want you. That's the one thing last night proved. That won't change even if you're married to someone else. Marrying someone else would be the worst thing you ever did to yourself, or to some poor guy. Don't think I'd let you go, either. I'm not a gentleman like your precious Chuck."

"Geoff, what are you talking about? We've never been anything but childhood playmates. What makes you think you can charge in here like gangbusters and talk to me like that? Our promising to get married as kids doesn't mean a thing."

Why had she mentioned that? she wondered. Suddenly her head hurt.

"So you do remember that?" he said at her back.

"That was kids' talk."

"True. But last night we weren't kids talking."

"What do you want, Geoff? Why did you come?"

"You asked me to come to your wedding."

"Yes, you're right. Just remember that's exactly why I invited you—to attend my wedding."

Her heart told her that it wasn't Geoff who was in danger of forgetting—it was her.

Chapter Four

It was early morning several weeks later and Sara's emotions were in a jumbled quagmire of anxiety, doubt, guilt, and other feelings for which she had no name. There was no use denying what was happening to her. Just as she'd been on the verge of becoming engaged to Chuck, she realized that it was Geoff she wanted.

It was the most insane thing that had ever happened to her. Although, she had loved Geoff from childhood, she was in no doubt as to his problem with women. From early adolescence, Geoff had been an incredible womanizer. They had lost contact during that period, but she'd heard her parents talk. His parents had actually seemed to encourage this. As far as she knew, Geoff had never maintained any longterm relationship. She wondered if he was even capable of such a thing. By allowing herself to become attracted to him, she had fallen into one of the worst situations possible. How easily it could sound a death knell to any friendship between them.

She was too aware of him as a male. But she kept reminding herself that he was Geoff, a childhood friend. True, she'd adored him as a kid, but he'd always been annoyed with her hanging around him. Aside from their kiss on that first night there had never been even a hint of any other type of relationship. And nothing had happened since to make her believe their relationship had changed.

There was no denying the attraction on her side—it was indisputable. And, although she was no expert on men, she was pretty sure that what she had felt from his side of that kiss had been real. He wanted her. But that was Geoff's usual approach. He desired her, while *she* was totally smitten with him.

Sara was the only one up at that time because she'd gotten into the habit of rising early and leaving the house before Geoff woke. She'd heard the delivery boy throw the paper against the steps while she was sitting in the kitchen with her coffee. She went to the door and retrieved the dailies that had been delivered. There was a *New York Times* and a *Wall Street Journal* in the batch—both Geoff's.

Edna had already complained about Geoff telephoning his New York trader sometimes several times a day, although he scrupulously paid for the calls. Sara laid the papers on the small table in the hallway and returned to sit in the kitchen.

She sipped her coffee, wishing the headache that had begun that morning before she'd even gotten out of bed would ease. She knew the coffee wouldn't help. Certainly the first cup hadn't, nor had the aspirin that she'd taken when she'd finally forced herself out of bed. She took her cup to the sink and rinsed it out.

It was guilt, she finally admitted as she stared at the running water. The pain hammered behind her eyes. Just thinking about him caused her stomach to squeeze with nervousness—and her spirits to rise. Sometimes she couldn't help repeating his name to herself. She was on the verge of whispering it just then.

"Good morning," Geoff's husky male voice said behind her.

As she swirled around, the cup slipped from her hand, shattering in the porcelain sink. Geoff stood there barefoot without a shirt. He had just come out of the bathroom. Her mouth went dry. There were droplets of water on his shoulders which he had missed when toweling dry. He was so incredibly beautiful. His just-shampooed hair was unbraided, and it was a huge, crinkly, curly mass. He looked like an Ethiopian highlander or a Fiji Islander. There were so many places in the world from whence he could have come. She stood stark still before realizing how strange she must appear.

Her heart raced as if she'd just run a mile. She rubbed the goosebumps that rose on her arms.

"Where have you been hiding? I've barely seen you in weeks."

"Yes . . . I've been . . . so busy what with the job and school, and helping out at the center . . ." she babbled.

She felt incredibly foolish, and frightened, too, by the instant physical attraction to this new Geoff. She feared that he might be right, that she could neither continue to see Chuck or marry him. All her efforts to avoid him seemed to go up in smoke at one glance.

He stepped forward, quickly grabbing her hand. Then he wrapped the towel that had been around his neck to cover her hand. It wasn't until that moment that she'd noticed she was bleeding—she'd cut herself on the shards of the broken cup.

"Thank you," she said, wishing she could move away from him. The close proximity made her confused.

He looked at the cut carefully. "Just a superficial scratch," he reassured. "Come into the bathroom and I'll fix it."

"I can do it. I have to leave or I'll be late," she said, pulling back from him.

"I'll only take a minute."

"No!"

He let her go. Her face flamed hot and she dragged her gaze away and pushed past him to rush upstairs, where she went into the bathroom. Once there, she closed the door and leaned against it. When she managed to settle down, she removed the towel. Her hand was no longer bleeding and she applied a Band-Aid.

Geoff watched her rush upstairs. He was aware of her late hours, for he'd been trying to catch up with her. The few times he'd seen her come in she'd appeared tired and worn out, and he hadn't tried to delay her retiring into her room. She taught at an experimental grade school, a lab school, that was located on campus and connected with their teacher's college. During the summer months, she worked at their day camp program for grade school children.

In the meantime, Geoff had made all the correct moves. He registered for classes. That none of the courses particularly interested him was something he didn't think of much. He had come back for Sara, not for school.

He couldn't seem to concentrate on anything else. He was too focused on her. He didn't see her as much as he'd thought he would. She was always going someplace, seeing someone—seeing Chuck.

On a warm July day, not too long after the incident in the kitchen, he decided to attend classes. The term hadn't been in session long, and it already was rare for him to go. At first he'd been more vigilant, but that was mostly in hopes of seeing Sara on the campus.

As for the classes, he preferred simply reading the textbooks and taking the exams at the end of the course. Halfheartedly, he'd brought a rather dogeared sheath of papers, just in case he took notes. In truth, his only reason for going was the possibility of seeing Sara. He'd walked past the building where she worked several times to no avail.

He was frustrated and had reached the point of feeling that it was a hopeless situation. But this day he hoped his chances of seeing her would be better than they had been at the house. It seemed crazy that two people who lived in the same house saw each other so rarely.

He was also scared, scared that he'd moved on her too quickly on the first night, or that he'd come back too late—or that she'd marry Chuck. Just the thought made his gut clench.

During the restless months that he'd been there, he'd toured Middletown and the surrounding areas on his bike. There wasn't much to see. Research on a long list of new companies to invest in had also been done. To earn extra money, he'd worked a few odd jobs.

The class scheduled for that morning promised to be a dull one, because the instructor was not well informed. The man never asked him any questions, because in truth he knew more than the instructor. Everyone had realized that at the last quiz, including the professor. Geoff was glad, because it meant he could drowse along through class.

He grew increasingly disinterested during the lecture. To make matters worse it was hot, and all the students looked listless. He glanced around, recognizing that most of the others were younger than he. He wondered if anyone could see how edgy he was and noticed one pretty girl watching him. When they made eye-contact, she smiled— invitingly, he thought. He stared for a moment before nodding and turning away.

Too bad, he thought. He could use a woman right about now. But he was sick to death of running with random women.

No more—now it had to be Sara—his Sara. No one else would do. He needed something to anchor his life, and running after women wouldn't do that.

Funny, the change that had occurred in him since he'd received Sara's letter. It hadn't been that long, he admitted, but it had been longer than any time since he was a kid. Since he was thirteen—since Hugo—but no, it was better not to think of that.

Later, he was walking along, planning to pick up his bike and do a little touring, when he spied a slim, dark woman with a graceful curve to her back as she leaned over to peer at the sidewalk. She looked so like Sara that his heart thumped. It wasn't the first time that he'd thought he had seen her. Much too frequently, he'd imagined that some stranger was Sara.

As he moved closer, he realized that it *was* Sara. She stood almost a block away near a bus stop. He sped up to reach her before the bus came and smiled at the thought.

Just before he reached her, she went down to sit on her heels, now getting a better look at whatever had caught her attention. She hadn't seen him approach and as far as he could see, she was engrossed in the wild flowers that grew at the roadside.

Geoff waited for her to stand, but when several seconds passed without her doing so he went down on his heels and spoke. "Hi."

She looked up, startled. "Geoffrey," she said, and then smiled her recognition. "Hi."

The smile nearly knocked him off his feet. It made his chest tight. The sun beamed down with an intensity that he felt beneath his shirt and the sound of cicadas filled the air around them. It sounded almost as if they were laughing at him.

"Look," she said, with another smile and pointed at the yellow blooms.

It took him a few seconds to drag his eyes away from her to gaze down. So thrown that he could hardly focus, he felt happy and lighthearted that he'd finally caught up with her and wanted to laugh with the cicadas. He looked back at her, puzzled and wondering what she expected him to say. Although he wanted to please her, it was only a small patch of flowers. It was she who was the miracle.

"No, really. *Look*," she insisted.

Then he remembered her doing the same thing that first night in the backyard. He did laugh, but he also looked more closely at the one tiny blossom that she indicated. And that's when he suddenly realized how perfect it was. The minute flower was perfectly formed, and there at its center was an even smaller black insect. The insect was clearly defined against the bright color with its sucker extended, extracting nectar from the flower's center. Suddenly he had a stunning moment of knowledge, an incredible revelation of how precious life was. It was a gut communication between him, the yellow flower, and the insect.

He was awed.

The world was teeming with life. He'd always known this on an intellectual level, but at that moment in time he knew it in his heart.

Gazing up at her again, suddenly he realized how much he needed her. How vital she was to his life. He admitted to himself that he had never wanted anything or anyone as much as he wanted Sara.

She looked rattled, probably by his direct prolonged gaze, he thought. Despite this, she stood up as gracefully and fluidly as a dancer. Standing, also, he was determined to remain in her presence for as long as she would allow.

Now that he'd found her, he didn't want to let go. He stood there at the bus stop waiting with her. He could barely keep the silly grin that he'd felt from showing on his face. Their talk was desultory at best. He wondered what had happened to her car but he was almost afraid to mention it, for fear she'd make him leave. When the bus came, he waited for her to get on, planning to follow. He'd go with her no matter where she led. Even if she led him into the fires of Hades, he'd go.

He would willingly die for her.

She also waited for him to enter. When he didn't, she motioned as if to indicate that he should go on.

"I wasn't waiting for the bus . . ." he mumbled.

"I thought you were . . ."

They spoke together and laughed when they realized the error.

"My car is over there," she said. "I was just going to pick it up."

"Can you give me a lift?" he said, thinking fast.

"Sure, if you're willing to go the Student Center with me and wait for a while."

It was exactly what he wanted to hear. "No problem," he interjected quickly and grinned happily.

"Where's your motorcycle?"

"Around," he answered, not wanting to admit that his Harley was parked in one of the student lots. He feared she'd rescind her offer to transport him. How could he explain that he was willing to walk anywhere with her, without thought to anything else in the world? She'd think he was crazy.

They went to her car, speaking mostly of small incidentals. It was hot as an oven inside the vehicle and she switched on the air-conditioning.

They had gone a few blocks before Sara turned briefly to him and said, "Do you still want to unite people?"

He knew she was referring to Edna's remark on that first night. "I hadn't thought of that in years until your mother mentioned it," he admitted.

"Oh," she said.

She sounded disappointed and he regretted his response. Geoff wanted her to smile at him and rushed to qualify his remark, grabbing at straws as he did. "Of course, in many ways, it *is* still a goal," he lied.

"You should never give up your dreams."

"Yes, I agree with you."

"You've certainly changed," she said after another moment of quiet.

He hadn't been uncomfortable in the silence, for he'd been at peace with himself now that he was with her. He'd been absorbed by the scent emanating from her. He thought that he could smell the sunshine coming off her healthy brown skin. Her remark caught him off guard.

"How so?" he asked.

"I remember when you used to do anything to avoid me."

He didn't know what she was talking about. "When was that?"

"Back when you hated girls," she answered.

It made him laugh. "Maybe I was at that stage when a

little boy realizes that in the end a woman will have a great deal of power over him. We're probably trying to delay the inevitable.'' This time they both laughed.

"A woman?" she said some time later. "Someone special?"

He'd been on the verge of denying it, but on second thought decided that a little competition might pique her interest. He smiled, evading the question and answered, "Maybe I'll tell you someday." To change the subject, he asked, "What do you do at the center?"

She shrugged. "Oh, I fill in. Various things. There are a lot of problems in our little microsociety here. Since the sixties we've had an upsurge of various difficulties. Students from troubled families. The incidence of suicide has increased, along with drug and alcohol use. Everyone suffers, but I think the children that I teach are the most seriously affected. Unfortunately, we see them down the road when they're older, college age. I want to help." She glanced at him, "Sorry, I don't mean to preach."

"It's okay. I can see you're very dedicated." Her words brought back that first night, and he remembered Edna speaking about his wanting to unite people and realized that once he'd been idealistic and high-minded, too. Almost as serious about this as Sara still was. But he wasn't that person anymore. He'd seen too much in Nam and other places. And now, he couldn't help himself but he didn't want Sara to be so close to other people's problems, either. She was too clean and wholesome. He feared she'd be besmirched. He wanted to protect her from the awfulness of what was truly happening out there. He had to mentally shake himself to speak. "Edna was right. You're very generous with your time."

"Don't listen to my mother. She doesn't mean any harm but I guess she's always been . . ." Geoffrey was curious to hear what she'd say, but respected her reluctance to criticize Edna. She seemed to think a long time before finishing her statement. ". . . very opinionated."

"I remember her as being very sure of what was right

or wrong. And she was pretty certain that I was a wrong one."

"She never means things the way they come out."

He was inclined to disagree. Edna had always been very capable of saying exactly what she meant. But he didn't want to pursue that. It wasn't Edna he wanted to talk about, it was Sara.

"How are *your* parents?" she asked.

"Okay, I guess," he answered, disinterested and not wanting to talk about his family, either.

"It's been a long time since I saw them. I guess your little sisters are big girls now. I've never even seen the youngest."

He shrugged, gazing at her as she drove. He wanted to reach out and touch her. She kept glancing at him as if trying to gauge his thoughts.

"I always remember your mother as a beautiful woman. But she used to scare me when I was a kid." She glanced at him again.

"Nora can be scary at times," he answered absently.

"I mean, she was so cool and unflappable."

"Yes, that too." He was bored with the topic already.

Sara glanced his way several times but didn't say anything right away. She looked puzzled. He wondered if he'd spoken too hastily.

Finally, with another quick glance, she said, "I've known you all my life, yet, somehow, I feel as if you've become a stranger."

"Is that why you've been avoiding me?"

She was flustered, and shifted her gaze away. "I haven't been avoiding you," she answered. He realized she was hedging. "It's just that I'm not sure of what to say to you anymore."

"Say what you want. I'm the same Geoffrey," he encouraged.

"Really, you *have* changed," she said.

And he had, he knew. He remembered kissing her in the yard. There had never been anything like that before.

But he was curious as to what she'd say. "How so?" he asked.

"I'm not sure. You just seem less open, somehow, while in other ways you're more approachable." Her voice rose at the end. Then she smiled and shook her head. "Am I making any sense?"

He didn't know what to say but wanted to reassure her. "I always thought I was an open book to you."

"It's like you've grown harder, less involved," she continued.

"I'm older."

"It's more than that. You don't really talk. Like you still haven't answered about your family. You sound as if you don't care, either."

"I haven't seen or talked to them in a while."

"What's a while?"

He didn't want to pursue it, but because it was Sara he wanted to please her in any way that he could. "A couple of years."

"While you were in Asia?"

"Longer."

"They've contacted you, of course?"

"They couldn't," he said, and looked away. He didn't have to tell her that but he didn't want to lie to her, either. Not if he could help it. He feared there would be times when he was going to lie, and he didn't want to do it unnecessarily. "They wouldn't know where to send anything. I've moved around a lot."

"But you've called them since you returned?"

He took a long time to answer. "No, I haven't."

She was right that he felt distant and aloof from his family. She was the only person he wanted to be close to.

"But you should," she insisted, sounding horrified. "They must be worried out of their minds."

It was a curious thought, and he seriously doubted it. Who would worry? Certainly not Hugo, his father. Hugo never stayed sober long enough to notice who was there.

Would Nora worry? Not likely, he decided. Nora's interest went to other things, such as her image or her portfolio.

They reached the center and he was relieved when the conversation dropped, but he was sorry that now he'd have to share her with others.

"You can come in. I only have to drop some papers. It won't take long," she said.

"Okay," he answered, wanting to remain with her.

Inside there were two people. One, a woman, was talking on the telephone. A man about his own age was at a coffee machine. Sara waved at the woman and went to speak with the man.

"Hi, Lloyd," she said. "How was your quiz?"

"Great," Lloyd answered, and his face lit up upon seeing her. Geoff's hackles rose at the other man's smile. He couldn't help the instant resentment that rose in his heart. He wanted to grab Sara and leave. "I got a B," the other man finished.

"Good for you," Sara answered. "I knew you could do it."

"How about some more sessions?" the man said.

"Sure. Call me later and we'll make a date."

Fortunately, it didn't take long for Sara to pick up the papers before returning to him. Soon they were back in her car.

"Who is he? Another boyfriend?" he asked.

She looked at him sideways before saying, "Suppose he was? Would you be shocked?"

"Why should I?" he said, trying to fake disinterest.

"He's not," she said, seemingly already tired of the game. "I tutor him."

"Tutor? More volunteering?"

"Yes."

"You're teaching, working for your master's, and volunteering on several projects?"

"I have the time. I'm only working part-time and taking a few credits. I don't have many expenses, living with my parents. Once I've gotten my master's, things will be different. It's not the hardship that it sounds."

"What subjects do you tutor?"

"Mostly English," she said.

"That was never one of my favorites."

She looked at him and smiled. "I remember you as a whiz in everything. I used to envy you."

"Envy *me?*"

"Life was always easy for you. You always seemed to land on your feet."

"That was an illusion," he said.

"Maybe so, but still with your marks you don't need any tutoring. I remember how fantastic you were, especially in math and science."

"I used to hate English, though. And now, it's caught up with me. I've been out of school for a long time, and I've fallen behind. A little work in English would be a big help."

"Well . . ." she paused.

"You'd be a big help, and I'd really appreciate it." He'd spoken quickly to take advantage of her small hesitation.

"Okay, we'll see how much help you need. Somehow, I doubt you can't handle this on your own."

"If you think that I can, then you can quit."

There was no further talk on the ride to the house.

A few days later Geoff got in one evening, looked at the books he carried and then at the graphs spread over his bed. He knew he should start on an assignment from one of his classes. But the graphs were like a lure, enticing him to work on them instead.

He glanced at his watch. It was too soon to call his broker. The man would be in transit, at neither his office or at home yet. His frustration mounted whenever he thought of how long it took him to contact the trader. There had to be a better way.

He gave in to the temptation to work on the graphs and tossed the books into the corner. His guitar was on the bed and he pushed it aside before sitting down to study a graph.

Some time later, he was still sprawled on the bed, surrounded by newspapers and books, when he heard a tap at the door.

"Yes?" he called, hoping it was Sara.

The door opened and Sara stood there, looking tired and uncomfortable. She wore a pink and white cotton dress with straps over her shoulders. She brought the wonderful balmy weather in with her. His heart leapt at seeing her.

"Studying? I'll come back later," she said. Her glance lingered on the papers on the bed, lighting up with curiosity.

"Come in," he said, hastily getting up and pushing everything aside.

She walked in, and he went to close the door. She stopped him, saying, "Better leave it open. You know my mother's an old-fashioned woman."

"I'm surprised you let her get away with treating you like a kid. But then, knowing Edna, I guess I'm not that surprised." They chuckled.

"Judith always says that we both should have run away to be hippies when we were teenagers. Somehow, that idea never sounded terribly appealing to me."

"You'd have been perfectly at home—bare feet and all," he said, looking down. Anyway, we leave the door open and we'll be above reproach," he said, feeling foolish but thinking Edna was indeed a wise woman.

"What are you studying?"

"I wasn't studying," he answered and glanced ruefully at the books he'd thrown aside earlier. "I was going over some of the market changes in the past week."

"Oh." She walked to the bed. She touched the guitar, saying, "You know, I can hear you playing sometimes."

"Does it disturb you?"

"Oh, no. I love it." She took a deep breath and changed the subject. "I was going to suggest that if you were ready we could begin the tutoring this evening."

His heart jumped into his mouth. "Sounds good to me."

She tilted her head to look at the papers and he was enchanted with the movement. But he'd thought she was disappointed when he'd said they were stock market information.

She sounded rueful when she spoke, "All of this is Greek to me."

"It's pretty easy once you know the codes," he explained.

"Anyway." She stepped back and turned to him with both arms behind her back. She looked like a woman with something very serious on her mind. "There *is* something else that I came to talk about before we begin."

"Ok-ay." He drew the sounds out, feeling uneasy. His mind raced through all the things she could say to him. He wondered if she realized how obsessed he'd become with her. She might even want to send him away. And that thought made his heart stop.

"I want you to come with me," she said, backing out of his room.

He followed, wondering what he'd done wrong, if she were displeased with him. She stopped in front of the telephone mounted on the wall. There, she pulled a slip of paper from her pocket.

"I want you to call your parents," she said, handing him the piece of paper.

Chapter Five

He glanced at his parents' phone number written there, feeling and probably, he thought, looking stupid. Then, realizing that he was safe, that she wasn't going to send him away, he exhaled in relief.

However, the last thing he needed was to talk to Hugo or Nora. He wanted to balk.

"Now," Sara emphasized, probably because she saw the reluctance on his face.

He had already promised himself that he'd do anything to win her, so without another thought he picked up the receiver and started dialing. She'd given him the number but he didn't need it. True, it had been years, but he hadn't forgotten.

"Mom?" he said when he heard Nora's voice.

"Geoffrey?" She sounded shocked. "Is anything wrong?"

"No, I'm fine. I called to say I'm back in the States."

"Where?" Nora sounded very glad, and it surprised him.

"I'm in Middletown," he said, and glanced at Sara who stood there, listening to every word.

"Middletown?" Now she sounded puzzled.

"I'm with the Turners."

"What are you doing up there?"

The conversation went on as he had to explain, and clue her in on some of the things that had happened. He didn't explain much of why he was there, but he could hear the bewilderment in her voice. Then he spoke to Hugo, who—as was to be expected—was drunk and not quite coherent. It was with his little sisters that he was surprised. They actually seemed to remember him. He felt happy, hearing their little girl squeals, and suddenly realized how much he'd missed them. Then Nora was back on the phone.

"Is Martin or . . . Edna there?"

"No, they're at church on Wednesday nights. Sara's here," he said, regretting it immediately.

"Little Sara?" Nora said, and it sounded as if she suddenly understood something better. "Let me speak with her."

"Well—" He glanced at Sara, who read something in his eyes, for she suddenly looked slightly tense. He didn't want to give the phone to her. He turned away, planning to fob Nora off with some pretext. "Look, Mom, Sara is very busy. She can't talk with—"

Suddenly, Sara touched him and he glanced back at her. She motioned that she'd speak to his mother and took the receiver from him. He felt as if he'd just led the lamb to the slaughter.

"Hello, Nora," Sara said.

"Who's that?" Sara heard Geoff's father's querulous voice in the background.

"It's Sara, Martin's daughter," Nora answered.

"Martin? Let me speak to Martin," Hugo said, his voice slightly slurred.

"It's not Martin. Wait a minute, give me back the telephone," Nora said, and there seemed to be a little scuffle before Hugo came on the phone.

"Martin?" the man said, "You old son of a gun! What're you doing?"

Sara glanced at Geoff before saying, "Hello, Mr. McMillan. It's not Martin. It's Sara, Martin's oldest daughter."

Suddenly Geoff was galvanized beside her. He reached abruptly for the phone but instinctively, she turned away, foiling his efforts. Geoff seemed incredibly anxious, and although he didn't attempt to take the phone again he scowled, and became increasingly more jittery as she spoke with Hugo.

When Sara had mentioned his father's name, Geoff's response had been instantaneous. He'd acted to protect Sara from his father's unpredictable behavior. While there were times when the man could almost be charming, at other moments he would be incredibly crude and disruptive. He'd also feared Sara would be besmirched, fouled, in some way. The thought that she'd see him as Hugo's offspring shamed him. Sara was like a queen to him—a vulnerable flower. He didn't want Hugo to offend her.

Geoff never understood why his mother didn't take his sisters and leave Hugo. The last time he'd spoken with Nora he'd asked that exact question.

The urge to snatch the phone was so powerful that he kept clenching and unclenching his fists. But he didn't want to frighten Sara, and hoped his mother was still capable of controlling his father at the other end. Somehow, Nora had always managed this. Only God knew how she did it. He focused on Sara's response, listening carefully, knowing that the minute she looked strange he would remove the phone from her hand.

The incident brought back scenes from the past, and the old rage seeped into him, bringing with it frustration and hatred. He took several deep breaths.

Sara, who had thought that Hugo wouldn't remember her, was relieved when he said, "Yeah, haha! I remember you. Skinny little thing, right? You're Martin's oldest girl, my goddaughter?"

"That's right." She smiled, pleased that he did remember. Hugo had always called himself her godfather, although, the title was in name only. There had never been any official ceremony. She couldn't imagine Hugo participating in a church event.

"How's your Papa?"

"He's fine."

"Ain't seen him in years. How 'bout you?" he asked in a swift change of subject, "Did you grow up pretty?"

"Well . . ." She didn't know what to say. His words were innocent enough, but he sounded sly and knowing. There was a peculiar undertone about Hugo's question.

"You must have, if Geoff's there. That Geoff, ain't he something?"

She heard the innuendo. It made her uncomfortable but she decided that she was overreacting. When Geoff had tried to take the phone, she'd held on, thinking that he was only excited to speak with his father. She'd actually been teasing, but observing Geoff she wondered if her resistance had been such a good idea. Now she wanted to hand the handset over, but couldn't without it appearing rude to Hugo.

"I said, ain't that boy of mine something?" Hugo repeated when she didn't answer right away.

She responded as carefully as she could. "Yes, he is." Feeling a bit disconcerted, she turned back to Geoff and smiled.

Geoff wasn't sure of what his father had said, but he could see Sara's bemused expression and knew it was time to get her off the hook. He reached out and took the phone, and this time she allowed it.

"Dad, let me speak to Mom," Geoff said when he had the phone. He glanced at Sara and exhaled in relief.

"Haha!" His father's booming laugh echoed in his ear and he moved away from Sara, not wanting her to hear. "So that's why you're there. Little Sara. You getting any of that, Son?

Geoff felt himself seethe, but he didn't want Sara to suspect anything. "Let me speak to Mom," he repeated.

"Geoff's getting into Martin's Sara," Hugo yelled to whoever was standing nearby. Geoff shot a quick glance at Sara, worried that she could hear. The reality of how much he'd come to despise Hugo was brought home to him.

It wasn't long before he was able to end the conversation, and he reluctantly allowed Sara and Nora to speak briefly. By the time it was finished, he was sure that his parents knew that if not for Sara he'd have blown up. He'd managed to calm down, knowing that Sara would be shocked if she saw him in that mood.

She looked bemused, ill at ease. He feared she'd heard Hugo's remarks. It humiliated him. He'd have done anything to wipe that expression off her face.

After the call they went back to his room, kept the door open, and began their first tutoring session. He was still angry, and couldn't settle down.

They had been studying for close to an hour when things changed. Geoff knew it had been a mistake to believe they could study in his room. He had been determined that nothing could happen there in Martin's house, but now he wanted to throw all caution to the wind.

He picked up his guitar and began strumming idly. She didn't say anything but continued trying to focus on the work.

Sara's eyes traveled to Geoff, where he sat cross-legged. He was dressed in his usual outfit of jeans and T-shirt. She'd been annoyed when instead of looking at his book he had picked up his guitar, but she held her tongue. Geoff was bright enough to have no problems keeping track of two things at once. He strummed it absently as he watched her from under hooded eyes. It was quite unnerving.

She often felt she was dealing with a two-sided man. In one, he seemed eager to please, but the other side seemed distanced, dangerous, an angry man who would take advantage of any weakness. Somehow, she almost felt as if the telephone call to his parents had brought out that side of him.

Feeling so aware of his maleness, she grew warm and

overheated in the small room at the back of the house. And worse, she suspected that if he ever guessed her dilemma, he'd push them into an unwise intimacy. She had to retreat from that thought.

Everything would be all right, she reassured herself. She wasn't going to allow anything to happen. Intimacy between them would surely kill their friendship, and that she didn't want to ever happen. This was just a phase, she reassured herself. Geoff wasn't truly interested in her. She pulled her mind back to the play they had been reading.

"What do you think the author was trying to say here?" she asked, more to distract herself than anything.

He looked up at her, and for that split second, she could see each individual hair of his eyelashes. Beneath the lashes, his eyes seemed to hold the secrets of the universe. But it was his mouth that was her undoing. It was pure, molded sensuality. It made her think of love, poetry, and more. He no longer seemed to be Geoff from her childhood. He seemed to be a god. She couldn't breathe for a few seconds.

She started breathing again with a gasp and sudden heaving of her chest, which only made her behavior more erratic. Desperately, she wanted to draw his attention back to the book. Then she looked up and realized that he was watching her stare at his mouth. He gazed into her eyes and she looked back helplessly.

Geoff leaned toward her and softly touched his lips to hers. Her head began to spin and she lost track of where they were. Automatically, her hand fluttered up to touch his chest and he deepened the kiss, molding her mouth to his pleasure.

Her body felt so weak that his mouth almost made her move backward. He put his hands around her face to keep her steady. Heat suffused her body, especially localizing at the apex of her thighs. A tortured throb of need, so swift and strong that she moaned into his mouth, tormented her. He drew her closer and she could feel his heart speed up.

He shifted to take her into his arms, and she fell onto him as if all strength to resist had been drained away. Resist? That was a joke, because there was no chance that she was going to resist.

When his hands cupped her breasts, she pressed herself into his hands and another moan escaped her. Geoff pushed her to lie back on her bed, her head spun faster, and she pulled him down with her. He unclasped her hands from around his neck and placed them on his hard chest. She began to caress him, moving down to his taught abdomen. His skin was smooth and hot to her palms. His eyes closed, and his chest rose on a deep inhalation.

Then he leaned over her and kissed her moistly on her mouth. His tongue entered her mouth, plumbing its depth. He threaded his fingers through her hair and pulled her hair until her chin went back, leaving her throat exposed. His attention left her lips to alternately nip and kiss her throat. Now her stomach was clenched in delicious anticipation. There was something erotically dangerous about baring her throat to his marauding mouth. She felt as if she had put her fate in the care of a ravenous predator. But it didn't matter. Nothing mattered but that she wanted to give herself to this man. The fact that he seemed ready to devour her only added to her eagerness to be his.

"Geoff?" Was that her voice? she wondered. It shocked her with its strange, weakened quality.

Geoff felt himself nearing the point of no return. He had known when he started touching her that he was making a mistake, but was loathe to stop. He hadn't meant for this to happen here but he wanted her so much that he could barely control himself.

He forced himself to release her. A pulse jumped at her throat and she moaned when he pulled his mouth away. She trembled, and even as she drew away she drew him toward her. He had her! She was his—but not here. He realized he couldn't make love to her in Martin's house. It was too much like a betrayal.

When she said his name, he forced himself to let her

go. He was so hard and eager that he felt torn apart. His frustrated desire unnerved him.

He didn't want to totally betray Martin, who was a man of old-fashioned values. *Not in your father's house,* he should have said, but didn't. He intended to keep her for himself. She was so full of sunshine and laughter, and he wanted her so much. He was in torment.

His mind reeled with possibilities. How could he approach Martin? It was insane that he wanted to convince Martin, but he feared that he'd lose Sara if she didn't have her parents' approval.

When he'd withdrawn, she'd begun to move away from him. He desperately wanted to bring her back but knew that if he didn't allow her to go then, he wouldn't be able to allow it later.

Sara was still fuzzy from the passion that pushed everything else out of her head when Geoff moved away from her. She'd almost cried from the separation. But looking up at him, she thought he looked as shocked as she felt. What was this all about? The realization that if he hadn't stopped she would quite likely have allowed him to make love to her frightened her and made her lash out.

"Don't ever do that again!" Sara said, struggling to free her mind from the lethargy. Sitting up, she knew her reaction was unfair as soon as she'd spoken. She yanked her skirt down. She glanced toward the open door. He'd totally forgotten.

"Why not? We both wanted it."

"I'm not one of your women, Geoff. I . . . I know how you are."

"What the hell does that mean?" The swift anger should have alerted him that he was still operating on his hormones, but it didn't seem to help tonight.

"You can't use me to relieve your sex drive."

"You're kidding yourself. You wanted it as much as I did."

"That isn't true," she said, knowing she lied. "And you know that I'm almost engaged."

"If you marry that twerp, you'll be making the mistake of your life."

"Don't call him that. You're just jealous because you're not like him."

"Be like him? Why the hell would I want that? You think you love him? Well, you don't. If you did, you wouldn't have responded to me the way you just did."

"You don't know what you're talking about."

"I know exactly what I'm saying. I know when a women is ready, and you were more than ready."

"That's a lie!"

"Suit yourself," he said, turning away.

"This is not going to work," she said, indicating the books that lay in disarray. I can't tutor you if you act this way."

Geoff shrugged as indifferently as he could manage and picked up the guitar again. She turned and stalked out of his room without another word, leaving him there to fence with his own thoughts.

He wanted to kick himself for starting this tonight. He knew he'd moved too fast, but he couldn't seem to help himself when she was around. He hadn't felt so inept with a woman since he was thirteen, and he'd certainly never wanted one more than he wanted Sara. His need was so strong that he seemed unable to say or do the right thing.

Now, he'd just sent her away like a scalded rabbit, probably right into Chuck's arms. That thought so enraged him that he dumped the guitar onto the bed and decided that he'd better get out of the house before he made a complete fool of himself. Fortunately Martin and Edna hadn't come home during that time.

Two weeks later, Sara picked up the phone to hear Chuck suggest, "How about a movie?"

"Not tonight," Sara answered. "I'm too tired."

She had been avoiding Chuck because she was ambivalent about her feelings since responding so heatedly to

Geoff. For days, she'd anguished over what it could mean. Everyone expected her to marry Chuck—everyone except Geoff. She was so confused that she'd been walking around in a fog.

"You're working too hard. You should be focusing on your master's now."

"Maybe when I return to school in September, I'll cut down," she said.

"You need to get out. You've been too busy lately," he insisted. "Come on. We'll take a drive if you don't want to see a show."

"Well . . ."

"Come on. It'll be good for you."

"Okay," she agreed. A drive didn't sound so much like a date, she thought.

He picked her up and they drove along the lakeside. It was a nice way to spend the evening, and didn't require much from her. Neither of them had spoken much until he was parked in front of her house. As they walked to the porch, where they had often finished off their dates, she was on edge, thinking about Geoff. She had seen very little of him since the night they'd called his parents and he'd almost made love to her. She'd heard him go out that night but had been asleep before he'd returned.

Chuck moved to kiss her on the mouth and she turned her face, presenting her cheek. He paused and withdrew.

"Now what's wrong?" he asked, sounding annoyed.

"I don't feel like it."

"You never feel like it any more. Ever since. . . ." He glanced quickly at the house but didn't finish the sentence.

"We're not married, Chuck. I don't have to."

"That's a good point. When are we going to get married?"

It took her a long time to answer but finally she drew a deep breath and said, "Chuck, I can't do it. I can't marry you."

She realized that she'd already made the decision before she heard the words leave her mouth. She had been reluc-

tant, and feared that by not having admitted this in the
beginning she was leading him on, but she hadn't done
it deliberately. It was simply that Geoff had been right
when he'd insisted she wouldn't marry Chuck. And it had
taken her this long to accept it.

"What do you mean?" Chuck asked quietly.

"It would be a mistake. We're not right for each other."

"Why not?"

"I don't know. I'm so confused."

"As you've been since Geoff came."

"That's not fair, and it's not true, either. You knew I
was having doubts before," Sara said.

"Just jitters."

"No, that's *not* what it is. There's always been something
missing."

"What?"

She wanted to say passion, but bit her lip. "I don't
know," she finally equivocated, "I just know it's missing."

"How come you're just finding this out now?"

"It's been there all the time. That's why I didn't say yes
before."

"Well, I think we're a good match. We like the same
things. We get along well. We've worked on various church
committees together—"

"It's not enough."

"It used to be."

"No, it wasn't. I need more than that. *You* need more,
too. It isn't your fault—it's me. You deserve a woman who
knows what she wants."

"All right," he said, cutting her off. "Don't be patroniz-
ing about it. I know what *I* want."

"I'm sorry," she said, wringing her hands.

"Think it over. Don't make a decision right now."

"No, Chuck, I *have* thought it over. I feel as if I'd cheat
you, and you deserve someone who loves you." There,
she'd said it.

"And you don't?"

"I'll always love you—but not the way you deserve. I'll always admire and respect you—"

He cut her off. "Okay, I get the picture. It's Geoff, isn't it?"

"No!"

"Sara, it's okay if you don't marry me, but don't get involved with *him*. You're a softhearted, gentle girl. You need someone to take care of you."

"Chuck, I'm not a child and I'm not a weakling, either. You're wrong about Geoffrey. No one understands him. He's not what you think. He's good . . . but sometimes he hides it." She stopped, realizing that defending Geoff to Chuck wasn't what she had intended. "Geoff isn't the reason that I'm refusing your proposal. I told you that I wasn't sure when you first proposed. There's nothing like that between Geoff and me."

Actually, she wasn't sure anymore what there was between her and Geoff. At one time they'd been friends. but what was this new development? For herself, she knew that it was simply the girlish crush from her childhood, but what was going on with Geoff? Why was he doing this? What did he hope to gain? Could they ever be just friends again?

"Maybe not now, but if he has anything to do with it there will be," Chuck said.

"I know he's difficult at times, but that's just the way he is. It hasn't anything to do with me."

"We'll see," Chuck said.

Chuck took a deep breath and exhaled. He leaned back against the wall, looking out across the lawn.

"I'm going upstairs, she said, but stood there waiting. She wasn't sure what she expected, but she wanted closure somehow.

Chuck glanced at her once. Then he pushed off from the wall, and walked down the steps. Before heading toward his car he turned and said quietly, "I hope you know what you're doing."

On Saturday, almost a week later, she met Geoffrey one morning as she was leaving the house.

"How's the fiancé?" he said, sarcasm coming through the remark.

"He's fine," she said, suddenly afraid of this new Geoff. She hadn't told anyone about breaking up with Chuck yet, and certainly didn't want to tell Geoff.

He stared at her through hooded, sexy eyes. She was standing close to the wall, and he'd crowded her when his arm went over her. She turned her head, following his progress, but he only placed his palm against the wall behind her. When she turned her head back, he was nearer and leaning toward her. There was a strange menace as he came closer. She stared back, immobilized. She could smell his clean, healthy scent.

His kissed her with a driving force that pushed her head back under the insistence of that demand. After a moment of total acquiescence she tried to twist away, but he leaned into her, pushing her against the wall, captured from lips to thighs, while he deepened the kiss.

His hands moved on her, up and down—under her hair, caressing her nape, her throat. She felt lightheaded, as if she weren't breathing. Heat suffused her body and she trembled under his onslaught. His marauding exploration of her body became more possessive while his kiss became more urgent. His hands cupped her breasts, and she gasped.

She hadn't expected to ever experience the way Geoff made her feel. Her own physical reaction engulfed her, and she made no further resistance after that first attempt to escape. Her eyes closed and her hands rested against the heat of his flesh.

It was as if just the touch of her hands against him was communicating to her. The heat of him was beating into her, until they were united, almost as if one person. She felt the rhythm of their hearts, merging into one aching, unrelenting drumbeat. She arched against him, inviting him to take her further. All her senses were ready to join

with him. Her mouth allowed his tongue to enter, and
they were fused together further.

Her legs felt weak and she would have slid down the
wall had he not held her pinned there. When Geoff finally
lifted his head, his body was still pressed against hers,
anchoring her to the wall. Her head felt cloudy and she
wondered if she would faint.

Her knees gave out and she slid downward. He pulled
her upward, using his hands under her arms until she was
supported by the wall. She leaned there until she felt stable.
Geoff stepped backward, one hand held toward her to
catch her should she slide down again. She had never been
so humiliated in all her life.

He looked around furiously and then his eyes came back
to her. A cruelty rose in them and when he opened his
mouth to speak, she knew he was going to hurt her.

Sudden tears sprang to her eyes but she batted them
back. She refused to let Geoff see how much he hurt her.
She knew him only too well. Even though she hadn't seen
him in years, stories traveled. She knew he'd gone through
more women than she could imagine. When she'd spoken
to Hugo, she'd sensed that was what Hugo wanted to say.
Geoff was only playing with her, while she was more shaken
than she'd ever been in her life.

"Planning to take this to Chuck?" he said nastily.

Chapter Six

"What are you talking about?"

"Are you going to take this passion to Chuck? Are you going to make him the beneficiary of my arousing you?"

"You're disgusting. Do you know that?" she spat at him. "And if you don't stop this you can leave here right now, and I won't ever speak to you again."

"What's the matter? Am I too rough on you? Not enough like Chuck?"

"I don't want to talk about this."

"No, I'll bet you don't. Have you told him, yet?" She was bewildered. He searched her face and continued. "Have you told Chuck how much you want me?"

"I don't need this," she said, putting her palms over her ears as if she were still a child.

He pulled her hands away. "Want me to do it? Good old Chuck looks like an understanding man. Anyway, he ought to know you're a hot number by now."

Sara shook at the thought of Geoff telling someone what had happened between them today. "You'd do something like that?"

"Yes, maybe I'd do it to tear you away from him."

It was the last thing she expected him to say, and he looked surprised, too. But she knew it was simply Geoff having one of his old tantrums.

"Take your hands off me!"

"Whoa! I've got a tigress in my arms," he sneered. "What did I do?" Touch a nerve?"

"Leave me alone."

"You don't really mean that, do you?"

"Yes, I do."

He grabbed her and kissed her hard again, pressing her head backward. At first his hands roamed freely over her body and then he cupped her breast, flicking the nipples with a fingernail through her clothes. And even this contact caused her knees to weaken again. She shoved against him, but as she did he stepped back.

"I don't think you really want me to stop." He laughed. Pure contempt seemed to emanate from him.

She slapped him as hard as she could, and would have hit him with the other hand but he snared both and yanked her against him.

"Quit while you're still ahead," he threatened.

"I hate you."

He stood away from her, releasing her hands. "Sure, you do, baby." He laughed again as he walked away, heading toward his downstairs bedroom.

Trembling with impotent rage, she spoke before he could close his door. "For your information, and I hope you're happy for ruining everything since you've come, I broke up with Chuck. You break everything that you touch, *just like your father*." She wasn't sure why she'd said that, but she could see instantly that he was hurt and furious. He swung back toward her and he looked ready for murder. A hard satisfaction cut its icy path into her heart. "Why don't you move out and leave us alone?"

Before she could break down she escaped outside and sat in her car. Her hands trembled and it took her a long time before she could trust herself to drive.

His cruelty did make her admit one thing. While she

hadn't believed Geoff would make good his threat, she was glad that she'd broken up with Chuck.

Geoff watched her rush to escape him. Why had he said the things he'd spoken? he wondered. He hadn't realized that he would until he heard the words himself. She had looked as shocked as he'd felt. *Why was he threatening her? Was he that insane?* He wanted to break something, anything, and had actually looked around for something before he brought himself under control.

He'd never realized that a woman could hurt him as much as she'd done today. He felt as if she'd stuck a knife in him.

And of course, she was right, Geoff thought. Why had he attacked her? Because he was laced through with jealousy. Or maybe he just wanted to control her. But he remembered her as a little girl, and knew that while Sara might appear soft and yielding, she wasn't. She wouldn't put up with his trying to control her.

She had her moments, but she could be tough—very tough. As a kid, she'd been so passive, and let him lead, while she would be his willing follower. However, there was always the danger that for some irrelevancy she would turn and ambush him with blood in her eye. The memory almost took his mind off the cruel, hurtful words they'd just traded. It almost even made him smile.

Several days later, Sara opened the side door and entered the kitchen to find Edna preparing dinner for that night. She was so tired that she muttered a hasty greeting and moved through the kitchen quickly, stepping into the hallway. She would have immediately gone upstairs had not Edna spoken behind her.

"I saw Chuck at the mall, today," Edna said, having followed her into the hall. Sara stopped and turned to face her mother. Not knowing what to say, she waited for Edna to continue. "What do you have to say for yourself?"

"It's a long story, Mother."

"Didn't you think the fact that you broke your engagement was important enough to tell your father and me?"

"There *was* never any real engagement. You always knew that. And I was going to tell you—"

"When? Next month? Next year?"

"I'm just not up to talking about it now."

"Don't you know how much this will upset your father? Both of you girls suddenly acting like this? And don't think I don't know what's going on with Judith."

Sara suddenly remembered promising her sister to speak with their parents. It was just one more thing that she'd failed at this summer.

"And that Geoff moved out today—just left precipitously, taking all his belongings. All he could say was that he didn't want to disturb us when he worked through the night. Humph, some excuse. After all your father tried to do. He's staying at the Carlton Motel out on Route One," Edna said, changing the subject. Sara was too numb to react. In truth, she had expected something like this. "Geoff's the reason you and Chuck broke up, isn't he?"

"No," Sara said, but knew that her answer was too dispirited to convince anyone.

They both stopped when sound of Martin's key at the side door reached them. Sara stood at the foot of the stairs, wanting desperately to go to her room, but she waited. They turned to watch him enter the hall. Suddenly the small area was too close to contain the three of them, and Sara inhaled as if unable to get enough air.

Martin glanced at them, sensing the tension. "What's wrong here?" he asked mildly as he placed the newspaper he'd been carrying onto the hall table.

Edna spoke, "She's broken off her engagement with Chuck. What are you going to do?"

Martin's glance moved from Edna and briefly to Sara. Then he took off his hat and hung it on a peg on the wall before answering, "I don't see anything I *can* do about that. Edna."

He retrieved his paper and moved toward the living room. Edna was on his heels. Sara trailed after her parents.

"Is that all you've got to say?" Edna demanded, her anger shifting from her daughter to her husband.

"I didn't know it was a formal engagement. I thought it was something they were considering," Martin said.

"Can't you see what's happening?" Edna asked.

"Edna, it's their business. They're both grown. If they don't want to be married, this is the time for them to decide. Would you rather they were married before they realized it was a mistake?"

"You don't understand anything!" Edna raged and stormed back into the kitchen, where she commenced to bang pots around.

Martin glanced across the room at Sara. "Is there any chance that you'll go back together?" He looked so hopeful that she wanted to cry.

"No, Daddy."

He looked away from her momentarily before coming back to say, "Are you all right?"

"Yes."

"Do you want to talk about it?"

"Not now," she said, and her voice trembled slightly. Tears stung the back of her eyes.

Martin looked at her sadly for a moment before slowly sitting down in his favorite chair. She sensed that his disappointment over the broken engagement was monumental, perhaps even more than Edna's, but he was a quiet man. He laid the paper on his lap, unopened, and gazed down at it.

"Sometimes, I can't understand you young people at all. You're like a pale shadow of your old self, and Judith never comes home anymore. Now, Geoff, without any sensible explanation, just ups and moves out."

Not being able to bear any more, she said good-night and went upstairs.

That night she dreamed about Geoffrey, a dream so powerfully erotic that she awoke crying. For days, she could barely function, her thoughts dwelled on him so often. She found herself going into the room where he'd stayed just to look around.

She opened the closets, wanting to smell some residue of him, but Edna had cleaned and scoured the room. It was as if he'd never been there. Finally, one evening, she felt compelled to seek him out. Driving to the motel where he was registered, she wondered why she was doing this. True, she regretted what she'd said, but he'd been just as cruel to her.

She simply couldn't leave it as it had happened. She needed to explain, but wasn't certain what that would entail.

Am I kidding myself? What makes me think there's anything that I can say to Geoff?

At the door to his room she paused, making several abortive movements to knock before her knuckles made contact with the door.

Geoff's door flew open and he stood there, wearing well washed jeans and the black leather vest over his bare chest. She stepped into his arms and stood there, neither of them speaking.

His embrace was gentle and he said softly, "What took you so long? I've been waiting for you."

With his words, the truth of why she'd come hit her. She loved him—she'd always loved him, no matter what happened. To him, she would probably be just one more conquest, but if she couldn't have Geoff there would never be anyone else. That was how much power he had over her.

Trembling, she reached up to touch his cheek where his beard had begun to grow, and he took her hand and kissed her palm, running his tongue over it. She put both arms around his neck and drew him down to her. Going on tiptoe, she pressed her mouth to his. He placed both hands on her hips and drew her between his spread legs, where she could feel his erection pressing into her stomach. She kissed him, her tongue foraging in his sweet mouth, and his chest rose on a quick inhalation of breath.

His hands slid to her buttocks and he lifted her, stepping back from the open doorway. She realized that, using his foot, he'd kicked the door shut behind them. Then he slowly lowered her to her feet. Swiftly, he caught her up under the knees and carried her to the bed. It happened so suddenly that her mind was still in a whirl when he lowered her to the smooth sheets below.

He stood over her, gazing down with unabashed desire. Feeling an urgency that shocked her, she rose upward, beckoning him to her. Then she put her arms around him and pulled him to join her on the bed. They lay down still clothed, and crushed together from mouth to hip.

"I want you," he whispered huskily, his hand coming to caress her chin.

She clutched the vest and pulled it from his body, and he let her. She pressed her mouth against his small, flat nipples and heard his sharp intake of air. His forefinger ran across her lips, and she drew it into the recesses of her mouth and his eyes turned smokey. His fingertips played with her nipples through her blouse, and the feel of the fabric against the sensitive, hardened nubs made her pant.

"I love you," he said, his voice becoming more raspy, "I want you."

She stopped, her gaze flying wildly to his face. It was so unexpected that she was dumbfounded. It only made her want him more. He lifted the bottom of the shirt up a few inches. Then he unbuttoned her jeans.

She was hot to remove her clothes and to feel him take her in all his powerful heat. When she went to pull her shirt up, it caught in the links of her gold chain. She would have torn it away. He stopped her and had the presence of mind to efficiently untangle her hair before carefully rolling the lightweight sweater over her head. Her bra followed like magic.

She desperately tried to loosen the big silver buckle of his belt, becoming increasingly frustrated until he came to her rescue. And though he was hurried and his hands shook, he was more in control than she was.

By now she was like an animal in heat, wanting him more than she had ever imagined possible. He cupped her breasts, gently weighing them in his palms like two precious treasures, and lathed them with the balm of his mouth, alternating drawing upon both nipples. It drove her crazy. Her need became electrical, coursing through her body in shocking, exquisite waves of urgent pleasure.

He peeled her jeans off like a second skin, with his own following quickly. He rained hot, passionate kisses on her abdomen, moving downward to the tight curls that snuggled over her sex, where he buried his face. He found that most sensitive organ and gently stroked it until her flesh felt scorched. Unquenchable fires stirred as he worshipped her body with hot, passionate kisses. Her breath came in sharp gasps, and she moaned, unable to stop herself.

She thrashed beneath him when he slipped between her legs. He lifted her buttocks and pulled her closer. She arched up to meet him.

"I want you," he chanted like a pagan to a deity.

Then he thrust into her slippery, wet core, sheathing himself to the hilt. Then, after a moment of exquisite sensation, began the rhythmic dance of love, each potent advance and withdrawal turning her to melted desire. Catching his rhythm, she arched toward him, consumed by her own ardor, striving for that ultimate release. Her body was in the throes of the most powerful tension when suddenly she crested, with a cry at the unbridled pleasure.

Long moments later, she shuddered back into awareness. Before she could fully come to her senses, Geoff, who had not withdrawn, pushed himself into her farther, and she was rising again as he pushed and pulled her back to that crest again—this time more agonizing, more exquisite than before.

He didn't move, and they were still merged flesh to

flesh. He rested his forehead on the pillow beside her. She lie there totally satiated and near to dozing off. Her thoughts went to his saying that he loved her and she wondered if she dared hope. Geoff's saying those words didn't necessarily mean what she would mean by them. For him it could be something that he said to anyone while in the throes of passion.

"Was it Chuck?" he asked. "You've been making it with him?"

"What?"

"This wasn't your first time," he stated, and rose to stare into her eyes, his face a cold mask. She was bewildered, and wondered where this was going to take them. "Who else?"

"That isn't your business," she said, unwilling to believe they were arguing again. She tried to move from under him, noticing now how sweaty they were and suddenly feeling the sticky sheets enmeshing them.

"Let me up," she demanded, but he held her captive.

"I want to know. Tell me!"

"Don't do this. What did you expect? That I was waiting for you?"

"Yes! That's exactly what I expected."

"The last time I saw you, you were covered in black leather and driving that motorcycle straight to hell, and you seemed glued frontally to that redhead."

She'd thought she'd forgotten that. She'd told herself it didn't matter, but here it was. The memory had simply gone underground to jump out at her today.

It made him stop and he moved to release her, rising when she did. She jumped up and rushed to collect her clothes and then realized that she didn't want to dress in front of him, in her highly agitated state. She held her clothes in front of her.

She realized that she felt like a complete fool. She didn't know what to say, what position to take. Lord, she wished the last hour had never happened.

When she tried to pass him and get into the bathroom,

he barred her. He grabbed her upper arm and pulled her roughly to him.

"How many others?"

She attempted to disengage herself, but his powerful fingers bit into her arm. She'd never been more humiliated in her life, standing there, the two of them totally nude. She wanted to hit him, but knew she'd be no match for him. "Let me go!" She heard the pending tears in her voice, which only made her angrier.

He released her and she fled into the bathroom, where she hurriedly put on her clothes. Dressed, she at least felt slightly more in control. She opened the door, determined to leave. She was glad to see that he'd pulled on his jeans

"You didn't answer my question," he said when she stepped into the room.

"Geoff, this is the most irrational argument you've ever started. You, of all people, have no right to ask that of me."

"I have every right," he snarled, but he released her and she rubbed her arm.

"What about you? Everyone knows you've been through enough women to keep several men busy."

"We're not talking about me."

"Oh, I forgot. You're a man. You can do whatever you want. But I'm just a woman."

"That's right."

"Drop dead," she said.

"Why didn't Martin stop it?"

"Would you stop this? You sound medieval. I'm old enough."

"If you didn't want me, why did you call?"

"Call?"

"Your chatty little note? Why did you send it? You hadn't written in over three years, so why then?"

"You're beginning to sound like my mother. It was just a note."

"Why didn't you write before you went to bed with someone else?"

She grabbed up her purse and checked for her car keys. "Where are you going?" he demanded.

"Home!" she snapped back.

Sara realized that it was her fault. He didn't want her as she did him. Sex to Geoff was a simple, hedonistic pleasure, while she knew it meant more to her. Geoff had never learned how to relate to women. In truth, even if he had, she shouldn't have gotten involved. She needed time to reevaluate after the break-up with Chuck. She needed to adjust to what it meant. Despite her knowing Geoff since they were children, they were too different. He was into stocks, and bonds, while she was committed to people. She was like her father in that way.

She faced him coolly, waiting for him to speak.

"You use birth control?" he asked without preamble.

"Yes," she said.

It was like a dash of cold water in his face. *Of course, she would,* he thought. Sara was a smart woman, not an untried girl. But he hadn't expected her to be so composed about it.

"Don't let it worry you. I'm a big girl," she said, adding, "I can handle myself."

There wasn't much he could say to that. She walked past him and picked up her sweater and purse, heading for the door.

He followed and she rounded on him, saying, "I have my car. I'll get myself home."

"I'm going to follow you there."

"Why?" she demanded hotly.

"Because I want to," he answered.

She shrugged as she went to her car and started it up. Then, without another word, she pulled onto Route One, heading east. He tailed her to her house, seeing her into her front door, before turning back.

"To hell with this," he said, throwing his keys against the wall. *So you lose some and you win some.* He wanted to call the whole thing quits. Best to leave now. No woman was worth all this pain. But instead of packing and heading out, he lay atop the spread and had a cigarette. He chain-smoked several.

Sara spent the rest of the night, listening to records and trying not to castigate herself too harshly. She pulled out all her own favorite records and lined them up to play. There were The Temptations, Roberta Flack, The Chilites, Simpson and Ashford, The Commodores, Dionne Warwick, Billy Ocean, and every other performer that she'd ever cried along with.

Once, she remembered him saying that he loved her, but knew that was probably something that he said to every woman he took to bed.

The strained atmosphere of the house remained unabated during the next few days as Sara went about working and spending much of her spare time at the Student Center. When she arrived home at night, her parents were usually in bed or sitting in the living room, watching television. The time she spent with her family was mercifully short. She couldn't tolerate the tension or their unhappiness, and had deliberately waited until she thought her parents would be asleep.

It was her father's pain that she dreaded the most. She could see that Martin was still hurt, although he attempted to put a good face on things. He was not a man who would try to force his opinion on his children. Edna was a different matter. Whenever they were in the house together, her mother launched into another spate of angry questions.

Sara unlocked the side door quietly, walking through to the hallway. There was a lamp lit in the living room, but at a quick glance the room appeared unoccupied. She checked the mail and was at the foot of the stairs when she heard a small sound behind her.

"Sara?"

She swung around to find Judith standing there.

"Judith! When did you get here?" Her younger sister's

disheveled appearance shocked her. Judith's skin was ashen, and she looked tired and ill. She wore an old, battered, chenille robe. Judith's eyes were swollen as if she'd been crying, and she reached out, wrapping her arms around Sara. "What's wrong? Are you hurt?"

"No," Judith answered, stepping back and wiping her eyes with a crumpled tissue. "I'm all right, but I'm just so glad to see you." Judith clutched at her, pulling her into the living room. They sat together on the couch.

"Why are you crying?" Sara said, holding her sister.

"I broke up with Larry." Judith blew her nose.

"I'm so sorry. What happened?"

"And . . ." Judith started crying again, "I had an abortion."

"Oh, Judith. Why didn't you come to me?"

"Whatever for?" her sister said, taking a deep breath and drying her tears once more. "You can't solve everyone's problems."

"Does Mother know?" Sara said, remembering Edna's remarks from a few days ago. When Judith denied this, Sara said, "Judith, she knows something." Then, changing the subject, she said, "You need to talk about this. Don't try to stuff it away."

"You're right, but not now," Judith said. "Give me some time?"

"All right," Sara said, trying not to probe. She remembered telling her parents exactly what Judith said to her tonight about needing time. But Sara was genuinely worried about her sister, and that worry prompted her to say, "But we will talk about it, right?"

Judith nodded. Then, taking a deep breath, she settled back and said, "What's this I hear about you breaking your engagement?"

Sara moved back at the sudden change. "You know it wasn't a true engagement."

"Tell me about it." Judith curled up, wrapping her arms around her raised knees. "Help me take my mind off my own troubles. Besides, you shouldn't stuff it, either."

"I can't marry Chuck because . . ." Before fully realizing what she was going to say, she blurted out "Because I love Geoff."

"Geoffrey? Oh, Sara, even I know how crazy that is." They were both quiet for long moments before Judith spoke again, "Is that why he left? Have you two been lovers?"

Sara nodded, "Lovers is too glorified a word for what we've been." Now, *she* wanted to join Judith and have a good cry, herself, but, she had cried about as much as she was going to over that incident with Geoff. Now was time to cut her losses and move on.

"Everyone knows how hard he is on women," Judith said.

"I know, but I can't seem to help it."

"Lord, for once I don't envy you. At least with Larry, my problems are all finished. Give me a few weeks and I'll be over him. Although, I can't help regretting . . . you know . . ."

"Yes," Sara answered, putting her arms around her sister.

"But you," Judith said, laying her head on Sara's shoulder, "Will you ever get over Geoffrey?"

Chapter Seven

Later that night, Sara was in bed when she remembered confronting Geoff about his nineteenth birthday party. The incident had occurred five years ago, and Hugo had invited all of them to attend. She had been excited because it was good to see them, since the two families had grown apart over the years. Also, a visit with the McMillans always meant sophistication and even meeting celebrities.

Martin drove them to Manhattan, and although, she'd been born there, there was little that she remembered except its glamor and dirt. Judith told and retold, in perfect detail, every innocent word that Geoff had said to her on his last visit. But while Sara might have had the remnants of a crush, she was dating real flesh and blood men by then, so it didn't really mean that much. Admittedly, she had still been sending out the occasional note and receiving little in return, but after this party it was several years before she wrote again and then, only Christmas cards. Once or twice, he had responded with brief postcards. Geoff had never been much for writing.

While Sara had been excited about seeing Geoff, she had also been excited to see his whole family. She had changed a great deal. She had remained slim, but at least men paid attention to her because she had finally filled out and had breasts and hips now, such as they were. Also, she had a job and was a junior—talk about gaining status. She had even gone to Spain on her high school senior field trip, so she felt like a woman of the world. Anyway, it had to count for something, or so she thought.

Being all together again was truly great. Nora was as slim as ever, while Edna had put on a few pounds and had become rounded. Judith, at fifteen, had turned into a lush beauty.

Hugo and Dad spent a great deal of time laughing and patting each other's stomachs, though in truth Hugo didn't seem any bigger than the last time she'd seen him. At first Geoff wasn't there, and despite her having grown up so much her heart fell a little with disappointment.

Unfortunately, when Geoff did come in, she was even more disappointed. He was as gorgeous as ever—more so—but he had changed, too. He wore black leather and silver, and managed to look quite dangerous. His hair was puffed out in a huge, curly Afro. Judith was mesmerized, and it was only her determination not to be gauche that kept Sara from staring, too. Of course, he teased Judith, which was nothing new. The thing that really annoyed her was that this time, he had teased her, too. It was as if she had been relegated to being a little sister. It irked her, and not the least because she felt he was showing off for the woman that he had brought with him.

The woman was everything that Sara had always wanted to be, including older. She was beautiful with long, red hair. Hugo and Nora seemed to approve. Her own parents were somewhat reserved.

Sara expected that Judith would be merciless in her teasing when they got home. Judith and Sara had a good relationship—considering what she had seen of other sisters—but sometimes her younger sibling could be a real pain.

Geoff had received the motorcycle that he rode now. It

was a present from his parents, and with the leather outfit
he wore it really made quite a splash. She wouldn't be
sending out any more pen pal letters, she had thought
with a vague sense of regret. She was actually surprised
when she realized that Geoff's having a life so totally
removed from hers had put a pall on her fun that day.

As for the rest of her family, everyone except Judith
seemed *not* to enjoy that day as much as they had expected,
and all for different reasons. Her father was now a minister
in his own church, and her parents had outgrown the wild
party scene. They had become quite committed to their
own lives. They appeared to have forgotten that they had
once participated in the same sort of bashes. It was as if that
party, instead of bringing the two families closer, actually
sounded the death knell for their family get-togethers.

Sara had been on the verge of calling Geoff ever since
that night, and she had managed to refrain only with the
most determined resolution. *What a fool I am, waiting by
the phone like an obsessed teenager.* There was no reason to
call him. Not when he had made his feelings so clear. She
couldn't believe that it had all been about his not being
her first lover. That was too insane. There had to be
another reason.

Had he simply lost respect for her for giving in to him,
or had that been all that he truly wanted from her? It was
so shabby, she thought. Everyone knew about Geoff and
his women. As a kid, he'd had grown women run after
him. Everyone had laughed, thinking it funny—everyone
but her own parents. Now she had become one of his easy
conquests.

It had probably only been an impulse for Geoff, or maybe
he'd sensed her frustration. She regretted the incident
more than she'd thought possible. How could it not change
their relationship forever?

Because she was lonely and feeling out of sorts, she went
out with Bob Healy, one of her coworkers at the center.

They went to an open air concert, held in a nearby city. She was glad to have something to distract her. It wasn't a date. As confused as she'd been during the last few weeks, the last thing she needed was a date. Whatever it was, she'd wanted to go. True, it didn't do what she'd wanted. It didn't make her forget Geoff. Right in the midst of Bob's best efforts, Geoff's face kept drifting into her mind.

They stopped for burgers at a diner and discussed the concert. Even here, she was barely able to keep herself from daydreaming about Geoff. It wasn't easy, but it was a beginning, and she believed that it would get easier.

She was glad that she had gotten out of the house on that warm summer night. Glad until she happened to look across the diner and wound up staring right into Geoff's hooded, smoldering eyes. At first she thought it was her imagination, for she'd been seeing Geoff's face everywhere in the last few days. But then it registered that this time it wasn't her imagination.

He was sitting in a booth with a loud group of summer students who'd also attended the concert. There was a beautiful young woman with him, dressed in black leather with loads of silver jewelry. She had her head on his shoulder and her hand inside his vest, but he was staring narrow-eyed across the room at her and Bob. She looked away quickly, a mixture of emotions running through her.

She was glad to have seen him like this because it punched holes through all her illusions. This Geoff wasn't her childhood friend. He looked dangerous, exactly the type of man she avoided, a man out for trouble. She had to admit that she was jealous of his companion, but she needed it. It was proof positive that she had to get on with her life and stop mooning over him. She made herself a promise—she was going to stop obsessing over Geoffrey McMillan.

From that moment on, she religiously kept her thoughts from straying to him. She chatted with Bob as if her life depended upon her being titillating. Bob was puzzled, having never seen her in such an up mood before.

On the drive home, Bob looked into the rearview mirror and said, "There's a motorcycle behind us. He's been there since we left the diner."

Sara's heart lurched and an ominous dread descended upon her as she jerked around to look out the window.

There he was, a lone dark rider, coming up behind them.

The rider looked alien with the smokey shield of his helmet. It didn't have to be Geoff, she told herself. There were other summer students who had cycles. But she knew it was Geoff.

He picked up speed and came around Bob's side. There he motioned for Bob to pull over. One look at Geoff's face made her know that he was out of control. Bob hesitated and Geoff moved ahead and swerved in front of the car, forcing them to either slow down and stop or to plough into him. It was an insane, almost suicidal act. Bob braked suddenly. She screamed while Bob cursed.

Geoff got off the big Harley and walked slowly around to the driver's side. Sara found her heart pounding against her ribs. "Come out," Geoff snarled to Bob.

"What . . . what . . . ?" Bob stammered. "You stopped in front of me," Bob said, not understanding what the incident was about.

"Geoff, what's wrong with you?" she said, trying to head off what was happening. Fear made her heart race.

Bob's head snapped around to stare at her in confusion. "You know him?" She was too frightened to take her attention from Geoff, and only nodded spastically to Bob's question.

Geoff never acknowledged her question, but again demanded of Bob, "Come out."

"What does he want?" Bob said, his voice quavery.

"I don't know," she answered, feeling as terrified as Bob sounded. She couldn't believe the whole incident was somehow about her.

Geoff grabbed the car and began to rock it, shaking them from side to side. When Bob didn't come out, Geoff grabbed the other man's shirt front and said, "Are you coming out, or do I have to drag you out?"

Sara opened the passenger door and stepped out onto the tarmac. "Geoff, please, why are you doing this?"

When she was out of the automobile, Geoff looked across the car at her and released Bob. Then he slapped the top of the car and said, "Get out of here."

"You listen here . . ." Bob spluttered ineffectively.

Sara looked through the passenger window and said to the frightened man, "It's okay, Bob, you go on." She grabbed her purse and closed the door.

"You're going to stay here with him?" Bob said, shocked.

"He's a friend," she said.

"Friend? Well, it's your funeral."

"Yes," she answered, her voice fading.

Bob started the engine and reversed away from the Harley that lay directly in his path. He drove around Geoff and the bike, flooring the accelerator as soon as his way was clear. He left skid marks where he drove away.

"Crazy hoodlum!" Bob shouted when he'd moved some distance away.

For long moments after Bob was gone, Sara and Geoff stared at each other, not moving from where they stood. She had begun to cry the minute Geoff had swerved in front of them. Tears rolled down her face as she tried to wipe them away with her hands.

Finally, Geoff spoke. "Don't ever do that again," he said in an expressionless voice.

"I won't," she answered, somehow knowing exactly what he was talking about.

"Not ever."

"Not ever," she repeated, and knew that she had promised. She hadn't asked what he meant because she knew already.

She stumbled toward him, then, and rushed to pound on his chest, the tears coursing down her cheeks. He pulled her into his arms.

"He could have killed you!" she screamed. "He could

have killed you in a stupid macho accident. And it would have been your own fault.''

Geoff marveled at her rage. Looking at where the bike lay, he knew that she was right. It had been insane of him to challenge someone like that. He could have died if the other man hadn't had fast reflexes. It scared him. Suddenly, he went icy cold.

"Don't you ever do that again," she said, echoing him.

He almost couldn't believe he had done it. He didn't want to die—certainly not now with Sara in his arms—but even without Sara. Suddenly, he shuddered with the realization of how close he had come to death. More than anything, he wanted to live. He wanted to watch starry nights and small yellow flowers with minute insects obtaining nectar. She could teach him how to look at them. Even if he never had her for his own, he owed her for a gift he could never repay. She'd shown him that there was life out there. He wanted to live out every one of the days granted him, and if he could live it with this woman, it would only be made sweeter.

"I won't," he promised, and knew it was the truth.

Could a woman bring the stars? Yes, a woman could even bring life. He had too much to live for with this woman at his side.

Sara felt clean and resigned, as if after a prolonged cry. Her heart felt as if all things had already been fixed, yet she knew that the true fight was just beginning. He led her confidently to his motorcycle and handed her a helmet, which she snapped on. There was no longer any sign of the rage that had consumed him earlier.

She swung her leg over the seat and and sat behind Geoff.

"It's going to be all right," he reassured her upon viewing her saddened face.

She tried to smile back but she didn't answer. Instead, she wrapped her arms around him and pressed her face against his back. He started the engine and turned onto the highway. They were both silent for the entire ride.

When they slowed and took a turn, she put her head up and asked, "Where are we?"

"You're home," he said.

"Oh." She was disappointed. She'd been wishing that the ride would go on forever, or at least that they'd find some hide-a-way where they could be alone.

She got off and removed the helmet. Geoff got off, too.

"I'm going in with you."

He parked and put the kickstand down then hung the helmets on the handlebar.

"Okay."

"I'm going to speak with Martin."

That alarmed her. "What about?"

"Us. He needs to know."

"We can tell him some other time," she said in a near panic.

"I don't want to wait," Geoff insisted.

"You know how they are. Let me talk to them first . . ."

Before they could say more, the front door opened and Martin and Edna stood there, looking taut with worry.

"Where've you been?" her mother demanded.

"Judith's in the hospital," her father said in a tight, frightened voice.

"Why? What happened?" Sara said.

"She began to bleed," Edna said.

"Oh, no! Is she all right?"

"Yes, she's stable, but they're keeping her for observation. She should be home in a few days," Edna said.

"You knew about this . . . this thing with Judith?" Martin asked.

"I—"

"And you condoned it? You didn't even try to give her any counsel against it?"

"Dad, what could I do?"

Martin didn't answer. His glance suddenly went from her to Geoff and back. There was new knowledge in his eyes when he asked, "Where have you two been? Bob Healy was just here with a story about some bizarre incident on the highway."

"What's going on between you two?" Edna asked.

Sara cast a quick glance at Geoff, but Martin spoke before either of them could. He glared at Geoff, saying, "You bastard. So that's why you left my house, you snake in the grass. You defiler of women. You seduced my daughter in my own home."

"Dad, it didn't happen that way," Sara tried to interject.

"And you . . . " Martin said rounding on her, "of course, you never noticed your sister's plight. You were too busy with your lover, here. Both you and Judith have betrayed everything I stand for."

"Martin, I genuinely care about her . . ." Geoff said.

"You? Care about my daughter? When Bob Healy came by here tonight and said that my daughter had gotten on some motorcycle with a hoodlum—a bum—I didn't understand what he was saying. But now I know he was right. You are a bum."

It was the second time within an hour that someone had insulted Geoff, Sara thought. She could see how affected he was when he didn't bother to deny anything. His face closed up against Martin.

When she realized that he wouldn't defend himself, Sara spoke up. "Daddy, that isn't true."

"She's no match for you," Martin went on. "You took advantage of her. How dare you tell me you care? What could you do for her? Your parents are still supporting you."

"Martin . . ." her mother attempted to cut in.

"No," he turned on Edna, "don't you try to stop me. You know it's true."

"People aren't perfect, Martin," Edna said, wringing her hands.

Sara was floored by the sudden turnabout in attitude between her parents. Now, it was Martin who was Geoff's detractor, while Edna appeared more understanding. If the scene before her had been less chaotic, she would have spent more time puzzling over it. As it was, she was too busy trying to contain the argument.

It also hurt to see her parents argue over something that she had done. It almost scared her as much as it used to when she was a child.

"My own daughters?" Martin said, disbelief tingeing his voice. He turned to Edna, saying, "Did you know about this? How could you have let it happen?"

Edna sounded fatalistic when she said, "What more could I have done? I tried to tell you, but you never listen."

"How was I supposed to take that foolish mumbo-jumbo of yours as true?"

"You don't know everything, Martin. Let it go," Edna pleaded.

"Dad, I love Geoffrey," Sara said.

"Be silent," Martin said to her.

"You have to understand. I'm a woman and I love him."

"No!" he exclaimed. "If you want him this much then leave here—go with him. Don't come back until you've come to your senses."

"Martin, don't . . ." Edna cried.

"Go," he repeated. "It will all come to no good, and you'll be punished for being a bad example for your little sister."

Suddenly, Edna said, "Stop! You ain't God, Martin! You have no right to say that."

Edna's statement effectively brought all of the fight to an end. Sara ran upstairs and grabbed a few things from her room. She left with Geoff that night and moved in to share his small quarters.

They were both quiet when they entered into the motel room. Geoff was glad that she was with him, but he knew the fight with her family had cost her dearly. It had hurt him, too. He understood Martin more than he wanted to admit, and he regretted that the friendship between him and the older man was damaged. Yet, he wanted Sara with every fiber in his being, and he'd sacrifice a lot more for her if it came to that.

Sara looked around at the small place, made even smaller by the clutter of charts, graphs, and books spread over every surface. He looked around, too, seeing it through her eyes, and realized he would soon have to find better living quarters for them. With her here, a lot would have to change.

"Do you know why your marks aren't top rate?" Sounding tired and dispirited, she answered her own question. "Because you spend all your time with these things!"

"Is it so important to you that my marks be tops?" He said.

"Geoff, we're not kids, and we've got to make a living. Besides, you always made good marks. You were ahead, intellectually gifted."

He inhaled and released the air, allowing his chest to rise and fall. "You're right," he agreed. "I guess you'll have to tutor me some more."

This ended with their going to bed. Where he tried to comfort her for the loss she'd suffered that night.

Later, he lay there, remembering the harsh words that had been said that night and Sara's saying that she loved him. It made his chest tight. The way she'd stood up for him had been so remarkable that he'd been too choked up to say anything.

He wouldn't let her down. She was right. They weren't children. He'd register for the master's program. Sara deserved the best, and he would see to it that she got it. She'd made a big sacrifice that night, and he wouldn't let it be for nothing. He knew he had to change if he wanted to keep their love viable.

It was weeks later, on a warm, Indian summer Saturday afternoon that Sara was working in the kitchen of their new apartment. She glanced in on Geoff as he was studying. He was lying on the floor, almost under the card table that they ate their meals on. He was so engrossed that he wasn't aware of her presence. She smiled as she returned to the kitchen.

Scattered on the table over his head were his papers for stock market quotes, etc. He often kept the place a mess, and she suspected that the hobby took a great deal of the time when he should have been studying. It was good that he had such high energy levels as well as being brilliant. She wondered how he'd manage otherwise.

What could she say? Although her salary covered their living expenses, the amount that he made from his trading usually came just at the right times. She shook her head and continued into their tiny kitchen. The dishwater that she'd left in the pan was cooling and she poured it out, adding more hot water.

As she swirled the dishes in the liquid, she realized that although she was tired, she was happy. *Doesn't take much to make me happy,* she thought, *just Geoff and maybe a baby in a few years.*

"Hey, Sara," Geoff called. "Come here a minute."

She peeped around the door before answering. He looked so serious, not glancing up from the papers and books in front of him. He was lying on his side, one hand propping up his head.

"What can I do for you?" she asked.

"Tell me what you make of this," he said, pointing at something in the book.

"Surely in your intellectual conceit, you don't need li'l old me to help," she teased.

In order to see it, she would have to get down to his level. She was drying a dish and took it with her as she lowered herself to her knees. She leaned over him to look at the page.

He grabbed her and pulled her over to lie on her back. The action was sudden and she started giggling.

"Conceit, huh?" he said before kissing her slowly and deeply, and it took her breath away.

"I thought you wanted me to help," she said in a breathy whisper.

"I do. I want you to help in the way you know so well," Geoff said.

He hitched up her T-shirt and buried his head between her breasts. She had no bra on and he sucked her nipple deep into the moist recesses of his mouth. Her hands held onto his head and she sighed. An instant heat coiled from her female core, spreading wonderfully outward. His hand sought entry at the top of her jeans, and when that failed he started unbuttoning them. It was hard going, for the fabric was tough.

Someone knocked at the door and they both stopped, listening. She raised up to answer and he kissed her, effectively sealing her mouth.

"Shush," he hissed when he drew back. "If we're nice and quiet they'll go away."

"I don't think so. Not with that paper thin door. Chances are they've already heard us. Besides, it's probably only Saul," she said close to his ear, "coming to take you to practice your golf swing." Saul was a classmate of Geoff's, also interested in the stock market.

"Perish the thought. You know I hate that game," he whispered.

"But Saul says you have to be good at it if you're going to wheel and deal in those monied halls you're both dreaming about."

"What does Saul know?" The knock came again, more insistent this time. Geoff buried himself deeper against her, holding her tightly when she tried to rise. "You see, Saul doesn't even know how to go away when he's not wanted."

He tried to kiss her again. "Sex fiend!" she hissed. Laughing, she eluded him this time, crawling under the table before rising. She hastened to answer the door for their insistent visitor, who was knocking harder by now.

She was still buttoning her jeans when she opened the door and found the whole McMillan family standing there. Hurriedly, Sara straightened her disreputable T-shirt and tried to smooth her hair down.

"Why Sara, you look positively radiant," Nora said.

Chapter Eight

"That's my girl! She's beautiful!" Hugo grabbed her in a bone crushing bear hug and swung her off her feet, making a full circle. She was dizzy when he held her close and kissed her moistly on the mouth. He smelled of alcohol. She pulled back instinctively.

"What did I tell you? Didn't I say she's the reason Geoff's here?' You know Geoff. A chip off the old block. No way he'd let a pretty girl like this go without his picking. Boy's been through every female—"

"Dad," Geoff interrupted. Upon seeing his parents, he'd quickly gotten up from the floor. He moved to his father and physically stopped the spin that Hugo had put them into. Geoff took her out of his father's embrace. It was a good thing because, although Hugo's grip was strong, his equilibrium was questionable.

"Sure, sure, Son," Hugo said, looking a bit foolishly at Geoff as he stumbled.

Nora deftly guided him into a chair. Soon he was laughing, enjoying the incident more than anyone else.

Geoff's face was a study in iron control. Sara, glancing at this cooly distant Geoff, at first assumed that he was embarrassed by his father's drunkenness. But she wasn't totally convinced that was the only thing causing his change of demeanor. Geoff didn't remove his hands from her waist until he'd drawn her to stand a few feet away from Hugo.

Nora pointedly stared at the proprietary arm that Geoff had placed around her waist. Sara felt foolish and gauche in front of the incredibly well turned out Nora. Nora had her own style—a sort of glamorous punk that she wore well on her reed slim frame. Her short bleached hair was cut in a shag. Showing under her short skirt and long expanse of leg were fine, calfskin boots. It seemed the older woman hadn't changed in all the years that had passed. She had a Scandinavian beauty. Her skin was as smooth as a girl's and she looked years younger than her age. Nora Stone-McMillan was still a very beautiful woman.

Sara had immediately fallen in love with Geoff's sisters. She remembered the older girl, Alexis, from before. Now there was a second daughter who was four years old. They called her Lizzibit. Sara remembered Edna being scandalized when she'd first heard this. Edna complained about Hugo and Nora burdening the child with a foolish name. Sara was inclined to agree.

Sara knew quite a bit about the McMillans from listening to her parents' talk. Nora had been born with the proverbial silver spoon in her mouth. Her family was old New York, and well respected. She had been a pampered daughter, groomed to make an advantageous marriage into one of the other old New York families, and from there reign among the elite. Her name somehow had still been in the social register until recently. That was probably due more to Nora's influence than anything else. However, neither her husband nor any of her children had ever been registered.

Nora and Hugo had met and fallen in love twenty-five years ago, although it was a time when interracial love affairs were more frowned upon. Hugo had been a world-renowned musician with a fantastic talent. He was taking

the world by storm and everything went well, even though
Nora had initially been ostracized by her family.

They'd traveled all over the world and when Geoff had
been born they'd either dragged him with them or left
him with friends and servants. Edna had been one of the
people who'd frequently taken Geoff in when Nora wandered off, following Hugo. Their two little girls had been
born years later. Geoff was already seventeen by the time
Alexis arrived, and Lizzibit came two years later.

Then Hugo had an accident that ended his career. Everyone thought the flamboyant couple would fade into obscu-
rity, but the Stone-McMillan's surprised them. And it was
Nora who surprised them the most. She took the royalties
from Hugo's last song, "Somewhere in Time," and
invested them. The song became a classic. Within a short
time, they were wealthier than ever. Sara suspected Geoff
had inherited his mother's flair for making money.

"Would you like some coffee?" Sara asked when they'd
come in and found seats.

"Yes, that would be nice," Nora answered, finding a
chair for herself.

"Not me," Hugo said, sitting in the only comfortable
seat they had. "I brought my own refreshments." He waved
a silver flask that he pulled from his pocket.

Sara escaped into the small kitchen alcove and made
coffee. She managed to rustle up cocoa for the two girls.

When Sara'd served everyone Nora took her cup and
said, "I'm surprised to see the two of you here like this.
She waved one lovely, manicured hand. When did this
occur? I know you've been friends all your lives, but it was
more like brother and sister than . . ." Nora's voice trailed
off as she arched one eyebrow.

"Things sort of happened quickly, I guess," Sara said
lamely.

"And it's nobody's business," Geoff added.

"Whatever happened to the fiancé?" Nora asked. Sara's
head snapped up, surprised that Nora knew about Chuck.

"Oh, yes, your mother told us all about it. I was under the impression that you'd be married by now."

Sara's face felt flushed and she said a silent prayer of gratitude that she was too dark to blush.

"There's no engagement," Geoff answered bluntly.

Sara's gaze flew to him, knowing that he wanted to protect her from his parents' curiosity, but she knew there was no escape. His parents had every right to be bewildered by this turn of events. She also suspected that no matter how Geoff fought they would ask their questions—either today or later. There would be no evading Nora and Hugo's quest for information.

"I sort of guessed at that, but—" Nora responded cooly to Geoff before turning to face Sara. Her head was tilted imperviously when she asked, "*You* can see our predicament, can't you?"

"Well, *I* can't," Geoff cut in again, determined to save Sara. "There's no predicament. We want to be together."

"Well, Son, now how's Martin and Edna taking this?" Hugo asked.

It was a good question, and showed that Hugo wasn't quite as out of it as she'd thought, she realized.

Geoffrey's eyes found hers and she could see his anger rising. She realized that he hesitated only because of her presence. But she knew something that Geoff could refuse to recognize. She knew that they couldn't just cut everyone out of their lives as Geoff wanted to. Both of their families would need time to get used to their living together.

"Sara, would you mind, Darling, if we had a little talk in private with Geoff? It's been so long since we've seen our only son—my prettyboy," Nora said.

At Nora's use of the term, Sara vaguely remembered hearing the older woman use the nickname when they were much younger. Somehow, it seemed terribly wrong.

"Anything you want to say can be said in front of Sara," Geoff answered before she could speak.

"No," Sara said, and looked pointedly at Geoff. "I don't mind at all." She stood up to go into the bedroom.

"And would you take the girls, too?" Nora requested, smiling.

"Of course," Sara responded.

She took Alexis and Lizzibit with her and pulled the door closed. They were adorable little girls, and Sara was grateful for the distraction. She found a certain delightful innocence about the children, and wondered why it surprised her. It was rare to find that children had escaped being pushed into an early precocity. Something told her that only Nora's strong personality had prevented this.

She talked to the children while part of her strained to hear what was being said in the other room. Despite this, she thoroughly enjoyed the time spent with them.

Just as with Geoff, his sisters had their mother's beauty. While Geoff's coloring was midway between his parents, much of theirs came from Nora. It was as if Nora's tea rose coloring combined with Hugo's mahogany to create their pale, rose-touched beige.

Alexis became more talkative when no longer under her parents' scrutiny. Sara asked her about schoolwork. Due to her work, Sara felt quite comfortable talking with children. Alexis was so eager to share her progress than Sara wondered if anyone had ever asked her about this.

Before more than a few minutes had passed, Geoff opened the door, and indicated she should return to the other room. "Come back. Talk's over," was all he said.

On her return, she could see that both Geoff and Nora looked tight-lipped. Hugo, however, appeared unperturbed, and had sunk further into his chair.

She sat, and the four of them talked sporadically about old times. Here, Hugo perked up and joined in, though his speech was becoming more slurred and disjointed.

Some time later, Nora opened her fine leather purse. She rummaged around for a moment before exclaiming, "Oh, I've run out of cigarettes. Do you mind going to buy me a pack, Geoff?"

He turned quickly, a knowing look on his face. Sara knew that Nora was trying to get him out of the house so she could talk, and it frightened her. She also knew that Geoffrey recognized Nora's ploy.

"Pretty please, my prettyboy." Nora reached to touch his face and he turned his head to avoid her touch.

Sara could see that Geoff was going to balk. To forestall his bald refusal, she hurried to say, "Yes, and could you pick up some wild rice for dinner?" Geoff's anger at being outmaneuvered was quite apparent. He scowled as he stood up, preparing to leave.

Immediately, the two girls jumped up. "Can we go too, Mommy?" They grabbed Geoffrey's hands.

Geoffrey seemed both bemused and pleased at the girls' enthusiasm, but he was reluctant to leave Nora and Sara alone.

"Of course," Nora answered and looking at Hugo, said, "Why don't you go too, darling? You and Geoffrey can have a little men's talk."

Once they were alone, Nora opened her purse again, and this time without any problems, she found a gold cigarette case and extracted one, which she lit up, using a slim gold lighter. She blew smoke out and then smiled artfully at Sara. "You don't mind, do you? My sending them away?"

"Oh, no," Sara said and found she had a strong urge to do something that she hadn't done since she was a child. She wanted to bite her nails.

"I thought we girls should have a chat," Nora explained. "I was a little surprised to see you here with Geoff. Oh, I know the effect he has on women, but I always saw *you* as the marrying kind. I hope you don't expect that from him?"

Sara straightened her spine and answered, "We have no plans to get married."

"Good. Aren't you older than he?"

"Only by a year," Sara hastened to add.

"But a year can be a lot. A woman at twenty-five is ripe to marry and start a family. But a man at twenty-four . . ." She held her arms out and shrugged. "You love him, I can see it. Be careful, Geoff has always tired quickly of his women. You could be hurt."

Sara realized that Nora's warning wasn't to be mistaken for any concern for her. It was more a mother's saying that no one was good enough for her son.

She took a deep breath and said, "I don't expect anything from Geoff."

"Good. Then you won't be disappointed. You're not like his other women. Most of them were—what do I want to say—more colorful? It's not that you're not attractive, for you are, in a sort of insipid way. No, wait. Insipid. That's not a good word. You'll have to excuse me—vocabulary was never my forte. I mean you're pretty in an understated way." Somehow, Sara felt that Nora meant exactly what she'd said at first.

Nora went on, "I always hoped he'd go into music like Hugo, but I guess he didn't want to do that. Too bad, but sometimes boys rebel against their fathers. The trading's good, though and I can help him there." She sounded proud. "I've always been able to smell the winners. That comes from my side of the family. My father was one of the best of all times."

"Yes, I've heard that."

"But what's this talk about economics and banking? I can't believe Geoff would want to go into such a stodgy field. It's the antithesis of everything he's ever been exposed to. Was that *your* idea?"

"No. It was totally Geoff's decision."

"I guess he's trying to change, but chances are it won't work. The first good-looking woman that passes will probably distract him from this new quest."

Nora's remark about good-looking women stung deeply but Sara chose to ignore it, saying only, "Geoff could do anything he wanted. He could have anything he wanted too."

"I agree." Nora looked at her as if trying to figure out what Geoff saw in her. Sara squirmed under the older woman's assessing glance.

"You don't think moving in with him was unwise?"

"Unwise?"

Sex is a funny thing. It can ruin a friendship." Nora had just touched a raw nerve, Sara thought. "When he leaves, you'll have nothing. It's impossible to go back to being just friends."

When he leaves. . . . the words were like knives in Sara's heart. She felt bombarded, and it was with great relief that she heard Geoff race through the front entrance and bang into the apartment. He shoved the cigarettes at Nora and scrutinized her face. She smiled as cheerfully at him as she could, determined to look unfazed despite feeling as if her heart would break. There was no way she could fight his mother, she realized.

She would remain with Geoff for as long as he wanted, but she had no illusions as to what the outcome would be. Nora was right. Geoff had never been inclined to long relationships. But it still hurt to know how much Nora was against their being together. It hurt especially because it came on top of her own parents' disapproval.

After the McMillans left Geoff turned to her, saying, "All right, what did she say?"

"Nora?" she asked, trying to stall.

"Of course, Nora. Don't try to hide it from me. You're as transparent as glass."

"I don't know what you're talking about."

"Then tell me why you're moping around like that. I want to know."

"She didn't say anything."

"Don't tell me that. I know her. There's nothing she likes more than stirring up trouble."

"It wasn't important."

"Let me be the judge of that."

"She said you got your ability in the stock market from her and her side of the family."

"That's a joke. She's no trader."

"That's not true. She did make a lot of money in the market."

"Using insider information. Anyone can do that."

"Oh, why can't you give credit where it's due?"

"You're stalling. That's not what's got your nose out of joint."

"She said you weren't the marrying type."

"So?"

"I told you it was nothing. I already knew that."

"But you let it hurt you," he accused, and she couldn't hide that he was right. "What a bitch!"

"Don't call her that. She's your mother. She's right, and she's only expressing how she feels."

"Who cares about what *she* feels?"

He saw red. He felt impotent, stymied. He was so enraged with his parents for coming and upsetting Sara that all he wanted to do was break things. He wanted to hit out at something. He reached for the lamp on the card table and before he had thought, he'd hurled it against the wall. The glazed china shattered, with a spray of sharp shards falling to the floor. It left a dent in the wall.

He'd heard her cry out but it didn't deter him. The sudden act had released some of his frustration, but it was only a beginning. He grabbed up a chair and heaved it through the window into their private backyard. The glass pane exploded outward as the chair sailed through.

That afforded him a moment of pure gratification. He picked up a group of small bric-a-brac and sailed them against the wall, all in a white hot heat. He would have gone on, but he caught sight of her rushing to the closet from the corner of his eye.

Sara cried out at the first crashing noise, stunned by his sudden erratic behavior. In trying to move away, the back of her legs hit on a chair and she sank heavily into it before covering her face. She could hear him tossing other items but was too distraught to raise her head. She remembered his rare violent temper as a child, and how she'd always been terrified by it.

Standing up hastily, she almost toppled the chair. She

went to the closet, where she grabbed two suitcases stored on the top shelf and pulled a bunch of hangers off the rod. Lugging everything toward the bed, she dropped various items, almost tripping over them in her desperation. At the bed, she tossed everything atop the coverlet and began frantically to throw clothes into the suitcases.

Suddenly, Geoff was there, touching her shoulder. She flinched, gave a shrill cry, and fought him off. He grabbed her hands and held her so that she couldn't hit him any more. His strength being superior, it was simple for him to pull her into his arms. Although she realized that he was trying to calm her, she couldn't seem to stop struggling and flailing against him.

Despite the gentle way he held her, his voice was harsh as he demanded, "What's wrong with you?"

"I can't stand it! I can't stay here." Her words came out shaky, almost incoherent.

"What are you talking about?" Geoff asked.

Geoff was alarmed by her behavior. *Why is she packing her clothes?* he thought. A sudden sense of doom descended upon him.

"You have no discipline, no self-control," she railed at him.

She was shaken, and he wondered if she was going to fall. He realized that she, too, had totally thrown off all self-discipline at that moment. His holding her seemed to make her even more upset, so he let her go and she moved so quickly away that she did almost fall.

"I can't live with you. I won't stay here with you breaking things." His mouth went dry.

"Okay, just calm down," he said and carefully pulled her to sit upon his is lap as he sank to the bed. "Tell me what's wrong."

"I'm afraid of you when you act like this." The truth of her words hit him like a blow. She began to cry.

"Afraid of *me*?" He was shocked. It tore at him to see her tears. "I'd never hurt you. I thought you of all people would understand me."

"Why should I?" she snapped back, getting angry now. He preferred her anger to her tears. When she twisted away from him, he allowed her to escape. She jumped up, and commenced to pack again. "You think with all your troubles with women that you can treat me worse than them?"

"What troubles are you talking about?" His heart started thudding against his ribs. He watched her rush about, picking up her things, wich she threw into the bag.

"I know they've been bouncing you out on your butt."

"More like me bouncing them." He'd said it because she'd piqued his pride. But he knew it was the wrong thing, and regretted it immediately when she stopped and glared at him.

"There, you've said it. I won't tolerate your violence."

"What violence? I've never hit a woman." Now he could feel his own anger rising again.

"Big deal, Mr. Macho Man. I'm going home."

"That's right, run back to your parents. Your precious Mommy and Daddy. Butter wouldn't melt in any of your mouths." It sounded so foolish that he wished he could take the words back. Heck, he wished he could take the whole day back, beginning with Nora and Hugo knocking at the door.

"My mother said you're undisciplined. That you've always been so."

That hurt, for some reason, and he wanted to strike back at her. "You want to hear what Nora said about you? That you're a perennial virgin. *That's* a big joke, isn't it?"

"Your mother hasn't seen me in years. Why should I listen to her?"

"You're right. So, give me a reason why I should care what *your* family says about me?"

"Don't try to twist me up."

"What else does your mother say about my lack of discipline?" He had to be a glutton for punishment, he thought, asking that one.

"She says that you'll never get your life straightened out if you don't start to control your behavior."

"And of course being as she's such a psychic—"

"She never said she was psychic. But she is good at reading people."

He went and sat. "Don't leave me," he said. It tore him up to continue, but he couldn't allow his pride to drive her away. He took another deep breath and ploughed in. "Edna is right. Sometimes I do feel like breaking things. But it's true, I never hit a woman."

"Have you hit men?"

"What the hell's wrong with you? I've fought when I had to. A man doesn't always have a choice." He put his head in his hands. "I'd never hurt you. That's what counts."

"It's not enough. We can't create a life under this cloud of pending violence. Our whole relationship will suffer. You can't always act out your rage."

"Sounds like something from Psych One-Oh-One."

"You know I'm right. It's too disruptive. . . ."

She picked up both bags and started walking to the door. For a moment he sat there, furious that she'd leave so easily. Then he had to act.

"Wait." He followed her to the door. "Okay, I'll stop."

"Why would you stop now?"

"Because I want to." He wanted to say that he'd do anything to keep her from walking through the door, but his pride kept him from admitting that. She looked torn for a moment.

"Can you? Just like that?"

"I can do anything I want," he bluffed.

"I want a normal life, not to live with a madman—"

"You've already said that," he cut in.

"I could have married Chuck."

He knew how much power she had over him by the agony those words caused. But he didn't strike back. The only thing he could do was say, "You couldn't have, Sara. Not just for me, but for yourself."

"You don't know what I could have done," she said, sounding sulky now.

"Maybe not," he admitted. Then he continued, "But you could marry *me*."

Chapter Nine

"No," she said, and her glance swung to his face. "Surely you wouldn't go that far just to defy your mother."

He knew that she hadn't expected him to say that. His words had shocked him, too. They'd come out as naturally as if he'd been thinking them all the time. It made him realize that he had indeed been doing just that.

He couldn't lose her, he dare not. He couldn't go back to what he'd been. He knew if he'd kept it up he'd have soon been suicidal. His life had been too empty, too lonely, too soul destroying. Maybe it would have done him well to think of what was wrong with him, but it didn't matter what the problem was, or had been. All he knew was that he had to change it or he'd be destroyed. Maybe he'd be like Hugo, and God knew he couldn't tolerate that.

"Forget my mother—," He cradled her face in his hands. "It's going to be all right."

"I know you've never done anything like this before."

"So what? You know I never do anything I don't want," he said.

"I feel as if I'm changing you," she said.

"You're not. This is something that I want very much. I won't disappoint you."

She slid down the wall and buried her face in her upraised knees and started crying again. He went down with her, almost afraid to touch her for fear she'd refuse him and leave.

"Your mother would never forgive me," she said, her face awash with tears.

"She'll have nothing to say about it. Believe me."

"You musn't hate her. She loves you. That's what the whole thing was all about."

"Nora never loved anyone except Hugo. She never had any interest in anyone but him."

"That isn't true. She loves all of you." She scrubbed the tears away and seemed on the verge of hiccups. She looked young and endearing.

"Well, I hope she's doing better for those girls than she ever did for me," he said.

"Why . . . why does she call you 'prettyboy?'"

"Shh," he said, putting his hand to her mouth. "Don't say that. It's Nora's craziness. Don't ever say that again."

"All right," she said. He kissed her, and she allowed him. He moved closer to cuddle her. "I'm not going to be a biker babe," she said.

"I know." He wanted to smile, trying to see Sara in that role.

"Or one of those earth mother types, following you all over the world and sleeping in the streets."

"I don't expect you to."

"That's what you've been doing."

"Not exactly."

"I want a normal life. I want children and a home," she said and he breathed in relief, realizing that she'd already accepted his proposal.

"I agree totally," he said.

"Geoff, do you love me?"

"Of course I do. Why do you think I'm willing to marry you?"

Sara realized that it wasn't quite what she'd wanted to hear, and she regretted asking. He'd said it too offhandedly. She knew that he loved her as a friend because they went back so far, but she wondered if he was *in love* with her. She also knew that he loved going to bed with her, but he'd never offered to say the words, except when they were in bed. She pushed the thought away. The last thing she needed was to become one of those women who constantly needed reassurances.

It was bad enough that she loved him as much as she did. In most relationships, one partner always loved more than the other. She had no doubt that in their relationship, she was that partner.

"I have no intention of exposing my children to life's seamy side. My life can't just be about having a good time. I want to grab all the opportunities out there, and I want to help others do the same thing. I owe it to my ancestors."

"I know what you're trying to say."

"Do you truly? I know what I want to do with my life. I want to be productive, not just self-indulgent and to live for the moment."

"But it's all right if you hate shoes?" He smiled at her.

It was an attempt to make her smile. She wiped her eyes again and blew her nose, wondering what she looked like.

"Do I sound silly and shallow?"

"No, you sound like my Sara."

"I was always telling you what to do, wasn't I?"

"Yeah, but you had a few good moments."

"When?" she asked.

"You made great mud pies." Now she did laugh. "Sara, you won't have to do anything that you don't want. If you're unhappy, all you have to do is say so, okay?"

"Sure, but I never said no to you. Will I be able to do it now?"

"Sure you will. Anyway, I don't remember you ever had trouble expressing yourself. Besides, don't ever pay any attention to my parents. It's not worth it. Hugo's a drunken sot, and if you give Nora an inch she'll take twenty leagues."

"Yard," she answered. "If you give her an inch, she'll take a yard."

"Okay. Feeling better, now?" She nodded and dried her eyes. "You'll never regret it," he said, taking her into his arms.

"There's something else, more important than anything." She looked him straight in the eye.

"Name it," he said.

"I won't be part of a harem. I won't tolerate other women. If you can't be faithful, don't even think about marrying me."

"It's a deal," he promised. "No other women."

She should be glad, she thought. She loved this man much more than she'd ever thought possible. Even more than she'd loved him all her life. Then, he'd only been her friend. Now he was her lover. But somehow, she felt as if marrying him would be a mistake. It wasn't something that she could explain. She felt as if Geoff were going past her on skis. She'd always felt that way. Was it wise to marry a man who was so different than she, even if she loved him as much as she did?

That evening, Geoff was getting ready for bed. His mind kept going over what Sara had said to him. She was right. He couldn't do the same things with her that he'd done before, being too selfish and going for himself only. She'd leave him. And he knew that the competition was stiff around her. He'd seen the way men followed her with their eyes. She could have any of them, most especially Chuck. Chuck would jump at the chance.

As he leaned over the sink, brushing his teeth, he happened to look into the mirror. *It was time,* he realized as he studied his reflection. He straightened up and left the bathroom, clicking the light switch as he did.

The next day, Sara went to pick up Geoff after his last class. She'd arrived a little late and walked around, searching for him. Students hurried to their classes. It was late October and the weather had turned cool, as if to prophesy that the winter would soon be upon them.

The sharp wind blew vivid red, gold, and brown leaves along the sidewalk. Wrought-iron benches lined the path along which she trod. Stomping her feet in an effort to keep warm in the dropping temperatures, she had walked the path twice looking for Geoff.

One hardy soul, a man, stood at the end of the path. She didn't pay much attention to him except to wonder at how still he was in the chilled weather. The next time she passed him, the man touched her on the shoulder and she jerked around, discovering that it was Geoff.

She gaped, disbelieving. He had cut the long braid and was wearing an oxford shirt and chinos. He didn't even have on his boots. She didn't know what to say.

"Well, don't you have anything to say, or are you going to stand there catching flies?" While it made her close her mouth, she still couldn't think of anything to say. Exasperated, he asked, "How do I look?"

"Great," she finally responded. *He always looks great,* she thought. "But I'm going to miss the hair."

He laughed. "Hate to give up your very own hoodlum?"

Sara knew, though it surprised her, that he had been annoyed by Bob Healy's remark, not to mention the things that her father had said.

"What are you going to wear when you ride your bike?" She had said it more in jest than anything else. But when his face became serious, she knew. "You've don't have the Harley, either?"

"No, it's time to move on from that," was all he said about the drastic changes that he'd made.

Several days later, Sara parked in front of her parents' house and sat there for a few moments before getting out. Then she zipped her parka and flung her backpack over her shoulder. The windchill factor was well below freezing.

She glanced upward at the gathering clouds, which foretold an early dusk and possibly a storm. From the darkening sky, she knew the daylight was working itself toward evening. Where had the hours gone? She took a deep breath and knew that she had to go in and speak with her parents.

Walking slowly from the old car over the walkway and up the stairs, she realized that the house seemed alien. Since moving in with Geoff, her childhood home seemed far away.

Inside the kitchen, she found Judith in the process of preparing dinner. They were both glad to see each other.

"Where's Mom?" Sara asked.

"She went to some women's meeting—or *ladies* meeting, as Mom calls it. She'll be here any minute, though. I've been chosen to cook tonight. Don't I look domesticated?" Judith asked as she went back to scraping carrots for stew.

"You look natural," Sara assured her.

"Oh, yuck!" Judith exclaimed. "And how are you two doing, living in sin and all that stuff?" Although Sara knew her sister had meant it in jest, it did not sit well. Judith understood her error by Sara's expression. "I'm sorry, Sara, but you shouldn't take it so seriously. Everyone does that now."

Sara shrugged it off. "How are you feeling?"

"Okay, I guess," Judith said.

"Not well enough to return to school?"

"I will, next term. Actually, I'm sorry I didn't go right back. It's been hell looking at Dad. He seems to blame himself as well as us."

"I know," Sara said. They were both quiet for a few moments before she said, "Geoff's asked me to marry him."

"You've got to be kidding! Geoff? I didn't think he had it in him," Judith said.

Glancing out the window, Sara gazed through the bare branches at the backyard. Although the leaves on the big maple were past their prime, some of them still clung to the limbs. Here it was almost the end of October, and the leaves hung on. *It's a good lesson,* she thought. She had to hang on now, too.

"Is this really what you want? Why marry him? Why not just live with him for a while?" Judith said.

"We want to get married. Both of us."

"But people don't do that anymore. Just think, you'll be living with the same man for the rest of your life."

"Yes," Sara said, "that's what I want. Are you turning against me, too?"

"No. You're my sister. Be happy." They hugged each other.

Sara felt that the weight of the world sometimes fell on her shoulders. Martin had called her his little peacemaker in the family because of this. She was willing to listen to others and to see their side of the story. She often felt as if she gave pieces of herself to those she loved. With the new coolness between the family members, she felt torn apart.

When Edna came home, Sara went and kissed her mother. Seeing her, she felt as if her childhood home was familiar grounds. Also, seeing Edna made her realize how much she missed her mother.

"Chuck's been seeing one of the Abrams girls. Melanie," Edna said.

Sara didn't answer at first, but she was glad. Chuck was a nice man and he deserved to date again. Melanie was a nice person. She hoped it would work out. Sometimes she felt guilty about Chuck, but Dad had been right. It was better to end it before they were married than to have met Geoff again afterward. That would have been a real disaster.

"Is Geoff still doing that trading thing?" Edna asked when Sara didn't answer.

"Yes," she answered reluctant. "He's also doing well in his studies."

"For him, what did you expect? Book learning always came easy for him. Will he keep up with it? That's the question."

"We've been discussing plans already—" Sara started.

"And you're still working at the center?"

"Yes, and we're doing—"

"You should be in school."

"I will be soon."

"Any woman who puts a man through school is a fool. In the end the man outgrows her and finds someone else in his new class," Edna pronounced.

"I don't believe that."

"You should, because it's true all too often."

"It won't happen to us."

"Did you know his father took him to prostitutes? 'Didn't want his son to be a sissy,' is what Hugo said."

"Geoff's not Hugo."

"How far from the tree does the acorn fall? He's got your nose so far open you can't see anything."

Lord, Sara thought. Her mother had always had a tart tongue, and it only got worse with time.

"You watch, he'll advance farther than you and he'll leave you behind."

"We love each other. We've always loved each other," Sara said. But she wondered how much did Geoffrey love her.

"You played together as kids, and now you both have the hots. That's not love. You two hadn't seen each other in years when he came back, and just as if he was entitled he broke up your engagement with Chuck. In the end, he'll think he's too good for you."

"What about you? You put Dad through divinity school, and you've always believed in him."

"That's different. I always helped your father in his life's work. How are you going to help with this stock market craziness, or with his banking? That is, if he ever goes into banking. I thought he was supposed to be a mathematician when he was a kid. You'll be more like a slave than a helpmate."

"I'm going," Sara said suddenly and stood up. She paused, hearing her father come in through the front. But as soon as he realized she was in the kitchen, he went into the den and closed the door. She felt totally stymied by that. Her mother caught her gazing at the door.

"What can you expect? You broke his heart."

"Is he going to hold this against me forever? I'm still his daughter."

"You were always his sunshine. Judith was the world beater, but you were his darling. You were going to stay near."

"I'm still near."

"Not for long. Only as long as Geoff allows. When he's ready to go, he'll snap his fingers and you'll run after him. Now the two of you have hurt him more than you can ever know. He feels it's God's judgement on him for his own sins."

"What sins? None of this is his fault."

"Who knows why things happen as they do?" Then in an abrupt change, Edna asked, "Why couldn't it have been Chuck?"

"I don't love Chuck."

"How do you know you love Geoff? He's only been back for a few months."

"He makes me feel alive. He wants me, he needs me. Chuck will find someone else, but not Geoffrey."

"Are you kidding? He'll have millions of women. He was already a womanizer when he was only a kid."

"You don't understand. If I had married Chuck, I would have been cheating him. I never loved him enough, and you know it. If I had, I'd have said yes right away. I wouldn't have written Geoff. I didn't hurt Chuck when I said no. I did us both a favor."

"The way he makes you feel?" Edna harped back on that. "You're talking about sex. That's all. You can't base a marriage on sex. For marriage, you pick a steady man. Wait a while."

"We've already made up our minds."

"I always knew it would come to this. You used to run home from school to be with him. It was the same with your father. He'd looked up to Hugo for so long. He couldn't see when the man turned bad. I worked so hard to get us free from Hugo and that woman, and all for nothing."

"Mom, don't feel that way. I know this is going to work."

"Are you crazy, wanting to marry him? He's undisciplined."

"No! He's just focused on what he does. He's very disciplined."

"He's unprincipled."

"That's not fair."

"He's been indulged all his life."

"Is that his fault? Can you blame *him* for his parents?" She'd rarely ever fought with her mother, and now here they were at each other's throats, she thought.

"He'll lead you a dog's life. He's got too much turbulence. There's a fire in him that could rage out of control at any time."

"I can help him."

"Don't marry a man to help him. Stupid women do that, and spend their lives in upheaval. You'll want children. You need a calm, stable man for children."

"We're going to wait. By the time we have children, we'll be in better straits."

"So, Ms. Sara Thing. You're going to do what God didn't. You're going to make him a better person."

"Mom, stop."

"You'd better think about it real hard." Then jumping back to what Sara had said earlier, Edna said, "You think that's all there is to life and love? You think the way you feel is what this is all about? You're wrong, and maybe I shouldn't say a thing to you. I hate him for what he's done to you."

"He's not doing anything to me."

"It's already done. You just can't see it yet. It's not that I have any favorites, but Judith, she's like me. You were always the one who brought us closer together. The daughter we could depend on."

"You can still depend on me. Marrying Geoff isn't going to change that."

"You think he'll share you? He'll consume your life. You're not going to have time for anything except him.

You'll spend your life trying to please him, and then find it was an impossible job."

"He's not what you think."

"That boy was always a handful. And now you want to make him your handful. You'll regret it. Maybe I should watch and wait until you find out for yourself. Life is not about feelings. It's about service and caring. Mark my words. You'll regret it. If there's one thing I know it's people. And I can see right through Geoffrey McMillan."

Suddenly, Sara was sick of the whole conversation. There was nothing she could say to convince Edna, and she knew it. "Mom, I'm going to marry Geoff, and I'm asking you to come to my wedding."

Edna wiped at her eyes with the dishtowel in her hands. "Okay," Edna said, sounding resigned. Then she put her arms around Sara and added, "Don't worry, your dad will be there, too." She was ready to leave when her mother came and spoke quietly, "He could do good things."

"Who?"

"Geoff," he mother answered, sucking her teeth.

"I thought you hated him," Sara said, totally bewildered by this sudden change.

"Of course, I don't hate him. But he's going to demand a lot of his mate, and he's going to take you through turbulent times. Don't say I didn't warn you."

"Did you speak with your family?" Geoff asked when she came home.

"I spoke with my mother and Judith."

"But not Martin," Geoff stated, knowing from her expression.

She shook her head but before she could stop herself, she started crying. Geoff came and put his arms around her, drawing her to him.

"Don't cry, baby. He'll come around as soon as I can pay his bride price."

"Oh, Geoff," she said, trying to draw away. "That's not true."

"Shhh," he hushed her, running a hand down her back soothingly. "Just relax. Everything will be all right."

They stayed that way for a long time, with him comforting her. Then she drew away, saying, "We must tell Hugo and Nora next."

After the scene in her parents' house today, she wasn't looking forward to facing Geoffrey's family. He pulled her close to him again. With her head tucked between his neck and shoulder, he said, "I've already told them."

"You did? When? What did you say?"

"Don't worry about it."

"Geoffrey, tell me."

"I called them on the phone today and said that we were getting married. I told them they could come if they were able to accept our decision, and if they couldn't accept it then . . . they weren't welcome."

"Oh, no. Now they'll blame me," Sara wailed.

"Not likely. They know me too well for that. Without you, they wouldn't have known where I was. Everyone knows that. I don't want to hear any more about this. Besides, I'm not letting them make you unhappy again. They can love it or lump it. Makes no difference to me."

It was a cold, blustery November day when Geoff and Sara were married at Martin's church. Her mother cried, while Nora was white as a sheet. Hugo dozed off with a gentle snore. Her father barely glanced at her. But Geoff was right. Although, she didn't believe that her father's reaction had anything to do with a bride price, she did believe that he'd come around sooner or later.

Aside from their families, few people attended. Among those was Saul Pessach, Geoff's school friend who was also very involved with the stock market. Attending with him was his new girlfriend, Myra. The couple actually seemed to enjoy themselves.

The only other people who seemed to enjoy the wedding were Geoff's sisters, Alexis and Lizzibit. Both girls were ecstatic, and appeared genuinely pleased to have gained a big sister. Afterward, Edna and Martin served lunch.

It was a strangely quiet gathering, except for Hugo. He'd brought several bottles of champagne and kept toasting them. The toasts became increasingly more risqué until her father managed to save the day by taking Hugo outside for a walk. Geoff was tight-lipped with fury, but managed to contain his temper. He'd become rather good at it, considering how new this was for him.

Not having a big wedding hurt more than she'd ever thought it would. All her life, she'd imagined herself wearing white at her wedding and walking down the aisle on her father's arm. She wanted to cry, but instead she straightened her shoulders. She wanted this, and she was going to make it work.

Book Two

Chapter Ten

Early April, 1989, Scarsdale, New York

Sara awoke that morning in the new house that they'd moved into only a few weeks before. The first thing she did was turn to look at Geoff, lying beside her. She never tired of looking at him. He needed a shave. There was a shadow of a beard on his chin and she had to stifle the urge to touch it. He would turn thirty-five this year and was still the most beautiful man she had ever seen. The years had planed his features, making him more handsome. Yes, he was a handsome man, yet no one could legitimately call him "prettyboy" again.

Success had eliminated the signs of rage he'd once carried around like a badge of honor. He was more completely in control of his world, now. With the anger sublimated into determination, Geoff had turned into a man of power and influence. He'd also been blessed with good fortune.

Suddenly she remembered that she'd dreamed during the night. She couldn't recall what it had been about, but she felt she'd been crying. For some reason, she thought of Nora, her mother-in-law, and Paula Stone-Weills, Geof-

frey's distant cousin and business assistant. She often felt
that Paula wanted to be more than a mere cousin to him.

Nora had been instrumental in Paula's coming into their
lives. Geoff's business was growing rapidly and he'd needed
another worker. It was Nora who'd voted for Paula. Geoff
hadn't seen Paula since she was a small girl. But Paula was
no longer a child, by any means. Sara wondered what Geoff
would have done had the two remained in contact years
ago, when he'd been so lethal to women? Would he have
slept with the other woman?

Sara sighed, not wanting to get into those thoughts. It
had never been wise for her to remember Geoff's womaniz-
ing phase. Such thoughts made her feel restless and frightened. She wondered if these ideas were the reason for her
recent feelings of being unfulfilled?

Then she remembered that Paula was only twenty-six.
Eleven years ago, she would have only been fifteen, much
too young to have caught Geoff's attention. Disgusted with
her imagination, she moved to get up.

Still half asleep, Geoff reached for her when she shifted.
Her movement disturbed him. She stopped, waiting for
him to be still, but when he didn't find her, his eyes opened.

"Where're you going?" he muttered.

"To check on the kids."

"Too early. Come back to bed." He dozed off and she
stood up.

One glance at the clock and she realized it was earlier
than she'd thought. The clock face nestled in a sculpture
of steel and had been a gift from Nora four months before,
on their anniversary. Steel, the gift for the eleventh anniversary—a symbol of strength. Considering how rocky their
marriage had been at its start, she smiled to think that the
symbol of steel wasn't as incongruous as it might have once
appeared.

Thinking of Nora made her remember that her mother-
in-law was planning a party with which she would be
expected to assist, as it would be given in her house. She

dreaded Nora's parties, and unfortunately the woman gave them at every opportunity.

The main reason for Sara's giving in had been that she knew it was Nora's way of making certain Geoffrey attended. Geoff's feelings toward Hugo had undergone little change over the years. He still avoided his father, which meant that he hardly ever saw them, and on the rare occassions when he allowed himself to visit, he seemed unable to remain in the same room with Hugo. It would be much more difficult for Geoff to avoid attending a party in his own home.

Despite the hour, she knew she wouldn't be able to sleep any longer. Pulling back the drapes, she gazed at the scene outside. It was not inspiring, and Sara accepted that today would be much as yesterday had been—cold and blustery, despite the fact that it was a few weeks into spring.

She remembered that an early spring had been predicted. According to the news media, the groundhog, had not seen his shadow. Sara wondered who was watching the groundhog, and if one didn't see *his* shadow did that mean that none of the others saw theirs, either? It was a peculiar thought, one of many that morning.

After donning a robe, she went to the children's rooms. There was still evidence of their recent move, with packing crates still sitting at various places. Somehow, she hadn't had time to finish setting things up. And the truth was that they needed more furniture for the huge house, which wasn't something she wanted to get in a hurry. She wanted it to be furnished perfectly, and that would take time and careful consideration.

She went to check on her daughter, Kamaria, first. Kamaria was a Swahili name, meaning *moonlight*. The name had been chosen by Geoff and her almost nine years ago, when they poured over books of baby's names. It had taken them a long time to agree, but in the end they'd both been satisfied. Somehow, it suited their daughter.

She'd been born the last year they lived in Middletown, a lovely child, inclined to be very contained and self-sufficient. Gently, Sara touched her daughter's short curly Afro, pausing to enjoy the moment.

Kamaria was a Daddy's Girl. And if she adored her father, Geoff thought the sun rose on her. This mutual admiration society had begun when the child was born. Geoff had still been in school, working on his master's while she'd taught grade school to support them. Geoff had done much of the caregiving during the child's earliest years. They certainly hadn't been able to afford a babysitter, so Geoff had been elected to do the job. During those days, he and Kamaria had been almost inseparable. He'd carried her on his back to his classes, on visits to the library, and anywhere else he needed to go.

Much of the change that had occurred in Geoff, Sara always believed, was due to his having the lion's share of caring for his small daughter. It had made him more patient and nurturing. The wild boy on a motorcycle had totally receded, leaving a caring husband and father behind. Although she knew that she loved Geoffrey without reservations, sometimes she missed that daredevil boy.

Kamaria had even totally won Nora over, which was something that Sara hadn't been able to accomplish. Sometimes, Sara felt left out of her daughter's life. Growing impatient with her mood that morning, Sara left her daughter's room to look in on Asa, their four-year-old son.

Asa lay sprawled out over the bed, leaving very little vacant space, the way Geoff slept. She pulled his covers up, pausing when he stirred and then went back to sleep.

It was funny, Sara thought, how things worked out. Kamaria was her first pregnancy, but she'd breezed through those nine months and the delivery had gone smoothly without a hitch. Who would have thought that? Everyone claimed the first birth was always the hardest, but that hadn't been true with her.

With Asa, her second pregnancy had been difficult. She had been in labor for thirty hours. He'd been in a transverse position. The doctors kept hoping that he would turn, but Asa had been too big to turn and they'd finally done a Caesarean section. By the time her son had been born, he'd looked angry and put out, while she'd been exhausted.

Geoff had been petrified. After Asa, he'd insisted there would be no more children. She's agreed, but sometimes she regretted that decision.

Things had been different in other ways for Asa, too. While Kamaria had been a quiet, restful child, those early months with Asa had been grueling. He'd been a difficult, colicky infant. It was fortunate for all of them that she'd been able to devote so much time to him. Geoff's business had already been launched and was doing well. There had been no further need for her to earn money, and Geoff had insisted that she should be home for the children. It had sounded like a good idea back then. She shook her head, not wanting to dwell on those thoughts, either, at this time.

Geoff hadn't had the same involvement during the second pregnancy that he'd had with the first. He'd been heavily invested in his business, and she had been much more on her own. It was she who had chosen the name Asa, meaning *falcon* in Yoruba.

However, Geoff had surprised her when he'd insisted on Asa's middle name being Martin. Geoff's gesture made her realize that he regretted the change in his relationship with her father. Although they'd made inroads, the old warmth had never returned in full force. She was gratified that her parents had been mollified by Geoff's gesture.

She was grieved more than she'd been able to admit by the distance that had sprung up between her and her parents. Her father wasn't a vindictive man, but he'd been hurt by the things that had occurred over eleven years before. Thinking about this brought sadness into her heart.

The fact that her son was still sleeping surprised Sara. Usually he awoke early and although he'd play quietly for a while, he'd be very active for the rest of the day. She stood there gazing at her five-year-old son, and within a short time she began to feel better. He was such a miracle that Sara felt as if her heart expanded. Unlike Kamaria, Asa had been born in New York after Geoff was established at Harlem Fidelity Bank.

After Asa's birth, she'd left her job with the New York City School System and had worked at home in Geoff's trading business. It had been an exciting time.

Asa kicked off the blanket again and coiled up into an amusing, pugnacious position with fists balled up. She smiled, thinking that for such a small bundle of humanity he had managed to take over the household since birth.

A sudden tingling over the nerve endings of her skin alerted her that Geoffrey had entered the room. She hadn't heard him but her senses were so tuned to him that often her first awareness was visceral. He stood behind her and placed his arms around her waist. She turned her head and he kissed her on the side of her mouth.

"Hmm," he sounded as he kissed her again, more deeply this time, his hands moving upward to close over her breasts. She responded immediately, as Geoff's touch always had that affect upon her.

"Shhh," she whispered, turning to move into his embrace.

"Afraid I'll wake the little tyrant?" Geoffrey whispered.

"Are you calling my little angel a tyrant?"

"You mean that devil boy?"

"Just like his daddy, he likes to be the center of attention."

"Hold that thought and come here. I want to show you something," he purred into her ear and led her out of Asa's room.

"I know exactly what you want to show me," she said, putting her hand under the terry robe he wore to touch his skin.

"Before he wakes up, I *would* like to be the center of your attention for a while." he said, trying to look innocent as he led her back into their bedroom.

"Do you have time for this?"

"I always have time for you," he said.

He kissed her softly, his tongue probing her mouth, and she put her hands under his robe, searching for the flat nubs on his chest. When she flicked a nail over them, he inhaled deeply and groaned. In response, his hands cupped her breasts as if weighing them in his palms. He bent to take first one taut nipple into his mouth and then the other. She arched her hips up to him as desire shot immediately to her feminine core, pressing her thighs against him, inviting him closer. His body heat tormented her.

He put his hands on her hip, sliding down to her mound and rubbing his fingers through the thatch of coarse, curly hair there. She pressed herself into his seeking fingers. He parted her fleshy lips and touched the small trembling flesh there. She gasped and pushed herself further into his hand.

They made slow progress back to their room as they eagerly touched and tasted each other every step of the way. Once their door was closed he tugged the robe off her shoulders, and she shrugged out of it in frustration to feel her flesh against his. She was on fire to be joined with him in the ritual of love. Her sex throbbed achingly. When she felt the bed at the back of her knees, she clasped her arms around his neck and pulled him down upon her. They were a tangle of legs and arms as they scrambled upward.

"That's my girl," he muttered into her ear and ran moist kisses down her throat to her breast, where he lathed her aching aureole with the wondrous balm of his mouth.

Her desire grew, driving her to clutch at him. She enclosed his manhood in her hands and he groaned louder. She drew him closer, feeling his hot, throbbing member as it eagerly sought union with her aching, moist body. When he felt himself against her feminine core, he sank deeply into her and stopped. They both held each other tightly and moaned in that exquisite initial moment of contact. She tightened around him. Then he began slowly to thrust into her, withdrawing and thrusting, driving her upward, closer and closer to climax. Heat emanated through her. She knew he was ready, but he drove her before him, before allowing himself release.

"I love you," she whispered mindlessly as her body frantically became more and more desperately close to release.

"Oh, yes?" he taunted. "Tell me more—tell me how much."

She gasped out a belly full of foolishness as he egged her on to further heights and when she crested, he followed swiftly behind her. In that moment, she called his name and he kissed her to dampen the sound. Afterward, they lay in each other's arms until their breathing slowed.

In their years of marriage they had made love so often that it could have easily become like a pleasant habit by now. She marveled that it was not so. Each time they joined it was different, new, exciting. It never failed to lift them to pinnacles of joy and wonder. It had never failed to be a wonderfully shared experience, to bind them closer every time. They had had the usual troubles during those times, and not every height was equal, but their physical love always managed to renew them.

Later, Geoffrey lay on his side with his head propped on one hand. He ran the tip of his finger down over her breast and down to her thigh.

"You know what I want?"

"Again?" she laughed and reached up to touch his face.

"Nothing I'd like more than to stay home today." He scratched at his beard. "We could leave the kids in Hannah's care and never get out of bed. We used to do that."

"Why don't you?" she asked, wistful for those bygone days.

"Today, as on every day, I am going to be busy earning our bacon."

"Or our daily bread?" she asked.

"No one can miss that you're a preacher's kid." His remark made her think of her father again, and she moved away. Geoffrey, not noticing her withdrawal, stretched, and she watched the interplay of muscles across his shoulders and chest. He continued, "If I stay home what about Harlem Fidelity?"

"Is that where you're going today?"

Harlem Fidelity Bank, where Geoff had first worked when they'd moved to Manhattan, was a small, black-owned bank. At the time he'd joined their staff, it was in financial straits and in danger of a hostile takeover. With Geoff's help, the bank had done incredibly well, managing to escape the unwanted merger. Geoff was on a roll when he introduced his methods to the bank.

This move was incredibly helpful to Geoff's reputation. In a few years, when he'd left them to open his own investment company, he'd taken the bank on as one of his clients.

When Geoff went on his own, his friend from school, Saul Pessach joined him as a partner. The two men had kept in close touch, and as the years passed their friendship grew. Saul Pessach became Geoff's trader.

"During the early hours." He rolled onto his back and put his hands behind his head. "I'll be talking with their investment department."

"Say hello to everyone for me," she said.

They entertained Geoff's customers frequently, and she'd become quite fond of the people who worked at Harlem Fidelity. Unfortunately, she was not particularly fond of some of his other clients.

"I will," he answered before adding, "however, the bank will only occupy part of my time today. There's also the Porters."

"Who?"

He sat up, throwing up his hands, exasperated. "Don't tell me you forgot." He rolled out of bed and pulled on his terry robe.

"No," she said, belatedly remembering the upscale couple he was talking about. "I just forgot their names."

"Well, please remember them by the time you come to the office."

"Don't I always?" She got up, too.

"Yes," he said, rounding the bed to take her into his arms. "You're a godsend, and I am grateful." He kissed her gently, but she'd lost the mood now.

Before he could remark on this, the telephone rang and Geoff reached to pick it up.

"Yeah, yeah," he said, impatiently to the caller, adding, "How can I forget?"

Sara realized it was his mother by his exasperated tone. He spoke briefly, then passed the handset to her and went to his closet. She watched him pick out clothes, which he chucked onto the bed as she spoke to Nora.

"Sara," Nora said, "I hope you remembered that Henry Morgan is coming to your housewarming?"

"Housewarming?" Sara said. *When did it become my house-warming?*

Sara had been annoyed when her mother-in-law had decided to give it at their new house, instead of her own apartment. But although Nora's apartment was huge, the new house was more spacious, and Sara had acquiesced.

Now, she wondered when it had become *her* party and not Nora's. Trust Nora to pull that one off.

"You know what I mean?" Nora asked."

"Yes," Sara answered, bringing herself back to the conversation.

"I like to include Henry whenever I can. I feel so sorry for him living in that hotel all the time. He's with that big company—"

"ICR," Sara supplied, thinking there was nothing to pity about Henry Morgan's living style. The hotel that Henry lived in was one of Manhattan's best. "Why can't Paula do some of this? She's family, too."

"Didn't I tell you?" Nora's voice was sweet as syrup— too sweet. "Paula isn't coming."

"No?" Sara couldn't help the suddenly optimistic glow that shot through her. Then, feeling guilty, she forced herself to ask, "Why not?"

"She'll be out of town that weekend."

That's one way to duck the work. "Oh, I see," Sara said. She dare not act disappointed, as it would have been absolutely hypocritical, and surely Nora would have known this.

"And don't forget Lizzibit's birthday party is coming up, too," Nora droned on. *Party, party, after insane party,* Sara thought. "She wants it to be for both your birthdays."

"Well . . ." Sara said, preparing to protest because she had no desire to celebrate this upcoming birthday.

"You can't disappoint the child," Nora cut in. "She's really looking forward to this."

"Yes, but—" Sara tried again, lamely, this time.

"Now, let me see," Nora cut in again. "Wasn't there something else?"

"Henry Morgan," Sara supplied, rolling her eyes heavenward. "I'll call him today."

With very little chatter, Nora soon hung up, leaving Sara holding the receiver. She put it down, determined to remain calm.

"You need to put your foot down when Nora does that ramrod crap that she knows so well," Geoff said, coming out of the bathroom with a towel tied around his waist.

"Lord, you have no idea how much I'd love to do just that."

"And what's this about Henry? Why are *you* calling him?"

"I promised her I'd see if he was coming to the party."

"I don't like him. He's a real sleaze bag."

"He's no worse than some of the others," Sara answered absently.

"Maybe, but he's got his own specialty, to my mind. If there's anything that Henry likes better than seducing the wives and lovers of his friends and business associates, I've never seen it," Geoff muttered.

"Probably money," she said, finishing Geoff's remark.

"What?"

"He probably likes money more than any of his other vices."

"All right, all right," Geoff said, "let's not get started on your favorite complaint. And let's not get off the subject. Why do you let Nora coerce you into doing these things?"

"She's doing it for you, Geoffrey. It's her way of bringing more clients into the business. Besides, it wouldn't hurt to have a housewarming."

"More excuses for another party, is what it is," he answered.

"That, too, I guess, but I'd feel guilty if I didn't help."

"She's manipulating you," he said, looking at ties. "And she'll probably stick you with all the work."

"It's just that . . . Nora is family, and I don't want any more . . . alienation than needs be."

"For Pete's sake. Who cares? If she doesn't like it, she can . . ." He stopped, probably realizing that she was speaking of her own family. "Baby, how many times do I have to tell you?" He hesitated again, appearing to chose his words carefully. "Nora's a troublemaker. She always was."

Sara knew that he'd hesitated, wanting to call Nora something worse, but restrained himself to keep from upsetting her. She'd never gotten used to Geoffrey's attitude toward his parents, although she agreed that Nora did cause a lot of problems and was inclined to interfere more often than not.

His words brought back her earlier thoughts. "How's your new assistant?" she asked.

"Paula?" he asked. "After a year, I don't consider her new anymore, but she's okay. As okay as I've told you before."

"Don't get touchy. Just asking," she said, then continued with, "According to Nora, Paula used to simply adore you."

Sara, that was a long time ago, when she was just a kid. Would you let it go?"

"I still don't understand why I couldn't have continued helping. We hardly see you anymore, you spend so much time at the office. Paula sees more of you than I do!"

"Sara." He stopped, that exasperated expression coming over his face again. "Haven't we discussed this at length? When I moved the office out of our home, part of the reason was to free you from those duties."

"Maybe I didn't want to be free."

"You did, then."

It was true, she thought, as far as it went. "I wanted more time with the kids, not to spend my life being a housewife."

"You don't," he corrected, "You have Hannah here, and now you're at that school almost as much as if you had a job. All that volunteering at the Maggie Ferguson School. Maybe you do too much."

"Oh, Geoff, I've only been doing that for the last six months, and it's good for me. It keeps my mind alert."

"I didn't say there was anything wrong with it, but if you were still working with me, it would be too much. Volunteering is better."

Suddenly, she knew why she was so jittery lately. She felt unneeded, aimless. She didn't mind volunteering, but sometimes it seemed such an unappreciated way to spend her time. She missed teaching. Teaching had been hard work, but it had been rewarding, too. While she had been working with Geoffrey she hadn't minded not teaching, but now she felt left out of the excitement.

She hadn't settled down, but had moved as Geoff's career needs dictated. Women always seemed to do that, and perhaps it was a mistake. She'd never looked back when they left Middletown, where she'd had a good job. Then, in the New York City public school system, she'd moved quickly from being a stand-in to full-time, but when Geoff needed more office staff, she'd quit her job and pitched in to help. It had seemed appropriate for her to assist in the fledgling business. Working with Geoffrey had been both exciting and challenging.

The business relied heavily on the computer, which had only come of age within the past few years. She'd rapidly become one of the experts in the area. Only a short while ago, the cost of the personal computer had been above most people's means, not to mention things such as video camera recording devices and cellular telephones. Being married to Geoff had kept her in the middle of the technology explosion. It was a time when anything seemed possible.

It had seemed a natural outcome that she should be the one who remained in the office, keeping an eye on the vagaries of the stock market. They had lived on Manhattan's Upper West Side and Geoff's office had been in the apartment. Those were the years when he always carried an extra shirt and tie in the car.

It was a miracle that he'd survived, for he always drove like a madman, with one arm steering the car and a quotrex—a machine similar to a portable radio that gave stock market quotes over the airwaves—in the other hand. He also kept in constant contact with Saul Pessach.

The two men had opened up the investment group together and Saul was often on the floor of the exchange while Geoff worked with the customers. They made a great team.

As for Geoff, of course, he thought this was better. He wanted to show that he could support his family without her working. Geoff had been good-natured about it, but she knew his pride had made him smart. Some of their conspicuous consumerism was caused by this same pride. He'd never forgotten being called a bum.

It was funny. Edna had always cautioned her against working to support their family. Her mother seemed totally unable to accept that many women worked in today's world. What Edna hadn't realized was how completely Geoff agreed with her opinion. He was the one who resented it.

There was another reason, too. She watched Geoff getting ready and thought that his mind was already on other things. She had her place in Geoff's life, but he was the center of hers. Someone always loved more in a relationship, and she'd come to accept she was that person. Geoffrey loved her in his own way, but she wondered how much.

These thoughts stopped when she heard a key turn in the lock. It was Hannah, the housekeeper. Hannah had been with them when they lived in Manhattan and she'd come with them when they'd moved. She was a mature, motherly type of woman with a warm touch with children. Since Geoffrey had hired her, the woman had proved worth her weight in gold. Sara glanced at the time again, realizing that she'd been daydreaming for the past few minutes.

Geoff went into the shower. She went to tell Hannah good morning before going into the room that would serve as their home office. Although, the rest of the house was still in the process of being organized, the office had been one of the first areas that they'd set up.

It had been almost two years, and still she missed that Geoffrey had moved everything into an outside separate office. She hadn't totally adjusted, and held on to the old days. It had been her idea to continue with a computer connected to the stock market quotes in the house. She turned it on although it was early. Quotes from the Nikkei market were running.

A few moments later, Geoff came. He'd gotten coffee and carried two cups, handing one to her.

"It's corrected from yesterday," she said, turning back to the numbers on the television screen.

"I told you so." He moved to study the screen over her shoulder. He stayed there for several long moments.

"Yes, you did." She smiled up at him. Then a frightening thought occurred and she glanced back hastily at the computer "You don't think it would repeat what happened before?"

"You mean our crash of eighty-seven? That's always a possibility, but no, I don't think that's going to happen any time soon. The market's recovering very well, and I believe it will break through the numbers and reach all new highs. I expect it to break the thousand points barrier within the next few years."

She smiled at his enthusiasm. Where the market was concerned, he always reacted like a young boy. "And of course, you'll make a bundle," she said.

"Naturally." He sounded pleased with himself. "You

need to trust your loving man, baby." Was he right, she wondered, was that all she really needed to do, trust him? Would he come through for her? Geoff had certainly come through for a lot of people on October 19, 1987, when the market had precipitously plunged. "I know exactly what to do if I see indications of that happening."

And he did, she knew. When the market dropped, many had sustained huge loses. Fortunes vanished. But not Geoff. His group had sailed through it unscathed. He'd been predicting such an event, and by the time it occurred Geoff's clients had been divested of all the troublesome holdings. Geoff's was one of the few groups that actually made money, something which had not escaped the notice of the news media. Since then Geoff's group had grown by leaps and bounds. His opinions were sought by many, and every word he uttered was news. Overnight, he had become something of a media star.

"I don't know how you do it—live under this much stress," she said.

"This is the time to do it, baby. Right now, the computer gives me an edge, but that's changing by the moment. Already the personal computer is available to more people. Soon, we'll all be equal. More people will have these in their living rooms."

"Your success isn't just having the computer. You're very good at this."

"Thanks for the vote of confidence," he said, touching the top of her head. "But you're right, it's always been more than just having a computer that crunches the numbers. A trader's longevity is his tenacity, his will to survive, and especially his reputation."

"I know," she said, repeating something he'd reiterated many times, "if you lose your reputation, it's all over.' "

"You're a quick study." He smiled. "Of course, there's the market itself. Its got to be able to pay off. As long as it does, the system can survive."

As he said that, she wondered if she wanted them to continue in the system. Many of his investors were black, middle-aged people, both male and female, who had worked hard, raising their children. And once the children were grown, they were surprised at how much of their paycheck was left at the end of the month. Now, left with these discretionary funds, they were looking for investments. With Geoffrey's soaring reputation, many of them had sought him out. Sara enjoyed entertaining some of these people, but that wasn't the whole of it.

It was a frenetic, crazy life-style and sometimes while the investors were so heavily involved with the materialistic that their spiritual existence seemed less substantial. It often appeared as if they spent their entire lives thinking of nothing except their bottom lines.

Chapter Eleven

Before Geoff left, she suddenly remembered that she'd forgotten to mention something that had happened at the school. She went and spoke to him as he finished dressing.

"The principal at the school asked me if you'd be interested in collecting some donations, too."

"Give me a break. When would I have time to do that?"

"You know what they say—if you want something done, ask a busy man."

"Yeah, all right, all right. Listen, that's highly improbable now."

"Just asking." She shrugged.

She walked him to the door and they kissed, more of a peck, in truth, but, he placed a finger under her chin and lifted her face to his, asking, "Are you all right?"

"Of course, I am," she answered, puzzled. "Why are you asking that?"

"I don't know," he frowned. "Sometimes, you seem more withdrawn."

She realized that he'd picked up on her earlier feelings, and stood on tiptoe to kiss his chin. "I'm fine," she said.

"Good. Stay that way." And he was gone.

Afterward, she had to mentally shake herself to eliminate the strange mood she'd been in that morning, realizing that it had been worse than she'd thought if Geoff had picked up on it. She was aided by the mad rush of getting herself and the children dressed. Kamaria was going to school, while she was scheduled to work today. Asa would be traveling with her.

She was taking a chance, knowing that she had to meet Geoff in the city later, to be driving all the way to Manhattan twice in one day, but she felt duty bound to go to the school, where she had been working to raise funds. Indeed, there was much unpacking still to do. She should have done that instead of going into the city, especially with Nora's party coming up.

She had to hurry her daughter, who often spent long moments looking in the mirror, and keep Asa on target as he played with his small car, rolling it across every surface he passed. The familiar activity made her remember how wonderful the years at home with her children had been.

Perhaps her discomfort had been caused by knowing that Asa was approaching the point when he'd be in school full-time, too. She would miss him, and maybe she needed to consider what the next phase of her life would be. She was buttoning Asa's shirt when the treacherous thought insinuated itself into her mind: *It wasn't until Paula started working with Geoff that this dissatisfaction began.*

The image made her feel so alone and frightened that she suddenly put her arms around Asa.

"Mommy, you're squeezing me too tight," he said absently, and then made childish motor sounds for his small car.

"Sorry, darling," she said, releasing him and straightening his small suspenders.

She helped the children put on their outerwear, wrapping scarves, finding earmuffs and tying shoelaces.

When they left the house the cold, wet wind whipped at their clothing. Despite their being dressed warmly, the wind seemed to find crevices to enter and chill various parts of their bodies. She had grown so tired of the freezing temperatures, and yearned for the warmth. Both children looked as fed up with the weather as she felt. She imagined they were tired of their padded snowsuits and galoshes, wanting to see the grass and run in the sunshine again.

At the posh grade school Kamaria attended, the child quickly found her best friend, Susan. The two little girls showed their glee at seeing each other with squeals and giggles.

Sara asked the child's mother, "Anne, would you mind picking Kamaria up this afternoon?"

"No problem. I'll take her to dancing school, too."

"Would that be too much trouble?" Sara asked, feeling slightly guilty.

"No way. Anyway, you always do it for me."

"Great. I'll tell Hannah to expect you. I really appreciate it."

"Hot date with the hubby?" Anne asked with one arched eyebrow.

"No such luck. I forgot I have to meet him for dinner with some of his clients."

"Mommy," Kamaria interrupted. "I want to stay with Susan tonight."

"Not tonight, Honey," Sara said as she tried to keep Asa from wriggling away.

"But I want to," Kamaria insisted, stamping her foot. "I want to be with Susan."

"I'll let you play with my cars," Asa offered.

"I *hate* playing with your old cars," the girl said to him. Then, turning to Sara, said, "I hate playing with him. He's just a baby."

"I'm not a baby," Asa insisted, his face screwed up to cry.

"Kamaria . . ." Sara started, thinking that the girl too frequently found a reason not to be home with Asa.

"It's okay with me," Anne cut in. "Tomorrow's Saturday. You could pick her up in the afternoon. And I know Susan would enjoy it."

Sara observed Kamaria's pleasure at Anne's offer and wondered if her daughter wasn't becoming too manipulative. There were times when her daughter reminded her very much of her mother-in-law. But one glance at her watch made her realize that if she hoped to get to the school she couldn't stand there arguing with Kamaria. Reluctantly, she turned to Anne, saying, "Okay, and thanks again."

Then she rushed Asa into his carseat in the rear and drove into Harlem, where the school was located. Asa enjoyed those days when they went into the school, and she preferred keeping him with her when she could. He needed the outing, and she always felt guilty when she left him with the housekeeper. Also, despite what Geoff always said, he didn't like his children being fobbed off on the servants, either. Sara wondered if it reminded him of his own childhood.

Geoff was sometimes impatient with their son. Although Asa was a terribly sweet child, he had periods of being hyperactive. When this occurred, it was difficult to deal with him. Sometimes, Sara wondered if Geoff saw himself in Asa, or if it was simply a case of his wanting a perfect life for his son.

Recalling how antsy she'd been that morning, she still wondered what it had been about. Her own accomplishments might not seem terribly grand when compared to Geoff's, but she loved the work she did.

The school had been started only a few years ago for inner city children. It was an ambitious project, set up on a shoestring budget. Despite this, they'd managed to survive. Crowded, lacking in funds, it provided a quality education covering preschool through eighth grade, and even taught music. The students consistently scored higher than those in the public schools.

The school was also involved with the families, giving parenting classes, instruction for high school equivalency certificates and other forms of adult education, including literacy classes. Although she wasn't teaching, she did occasionally fill in for absent instructors. It was incredibly rewarding, and she was proud to be affiliated with them. She hated to believe that she could become a person who equated her worth only by her paycheck.

Once at the school, she placed Asa in one of the preschool classes and headed for the office. There was a fund drive going on and she was working with other volunteers on this. Unfortunately, she wasn't the best fundraiser, often embarrassed by having to ask people for money, but she did her best. Sometimes her efforts seemed like small potatoes.

She checked her watch again, not wanting to stay past her time or be late to meet Geoff that evening. Then she picked up a phone and started making calls.

Hours later when she finally arrived home, she was exhausted. What she truly wanted to do was have a nice, relaxing bubble bath, but she had to get ready to meet Geoff.

Asa was also overtired, and when Hannah came to put him down for a nap, he fussed for a while. She took him herself, knowing that her son often responded better if she gave him a little extra attention. She helped him into his bed and sat near for a while. She even read him a story, letting him chose the book.

Soon, his eyelids began to droop but before he fell asleep, he put his hand on her cheek. She took the small fingers and kissed them, which made him laugh. Asa couldn't hold out much longer, and soon he closed his eyes and started breathing quietly. She was still holding Asa's small hand and glanced down as his fingers closed around hers. It made her remember the first time she'd realized that he was musically inclined. . . .

It had occurred only months before. They were still living in the old apartment, where a piano had been left by a previous tenant. Asa had climbed up onto the bench. Sitting at the desk, Sara had seen him and stood up slowly. She walked toward him, watching that he didn't fall. Like a little monkey, the boy was soon sitting with his hands on the keys, at first only banging. The noise was deafening, and she reached to take him down, but her reaction was delayed.

Suddenly, he looked incredibly absorbed in the sounds that issued from the instrument. Then, with head tilted to the side, he had seemed to be listening to something that she couldn't hear. He stopped banging and touched the keys with one finger, then looked at her and laughed.

She sat beside him and smiled, "You like that?" she said, and chucked him under the chin.

As if from nowhere he tapped three keys in succession, and she was totally arrested. It sounded almost like the first three notes of a popular melody that frequently aired on the radio. Hannah often listened to the radio as she worked, and Asa spent a great deal of time with the good-natured woman. Even Geoff occasionally played the song on the guitar, in those rare moments when he played to relax himself.

Asa had elicited the same sounds several times in a row as she stood holding her breath, waiting. Then, laughing loudly, he seemed to lose interest. He reached up to her, gesturing that he wanted to be picked up.

She swept him into her arms, "That's Mommy's little musician," she said and tickled his stomach. He went into squeals of giggles and she closed the piano.

The next day he had played those same keys again, actually adding a fourth note, making it seem even more that he was imitating the popular song. Then he moved on to something else.

After that incident, Asa became very interested in the piano and often wanted to play. She would open the top, for it absorbed him for long periods. Usually, all he did was bang, but soon true sounds began to emerge from the instrument.

Knowing that both of her son's grandfathers had been musicians, she also thought of Geoff's playing. Her father's words echoed in her memory—Hugo had been a genius. Had Asa inherited a talent similar to Hugo's? She had decided to enroll him in a preschool where he would have the opportunity to learn music. It was due to Asa that she'd found the Ferguson School.

The memories and sudden quiet were so wonderful that she allowed herself to relax, promising that it would only be for a few moments. It had been a hectic day, and the brief inactivity lulled her into a doze.

When she woke, it took a few moments to orient herself. She stared up at the ceiling before realizing she was in Asa's room. She glanced at her watch. Oh, no, it was almost three o'clock! Moving as quickly as she could, she slipped quietly out of Asa's bed and hastily went to her own room, to get dressed.

Hannah had pressed the dress Sara had asked for and hung it on the closet door. It was a soft, flowing aqua wool that showed her small waistline. She rushed into the shower, where she shampooed her hair and blow-dried it into softly framing her face. Gold hoop earrings and several gold chains were quickly put on. Although nervous, she carefully applied makeup with a steady hand.

She wasn't looking forward to the evening with Geoff's clients, but she wanted to look her best. Entertaining the stock market group was coming to be a job that she didn't enjoy. Her enthusiasm seemed to wane as time passed.

She finished the outfit with her full-length, sable mink coat, a gift from Geoff last Christmas. Geoff encouraged her to wear it. It was another part of the male pride thing. No one could look at that coat and believe Geoff wasn't doing very well by his family. Somehow, she realized that this was not the way she wanted to live. She wanted a simpler life.

It wasn't that she didn't admire what he'd done, for she did. The problem was that she was surprised at how well he'd done. She remembered his proposal, and how she'd feared they would live as vagabonds. That certainly hadn't happened. She'd been proven wrong. But sometimes she wondered if they truly needed so much money when it took Geoff away from his family so much.

Suddenly she realized that the strange mood she'd been

in earlier was returning. She pushed the disturbing
thoughts away and finished dressing. As luck would have
it by the time she was dressed and giving Hannah instruc-
tions, Asa was awake and fretful again.

"Don't you worry, Mrs. McMillan, I'll take care of him,"
Hannah said, trying to be reassuring.

"I'll just tell him good-bye," Sara said, feeling flustered
and frustrated as she went into the child's room.

Once she saw Asa's sleepy, tearful little face, she picked
him up, wanting to comfort her son. He didn't miss that
she was dressed to go out.

"Don't go out, Mommy," he begged querulously.

Hannah came into the room with a slice of orange. She
tried to coax Asa to come to her, using the fruit. He reached
out quickly and took it from the unsuspecting woman and
popped the fruit into his mouth. The sudden act made
them roar with laughter, and being the center of attention
made him more amenable.

However, when Sara handed the child to Hannah, she
realized that he'd messed up her dress and she would have
to change again. She anxiously glanced at the clock.

As she changed, she thought angrily of how Geoff
expected her to be the perfect corporation wife and how
hard she worked not to disappoint him. Added to that
were her efforts to maintain good relations with both their
families. Her life was a mad swirl of activity. Sometimes
she thought it was all meaningless and demented.

She rushed out of the house, the sound of Asa's heartfelt
cries following her through the door. "Never you mind,
He'll be just fine," Hannah commiserated. To Asa, she
said, "Won't you, snookums?"

More frustrated than ever, Sara jumped into her car.
Ordinarily, she would have called for a cab, but not today.
She was already running late, so she decided to drive to
the train station. It meant that Geoff would have to drop
her off later so that she could drive it home, and he would
be annoyed at that, but there was no help for it. Geoff's
office was located on Manhattan's Upper West Side. Once

in Manhattan, she hailed a cab. The short ride seemed to take forever in the early evening traffic.

She hurried into Geoff's office and he looked up and examined her quickly. After a small delay, he smiled. She could see that he appreciated her wearing the mink. She exhaled in relief. He wasn't as easy to please recently as he'd been in the past. Now she had to dress more sophisticatedly. She thought briefly of how she used to be more natural. That was no longer acceptable.

Geoff checked his watch. "You're late," he said.

"Asa woke just as I was getting ready to leave and I had to change."

His mouth tightened and she regretted mentioning the small delay. "You coddle him too much."

"He's just a little boy," she said too quickly, and was immediately sorry. They disagreed too much over Asa lately, she thought, and wondered what this meant.

"All right, not now," he chided. "The Porters will be here any minute."

"Where's Paula?" she asked, not having seen the woman in the outer office.

"Around here someplace," he answered absently, his attention on the papers in front of him.

"Let me freshen up," she said after laying her coat across the leather couch in Geoff's office.

She went into the lavatory, wondering if she'd gotten mussed in the mad dash to get out of the house and the short train ride. The cool, well made-up woman who stared back from the mirror surprised her. She looked calm and unflappable. What a joke. Using a paper towel, she moistened it with cold water and used it at pulse points.

"So, what time are the Porters—" Sara asked as she came out of the bathroom.

Sara stopped upon finding Paula Weills there. Paula was a beautiful woman, standing a sleek five-nine with gorgeous legs and clear, grey eyes. She wore a short, tweed miniskirt that barely seemed to cover the basics. The younger woman stood over Geoff, one slim hand with red tipped fingernails resting on his shoulder. The two of them shared a smile that looked incredibly intimate. Sarra almost gasped aloud.

Then Paula looked up, glimpsing Sara. "Oh, Sara," she said, tilting her head in such a way that her wheat-colored hair fell in a thick sheath away from her face. She raised one eyebrow knowingly and said, "I was just getting coffee for good old cousin Geoff here."

"Yes, I see," Sara said. She took a deep breath and, forcing herself to appear natural, said, "And how are you today?"

"Just fine." Paula treated her to a full array of exquisite porcelain caps. Paula asked Geoff, "Are you certain you don't want me to stay and help with the Porters?" Her voice sounded as if she'd asked the same question before.

"No," Geoff said, already back to perusing the papers. "Just show them in and then you can leave. Sara will take over, now."

"Okay." Paula's eyes met Sara's over Geoff's head.

Paula then sauntered to the door. The woman's habit of swinging her hair at the least provocation annoyed Sara, but she simply sat in one of the chairs in front of Geoff. Then, before Paula exited, she turned back and speaking to Sara, said, "Oh, would you like some coffee?"

"No, thank you," Sara said with a determined smile.

"Well, toodleloo." Paula waved her fingers at them and quietly closed the door behind her.

"I don't see how you get any work done with her all over you," Sara snapped, feeling shrewish.

"Paula? Ah, that's just her way. Probably a holdover from when she had a kiddy crush on me."

"Kiddy crush? Wasn't that a long time ago?" she said, but he simply grunted, obviously missing her attempt at sarcasm. She took a deep breath. Determined not to allow Paula to get under her skin, she said, "Tell me about the Porters."

Geoffrey looked up and sat back, relaxing. "Danny Porter's an old Harlem boy whose been living on the west coast. He's done well for himself, designing a sportswear line. Made a mint. Then he got homesick and returned here. Recently, he opened a store in Brooklyn that's doing well.''

"Where's it located? Does he have an account with your bank?"

"Harlem Fidelity's not my bank anymore, Sara."

"You know what I mean."

"Yes, he has an account. I'd like to get him to invest with the group.

"I figured that. And Pamela Porter," Sara said, pulling the name out of her memory. "What's she like?"

"I don't know. You met her at that cocktail party last week."

"We only spoke briefly," Sara answered.

They were able to talk for a few minutes before the Porters arrived. When she and Geoff greeted them, she thought, *It's as if we're a united front.* The idea took her aback. She wondered from where it had come. Of course she and Geoff were a united front.

They went to a wonderful restaurant in the neighborhood. The food was spectacular. The owner, a beautifully well turned-out black woman, came to their table, and Geoff introduced everyone.

Despite having met the Porters only once before and then briefly, she recognized that she didn't particularly like them. They were very like many of Geoff's clients, affected and even pretentious. The wife, Pamela, bordered on being obnoxious.

Although Sara admired Danny Porter's accomplishments, she became increasingly more uncomfortable as the couple drank their way through dinner. While it was not always true, many of the people Geoff dealt with lived strange, frenetic lives. They were usually too hyper, often teetering on the edge of control. The Porters were such a couple.

The evening went on longer than they expected, and Geoff was forced to babysit the couple as the night wore on. For one thing, it took him a long time to convince them not to drive in their intoxicated condition. Geoff had to make arrangements to park their car and see that they arrived home safely.

He was in a foul humor by the time he'd finished and they were in their own car, driving up the Hutchinson River Parkway toward Scarsdale. Then, with temper still frayed by his dealings with the Porters, he turned on her. "What was wrong with you tonight?" he demanded.

"Nothing," Sara answered, feeling sulky and spoiling for a fight herself.

"Don't give me that."

"Pamela threw up in the ladies' room."

"I see," he said after a moment of silence. "And?"

"And what?"

"You're too upset for that to have been all."

"As sick as she was, she was still drinking from a flask she was toting in her purse. Also, she was smoking in there, and was so careless with the match that she almost set fire to her hair. If it weren't for me and the rest room attendant, she might have had a serious accident. You don't think *that* was bad enough? Do I need to say she killed someone to get a rise from you?"

"I understand your annoyance—" Geoff started.

"It was more than just annoying. It was downright scary."

"Yes, I'm sure it was. And it *was* a good thing that you were there. But we're not in the business of policing people's moral behavior, and I wish you'd remember that."

"I wasn't policing anything, but wouldn't you think she'd be a bit more careful? And why do I have to be the understanding one? Why couldn't she consider that her behavior might offend me, or someone else, for that matter? I'm coming to hate doing this."

"Sara, remember that my work provides us with an income. You need to be more willing to help. I need my wife at my side. You always understood this before."

"I do, but I can't help resenting it sometimes. She was so stoned that she was dangerous. Maybe that's the point."

"It's not our business to say."

"So you've been telling me, and I'm not judging. It's simply that . . . oh, I don't know. But I feel as if something needs to be done about it."

"Something like what? Who do you think you are? God?"

"Why do we have to play nursemaids to all these prima donnas?" The timing was bad, but suddenly she thought, *In for a penny, in for a pound.* "I want to go back to work."

He didn't answer for a few moments. Finally he said, "What do you mean? You're already working at the school. You're there all the time."

"I mean back to teaching."

"What for? We don't need the money."

She looked at him quickly. "This is not about money. You know I always loved teaching."

"Why now? The kids are still too young. Asa isn't even in school, yet."

"I could enroll him for more hours."

"He's four years old. He needs his mother, not more hours at school."

She wondered if he remembered his own past, and how he'd started school so young. But this was different. Much of Geoff's childhood had been spent being shifted from one place to another while his parents were on the road. This wasn't true of Asa. She wouldn't be away for weeks or months at a time. Asa lived in a quiet, stable home and saw his parents daily.

"I think he'll benefit from it," she said. "Besides, I could probably get something part-time."

"If it isn't the money, what's the difference between what you're doing now and that?"

"I'm not teaching now. Mostly all I do is assist in the fundraising."

"That place needs good fundraisers, and both of the kids need you at home—accessible to them."

"I'm not moving anyplace. I'll still be accessible." She

knew her frustration was rising when she added, "What about what *I* need?"

"That's what this whole thing has been about, hasn't it?" he asked.

"What whole thing?"

"Your anger, your vague complaints, your dissatisfactions? You're bored, and you want to dump your responsibilities."

"That isn't true," she said.

"You're going to leave *your* children to teach other people's?"

"I'm not leaving my children." But she knew she was wasting her time. It was an issue that Geoff was too sensitive about.

"I'm not saying that you should never return to your career, but give the kids a few more years, that's all I'm asking. Then we'll talk about it," Geoff said, sounding so reasonable.

Another few years! She wasn't sure what she wanted to do, scream or cry. She decided to do neither, simply to think on it more. Maybe he was right, she realized, and maybe her restlessness was only some sort of personal insecurity.

The next morning, Saturday, Sara was in the house alone. Geoff had gone to the office for a few hours. They still hadn't made up from last night's argument, and she felt slightly depressed. Hannah had taken Asa to the park and Kamaria was still at her friend's house. Sara was at the back of the house unpacking some of the few remaining cartons.

The telephone rang and she ran to get it, frantically wondering where she'd left the portable handset. Her eagerness was partly due to her hope that it was Geoff. She wanted to make up, and she was hoping that he'd suggest their having lunch someplace. It was Nora.

"Let me speak with Geoff."

"He went to the office."

"On a Saturday? He works too hard. My poor pretty-boy," she complained. "I hope you appreciate all he does."

"Of course I do," Sara snapped. It always amazed her how Nora knew where to drive her nasty little barbs.

"Well, that's not why I called. I need Geoff to come immediately. Oh, never mind, I'll call him at the office."

"Is it an emergency?" Sara asked too late. Nora had hung up, leaving Sara still on the line. She set it on the receiver. Sara wondered if there was something truly wrong. Knowing Queen Nora, it was probably something that was urgent only to her.

At that moment, she heard the front door bang. "Sara!" Geoffrey bellowed.

Chapter Twelve

"Sara!" he yelled again and his voice seemed to reverberate through the house and bounce off the walls.

Jeez, she thought. Was he trying to get their neighbors up in arms before they'd even finished unpacking?

Something about the inflection of his voice made her hesitate to answer. It reminded her of something.

"In here," she called back finally, expecting him to join her.

She glanced up as he passed by the open doorway, acting as if he hadn't seen her. He dropped his shirt and went stomping around the house. Why hadn't he come into the room where she was? Doors banged along his route.

Suddenly it was as if a light flashed on. She remembered a scene in an old video movie they'd borrowed the week before. So, Mr. Geoff Stone-McMillan wanted his own personal reenactment. She wanted to laugh her head off. Obviously, he also wanted to make up their differences from last night. She'd show him a thing or two.

Gladly, she left the packing crates to peek out the door at Geoff's progress. Bits and pieces of his clothes had been dropped along the way. When he was out of view, she tiptoed to the stairs, where she sneaked upward as quietly as she could. She held her hand over her mouth to keep from laughing and giving her presence away.

She was almost at the top when she tripped. "Oops!"

Geoff's hand coming through the banister caught her ankle, "Aha!" he said, "so there you are, my pretty." He was down to his underwear.

"Ah!" she squealed, as excited as if the whole scene were real.

She managed to escape from his loose grip. Before moving on, she stopped to look at him over the banister.

"There's no escape, Ms. Sara, my pearl." He leered up at her.

Another old movie She ran as fast as she could to top the last few steps. "Now, you're mixing your metaphors," she said.

She laughed and ran for their bedroom, unbuttoning her blouse as she did. Inside the room, she shut the door and slipped from the jeans she'd been wearing. She heard him coming up the stairs with heavy, exaggerated steps and had another attack of the giggles that almost made her fall on her face as she slipped from her bikini panties.

He was truly hamming it up, stomping slowly down the hallway when she jumped into the bed and hurriedly posed herself so that she sat lounging on the pillows, facing the door with knees raised and opened. Not wearing a strip of clothing was partly the reason that her skin felt tingly. The other reason was that she'd begun to anticipate their being together.

The door flew open and Geoff stepped in, still in his briefs. "Aha, this must be the place." He walked to the bed, stripping off his shorts.

He joined her and moved on his knees until he was between her opened legs, already fully erect. His manhood bumped her thigh, hard and ready.

Then he addressed the next words to her feminine core. "Hello there, you little cute thing."

She wanted to laugh, but desire was swelling. Her body

didn't need any message from her to prepare itself for him. It was always ready. She knew she was moist, and a throbbing need began.

Geoff rose up and kissed her mouth. She shuddered as she put her arms around his neck, drawing him closer.

"I've been waiting for you," she said.

"Me too," he answered. "Going into the office was a wasted trip. I didn't get anything done because I was too busy thinking of this," he whispered in her ear, and his warm breath sent tremors through her.

"Oh, yes?"

"Now," he said. His hand went slowly, caressingly, down her side. "It's time for you to pay your rent."

"Rent? Are you the landlord?" she asked, running her hand through the hair on his chest.

"Me and my wife," he responded.

"Wife?" she played coy. "Will she mind?"

"Don't worry about her. She'll understand." He took her mouth in a long, soul-drugging kiss before drawling seductively, "Baby, am I not your loving man?"

"Oh, yes, you most certainly are."

"Don't you think I should be rewarded for that?" he asked.

"Absolutely.

"Come here."

"What do I have to do?"

"Start by giving your loving man a big hug and kiss."

She sat up, put her arms around him, and pressed her mouth to his. Then she gently guided him to lie down.

"Hmmm," he murmured when she mounted him. "If this is an attempt to kill the landlord, do carry on. I'm certain to die happy."

Slowly, she lowered herself upon him. "That's what I intend to do," she whispered, leaning forward to kiss him again. Her breasts above him caught his attention and he lavished attention upon them. It made her mindless.

Within a few short moments, she was caught up in the pure sensation of making love with her husband in the afternoon when he said in a husky, seductive voice, "Hey, you're cheating."

"What?" She tried to divorce her mind from what was happening to her body, with little success.

"This is supposed to be my reward," he said.

"For what?" she murmured, not quite able to focus on the game anymore.

"The rent, maybe? Anyway, if it's *my* reward, why are *you* making all that noise? I think you're having as much fun as I am."

If he'd expected her to laugh, he had to forget it. Her body took off and she accompanied it into ecstasy. At that moment she couldn't have cared less if Geoff wanted to horse around at such a sensitive moment. As always, he followed soon after, pushed by her sounds of pleasure to losing his own control.

They clung together until their breathing slowed. He rolled over on his back and lay quietly for a short time. However, when she started to rise, he snared her wrist. propped his head on one hand and leaned over her.

"Now," he began and paused.

"Again?" she shrieked.

"New house means a rent increase." He shrugged and leered at her.

"Oh, naughty landlord."

He leaned closer and kissed her slowly and lingeringly. The telephone rang, and although their mouths continued together, their bodies went tense.

"Ignore it," he said, drawing away slightly. He moved to kiss her again.

She wanted to let it ring as much as Geoff did, but suddenly she remembered the earlier cryptic conversation with Nora. "We can't."

"Yes, we can. Watch how I do it," he said, moving one hand to caress her hip.

"Your mother called," she said, ashamed that she'd forgotten.

"So what? She can wait." He sounded impatient, as he often did with Nora.

"She said it was urgent."

"Sure, I believe that," he snorted, but his hand stopped. Now she had his attention. "Sometimes, that woman rivals Edna in the psychic department. How can she always know when to mess up a good thing?"

"Don't complain. You're just greedy," she said.

"What's greedy about wanting another . . . ?" He spoke in mock indignation but she'd already picked up the handset and passed it to him after she heard Nora's voice.

"Yeah, yeah, right," Geoff said shortly into the phone as he glanced at her across the bed.

Her errant memory took that time to remind her that she hadn't called Henry as Nora had requested. *Oh, no,* she thought, and glanced anxiously at Geoff.

"No," he said, "Sara can't come to the phone. She's busy," and he turned away when she reached to take the handset. *"I'll* call Henry. Why should *Sara* do it? Besides, I couldn't care less whether he comes or not."

The night of the housewarming Sara heard a commotion at the door and glanced up to see the McMillans enter. Hugo and the two girls in were front, followed by Nora. Alongside of Nora, Sara spied Paula.

She had been overseeing the catering crew, keeping close to them, making certain that everything went well, and suddenly it all seemed perfectly ridiculous. As a matter of fact, she had actually been talking to the maitre d' when she'd stopped midsentence to gawk at the two women. It was such a cheap shot for Nora to say that Paula wasn't coming. What had she hoped to gain? But cheap or not, Sara was furious.

The two women were dressed to the nines. *Of course. Why not?* she thought. *I'm the one who's been knocking myself out for this party. They've had nothing but time to make themselves gorgeous.* Suddenly, she felt less secure with her own dress, but she just as quickly pushed that thought away. Sara glanced down at the black sheath that skimmed her body and was cut low in front. She looked good, and she was going to enjoy it.

As soon as they'd removed their coats, Paula immediately took Geoff's arm, and from there on the woman seemed glued to him.

"You were saying, Ms. McMillan?" the man prompted to recapture her attention.

Sara turned around and stared at him, having totally forgotten that she had been in the process of making a request that he tend to some minor duty. He looked at her as if he thought she had gone crazy. Geoff was right. She'd allowed Nora to dupe her into this, and then to have Paula, too, just seemed too much all of a sudden.

The whole thing was ridiculous. Here she was working like a fool for Nora's party while Paula was hanging on to her husband. She started laughing, and the poor man looked alarmed.

"James, you're the expert. Carry on," she said when she could stop the laughter. And this time, he looked truly alarmed. Never in all the years that she had been dealing with him had she given him carte blanche such as this.

She walked away, hobbled a bit by her long, narrow, black skirt. As she passed a waiter, she snatched a long-stemmed glass of champagne. Then, thinking better of it, grabbed another, and drank both quickly.

Just as she was passing Geoff, he happened to glance toward her. He looked shocked at the sight of her finishing the two glasses of champagne.

Somehow, he'd slipped out of Paula's clutches—only God knew how. Now on her trail, catching up with her immediately, he took her hands, removing both glasses.

"Why are you swilling that stuff like that? You know how fast it goes to your head."

She relinquished the glasses and stared at him. "Are you enjoying the party?" she asked, smiling brightly. Already she felt lightheaded.

"Do you think you've answered my question?" he responded, and glanced around surreptitiously.

"I don't need a father. I already have one." She had the urge to say more but managed, despite the alcohol, to close her mouth before she could.

His eyes widened in surprise. "What's going on?" he said through his teeth in an attempt not to be heard by their guests.

Now she wanted to stamp her foot. This was Geoff, the love of her life, the only man she had ever loved. The man that she had shared her life with for the last eleven years. No, make that the man to whom she had given the last eleven years of her life. The man who made the sun rise in the morning. The man whose every smile meant life for her. *Well*, she thought, *maybe Paula will see to it that there's no more of that.* She tried to extricate herself but he held on.

"Why are you asking me?" Sara spoke facetiously. "Ask your mother. She's the local expert on everything." She could see that her unexpected remark and attitude shocked him. He rarely heard her say anything negative about his mother. She was able to pull away from his detaining hand.

She walked away, grabbing another glass of champagne. She sensed rather than saw that Geoff had overcome his momentary shock and was now following in her wake to make her account for her words. Geoff was an American prince, and he wasn't used to Cinderella leaving the chimney. She giggled. The alcohol, which she never drank, was bypassing her stomach and going straight to her head.

Just as Geoff put a hand on her bare shoulder, she turned to the first available escape. It happened to be Henry Morgan.

She threw up her hand. Fortunately she had swilled down the champagne, because she'd probably have poured it all over the three of them.

"Henry! Dance with me," she said, and wrapped her arms around the man's neck.

Henry's eyebrows shot up, and looking at the sly smile on his face Sara wished she had found another rescuer. Henry was a real letch and was obviously pleased, probably sensing there might have been something going on between her and Geoff, for Geoff was right there.

Henry took the bait instantly and swept Sara into his arms. Then he took the empty glass and casually handed it to Geoff. Her husband looked murderous for a split second, and Henry looked as if he might be having second thoughts.

Sara went cold. Geoff had rarely ever shown jealousy, except for eleven years ago. He had terrified her then, and the memory never failed to raise the hair on her neck whenever she thought of it. Her heart had stopped at Geoff's furious glance. She could barely breathe.

Then Geoff's expression was quickly composed, and he smiled charmingly before stepping back. Air rushed into her lungs with a sharp pain. Henry went on because he had no idea what Geoff was capable of when in a jealous rage.

She had planned to get away as soon as they had put enough distance between themselves and Geoff. However, she could see that Geoff's eyes were glued to them. Now, she regretted the champagne, as her legs were a little rubbery and her stomach felt queasy. She took a deep breath, thinking that Geoff was right. She had always been a cheap high.

Geoff wasn't the only one watching her with Henry. There were quite a few other people staring, including Nora, who hadn't lost the smirk. Sara could just hear their little minds ticking: *Was there trouble brewing between the brilliant gorgeous Geoff Stone-McMillan and his devoted little slavey?*

All the attention only made her want to give them something to stare at. She laughed up into Henry's face, really trying to look fascinated, although she was beginning to have problems focusing. And when he decided to dip her, she feared she'd lose her dinner.

"Why, Sara," Henry said in his most seductive voice,

"why haven't we seen more of each other?" All she could manage was a giggle, because the man was so obvious that she wondered what women saw in him. Well, she had to admit he was handsome. "Why don't we have lunch sometime this week?" he went on.

"Lunch?" she gasped, just as he decided to dip her again. When she was vertical again, she grasped his arms, saying, "Henry, let's talk about it later. I don't feel very well."

A look of pure triumph came over his face. "Of course, my dear. Let me help you." Henry was leading her from the dance area toward the outside garden when Geoff confronted them.

She was feeling more ill and knew there was no place to run, because Geoff looked determined to collect her as if she were an errant child.

"Geoff, old boy," Henry said as Geoff carefully took her out of his arms, "Sara seems to be feeling a little under the weather. We were just looking for you."

Despite the words, Sara thought that Henry sounded terribly reluctant as the chance of their having a little tête-à-tête faded away in the presence of Geoff's poker face.

"Thank, you, Henry," Geoff said with his usual charm. "I'll handle it, now."

Sara was reluctant to be passed on to Geoff, but for a totally different reason. She hesitated at the fight they would have later. But, she realized, maybe this was best. Besides, she knew how to distract Geoff from his anger.

She wasn't the frightened girl she had been when they first met. She had learned early how vulnerable he was to her sexually. Of course, he had the same affect on her, but you couldn't have it all.

She threw her arms around Geoff's neck, and whispered in his ear, "Let's go to bed."

He stiffened. His arms came around her for support as he took her from Henry. When she looked up into his face, it had hardened. His anger had worsened. He led her away, saying to their guests, "Excuse us, Sara's not feeling too well."

Sara gazed at the people staring at them, thinking, *They already know that.* But everyone was kind, and now she was sorry that she had made such a stupid scene. They offered to help and wished her a quick recovery. She smiled, though her stomach was acting up worse. Nora and Paula took over the party as she exited the room on Geoff's arm.

As soon as they were in the bedroom, her stomach showed signs of going from ominous lurching to a full fledged eruption. She made a beeline to the bathroom. Geoff followed and held her head as she hung over the toilet, totally disgracing herself. For some reason, as helpless as she felt, she still didn't want him to see her in this position.

"Go back to the party," she told him.

"Be quiet," he said and placed a cool, wet cloth on her forehead. He sounded more patient than she had expected after the scene she had just caused.

His sweetness only saddened her. Geoff had always been capable of great kindness. Maybe his anger with her would have evaporated if he hadn't picked that moment to remember.

"What the devil made you make a fool of yourself with that damn Henry Morgan? And I don't know why I'm feeling sorry for you. It's your own fault. You never drink. What made you do it tonight?" he demanded.

Lord, she wanted to pour out everything to him at that moment—all her recent fears and insecurities. But she knew how foolish it would sound. Instead, she rinsed her mouth and walked around him to lie down on the bed.

"I want an answer. Have you been seeing him?"

"Are you still talking about Henry?" she asked just as a headache started.

"Who else did you think? Yes, Henry!"

"No. Of course not," she answered quickly. "Why are you asking that?"

She gazed at him, bewildered. It was unusual to see Geoff

losing his composure. It made her remember him as a
child, with the sudden, rare storms of wild tantrums.
They'd always had more to do with his possessiveness than
with anything else.

Also, she hadn't missed that he'd sounded surprised
when he'd asked, but certainly no more surprised than
she was at the question. *His* surprise, however, galled her.
He would be shocked if she were ever untrue. Geoff had
the utmost faith in her. Why shouldn't he? Aside from her
work at the school, she never did anything that wasn't
somehow involved with him or with someone in their families. And now that he was too busy to watch her, there was
Nora to do the job for him. Even his two teenage sisters
sometimes seemed like jailers. She shook those thoughts
away. Those thoughts were unfair.

Besides, she had never had any interest in other men,
and he knew that, too. In all the years, she'd never even
looked at another man. She believed he'd never been
unfaithful, too, but only because she truly felt that she'd
have known if there was ever another woman.

This didn't comfort her much. Sara remembered Nora
calling her insipid, and she'd come to feel just that. There
were times when she feared Geoff had been pressured
into marrying her, that his whole proposal had been done
almost on a dare, an effort to forestall Nora. He'd never
implied this, but it was an odd thought that sometimes
came to her on quiet moments. What had he known about
love? He'd just come back after years of silence and collected her like abandoned baggage.

She closed her eyes, pretending to be asleep, and he
left after a few minutes. Coward that she was, she didn't
relish the scene that would follow the party. She got up
and, although she was wobbly, managed to shower and
brush her teeth. Then she changed the sheets and put on
a new nightgown that Geoff had never seen.

She was trying to work quickly so that she would be ready
when he came to bed. But their bedroom began to look
like Grand Central Station, with Geoff's family wandering

in and out. It reminded her that her own parents never attended Nora's parties. *Smart,* she thought.

First it was his sisters, Alexis and Lizzibit, ages seventeen and fifteen respectively, who came to see her. Each girl had come alone, as they rarely went anyplace together. Alexis, looking far too sophisticated for her years, swayed in once. She held a fluted glass, from which she sipped.

"What's that?" Sara asked.

"Champagne," Alexis answered.

Sara wanted to say something, then didn't. She felt that her own behavior that night gave her no right to talk. *The girl worries me,* Sara thought, watching her young sister-in-law. Despite their good beginning, their relationship seemed to have waned in the last year. Possibly that was caused by Sara's working at the school, or by her being too distracted by her own problems.

Recently, she had begun to wonder if Alexis were actually avoiding her. The girl had become remote. And lately, she had felt a certain urgency about Alexis. She had always identified strongly with her.

The girls, as often seemed true with teenagers, had grown into their own beauty. However, Sara had noticed that Alexis's complexion had lost the rose hue. She appeared sallow.

"I thought you were going to bed," Alexis said.

"I am," Sara answered as she leaned into the mirror and puffed her hair with a small Afro pick. "I wanted to clean up first."

"I'm surprised you're still on your feet. You sure looked bombed," Alexis said, wandering around the bedroom.

Sara had another twinge of conscience. It was very wrong to have behaved as she had with the girls in attendance. "I'm sorry about that," Sara said.

"Why?" Alexis looked puzzled. "Everyone gets bombed at Mommy's parties."

Sara wanted to say more but decided to leave it alone. Instead, she picked out a special album to play when Geoff came, and set it on the player. Not turning the music on, she faced Alexis. Once again, she was aware of the changes that had occurred recently.

Unable to restrain herself, Sara said, "Alexis, are *you* feeling okay?"

"Sure, I am," Alexis snapped, sounding annoyed and added, "Well, if there's nothing wrong with you, I'll see you later."

Next came Lizzibit, who was a different case altogether. At fifteen, Lizzibit was short and still plagued by baby fat, while Sara knew that the girl longed to be tall and thin like her sister. The two girls had different personalities, also. Lizzibit had a natural serenity and sweet temper, while Alexis was prickly and easily offended.

It was easier to love Lizzibit, but Sara had always been scrupulously determined not to pick a favorite. She felt they had enough problems living with Nora and Hugo, and didn't want to add to the situation. As it was, both girls were proof that miracles happened. They maintained a sort of innocence despite their often unsettling lives, and although Alexis wasn't doing as well in school as she had in the past, she was still passing.

Sara climbed back into bed, glad to be horizontal again. She pulled the covers up to her chin. It was the second time the girl had drifted into the room.

"Sara, did you see Paula's new dress? Isn't it fabulous? She bought it specially for tonight."

This time, Sara was glad to talk. It gave her an opportunity to pump Lizzibit for information. However, she felt a little guilty when she said, "Really? When was that? I thought she wasn't coming tonight."

"Are you kidding? She and Mommy have been planning this for months."

"Oh," was all that Sara could say. Now she was sorry she'd questioned. Hearing that her suspicious were true was not comforting.

"You don't have to worry, anyway," Lizzibit said, picking up Sara's lipstick. "Do you think I could wear this color?" she asked, staring at herself in the mirror.

"It's not your color, honey. You need something with more pink in it." Then she couldn't help asking, "Worry? Why should I worry?"

"About Geoff, because he really loves you. He'd never look at anyone else. Geoff's not like—" The girl's voice trailed off as if she thought she had said too much.

Sara knew she was going to say that Geoff was not like Hugo, the notorious alcoholic skirt chaser. Only God knew how Nora had tolerated Hugo's philandering.

Their conversation moved on to Lizzibit's upcoming birthday party and the gifts that she expected.

"Why couldn't we live some place besides Manhattan? Then I could have a car," Lizzibit said.

"You'll have to wait for that one, I'm afraid," Sara said with a smile.

"That's not fair."

Unbidden, Sara remembered Alexis' sixteenth birthday and a cold chill went up her spine. It was two years ago, and both Hugo and Nora had presented Alexis, with much fanfare, a packet of birth control pills and a box of condoms.

Alexis had appeared bewildered for a few seconds but had quickly recovered and laughed it off. Sara remembered how shocked she had been, herself. Even Geoff, who was used to Hugo and Nora's gifts, had looked askance when she'd told him about it. Then Alexis had behaved as if everything was all right, although she had appeared a little subdued afterward.

"Anyway, let's talk about something else," Lizzibit said suddenly. She came to sit on the side of the bed. "What do you think about the name Liz? Or maybe Liza?"

"Why are you asking?" Sara asked.

"I hate my name." Lizzibit sulked. "It's so stupid. Can you see me spending my entire life as Lizzibit? I'd rather die."

"You don't have to do anything that drastic," Sara reassured her with a smile. "A simple name change would suffice. Lots of people do that."

"Have you decided whether you're going to have your birthday with me like last year?"

Sara held onto her smile for her young sister-in-law's sake. Just thinking about another party made Sara's head ache. Lizzibit would be sixteen, while she would be thirty-six. *Thirty-six,* Sara thought. It was positively scary. And what did she have to show for this latest passage of her adult life? Aside from the children, nothing.

Although Lizzibit continued to chatter, Sara found herself distracted by her thoughts. Throughout her marriage, she had abandoned various plans and diverted her energies to the demands of the children or to their families—or, most especially, to Geoff. It wasn't the birthday—thirty-six was not old, after all. She enjoyed her age. It was that the time had passed so quickly.

She pulled her attention back to Lizzibit. Not long afterward, the girl said, "I'm going back to see what's happening," and left.

It gave Sara chance to finish what she'd started. She moved slowly out of the bed, still feeling slightly peaked, and went to apply a little makeup, using the lipstick that her young sister-in-law had put back on the dresser. Then she quickly sprayed the room, using a perfume atomizer, after which she returned to bed.

"What is that smell? Perfume?" Nora hooted from the doorway only a few short minutes later.

Nora paused, a smirk settling upon her features. "It's so . . . ladylike." Nora made the word sound like a disease as it rolled off her lips. Paula, who had followed the older woman through the door, giggled.

Chapter Thirteen

Both Nora and Paula advanced to stand over her bed. The urge to slide down and pull the covers over her head was almost irresistible, but she squelched it. She was certainly in no mood to talk to either of them. As there was little possibility of avoiding it, she sat up, plumped the pillows at her back, and faced them.

"How are you feeling now?" Nora asked.

"Better," Sara said.

"Oh, my, you don't look it. You look tired." Nora peered closely before turning to Paula for confirmation. "Doesn't she?"

"Yes," the younger woman agreed. "You do look terribly sick."

Sara gritted her teeth, managing to bite back the cutting remark that came to mind. It would have been totally fruitless, anyway. Fortunately, they didn't stay long.

Later, Geoff came to check on her. It was the first time she'd seen him since their spat. By now she felt incredibly foolish, and regretted having abandoned the party. True, it was Nora's fête, but still it was in her house. All she wanted to do was make up with Geoff.

Sara heard the last of the party guests leave. Lizzibit ran in for a final hug. The girl seemed almost psychic for a split second, for she held on tightly and said, again, "Don't worry, Sara. It's going to be all right."

"Of course, it is, honey," Sara answered.

Within minutes of Lizzibit leaving her, she heard Geoff say good-bye to his family. He moved around for a while, talking to the caterers, and then he was standing in the doorway of their bedroom.

She could tell from his tight face that he was still angry with her but it was a contained anger, even cool. Her memory took her back to their first summer as lovers. His anger had been hot then, spilling over to touch anyone who came near. It was amazing how much he'd grown. It made her wonder if she had kept pace with him. Actually, in some ways they had almost switched places. He had been the wild one then. Now, it was she who skirted the edges of her own control.

Geoff didn't say anything but quietly removed his tie. Sitting up with her arms wrapped around her knees, she watched, always loving to look at him. He was handsome enough to sell magazines.

Geoff turned as he unbuttoned his shirt, saying, "What was that all about tonight?"

"Oh, Geoff, don't make a big thing about it. I simply felt under the weather. Aren't I entitled to a bad day?"

"Next time, don't fall into Henry's arms." He removed his pants, leaving himself in underwear only.

She stood up and put her arms around him, grateful that he'd let it lie. Their sex life had always been exceptionally good, and she was sure of herself in bed with him, but despite all her preparations for seduction he remained cool and disinterested. Her kisses went unanswered as he stood there, not moving despite her efforts.

It wasn't until she pushed a tentatively probing hand down the waistband of his shorts that she felt him respond. His whole body stiffened with a quick inhalation. Triumphant now, she led him to their scented bed. He took her into his arms and his mouth came down firmly to take hers in a drugging kiss. This was the one thing that had always been true, they were a perfect match for each other sexually.

This moment was no different. With his initial caress, she was caught up in the passion for him that controlled her life. A strange thought surfaced from the recesses of her mind—a thought that she hadn't realized was there.

Could she survive without him?

But why, she wondered, would she have to be without Geoffrey? Tears stung the back of her eyes, then quickly spilled over and ran down her face.

Some inner sense made Geoff aware that she was crying. "What's wrong with you?" he asked.

"Nothing," she said, and reached to draw him close again.

"Why are you crying? You rarely ever cry. Is this for Henry?" he demanded.

"No," she said.

Geoff realized that he wanted to believe her, but his stomach tightened in alarm. Wild thoughts raced through his mind. Lately, she seemed so restless, so full of discontent. *What's going on?* He knew Henry was an opportunist, but surely not his Sara. Suddenly, he realized how threatened he felt.

"You've spent the night playing up to another man and you think I'm going to play stand-in?" He heard the tight anger in his own voice and realized how scared he was at that moment.

"What about you spending your night with Paula?" The words rushed out of her mouth.

"Paula may have the remnants of an old kiddy crush, but it's Henry who loves seducing the wives of his business associates."

She turned her back to him, saying, "I don't know why you're so hard on him. He's not the only one. That whole group are all such creeps."

"I don't want to talk about this," he said to her back, and she felt him turn away from her.

She lay there aching for him. It was so rare for Geoff not to respond to any sexual gesture she might make that it took a few moments for her to accept the rejection. She almost reached out and touched him, but pride stayed her hand.

Geoff's rebuff was another blow on what had been a truly difficult day. Usually she could seduce him into better humor, and it didn't help that on this particular day Paula Stone-Weills had looked so incredibly beautiful.

Geoff lay there, stiff as a board, feeling annoyance invade his thoughts. He had never been more troubled than he had been when Sara fell into fell into Henry Morgan's arms. He'd known Henry for a long time, and had seen the man go after women. Just the idea of Sara making up to the man had rung every alarm bell in his body, a feeling that hadn't happened to him in a long time. The thoughts kept him awake long after Sara's breathing turned deep and rhythmic.

He took a deep breath and turned to glance at Sara. She had moved as far away from him as the bed would allow. He thought of how restless she had become these last few months. Edgy and dissatisfied, she seemed to be straining at the bit. Even her small innuendos about Paula Weills seemed suspicious. And lastly, the tears had undone him.

Suddenly, he thought how much he could use a cigarette just then. Funny, it had been eleven years since he'd had one, but occasionally the urge still came on him.

Sara woke early that next morning when Geoff got out of bed. She was surprised to realize that she'd fallen asleep immediately last night despite the words with Geoff. It had obviously been from a combination of fatigue, champagne, and worry over Nora and Paula. Once asleep, she'd been vaguely aware of troubling dreams. One in particular had wakened her in a sweat.

It was a dream in which Nora was grooming Paula to be Geoff's wife. And everyone, including Geoff, insisted that only Sara could plan the party to celebrate this event. Lord, she was getting fed up with Nora's parties.

Thinking back on their argument the night before, she wondered why he'd gotten so hot under the collar about Henry. While it was true that Geoff had never liked the man, she'd never given him any reason not to trust her. So what had been going on? Surely, her having too much champagne one time shouldn't have bothered him that much. She could see that Geoff was still angry, and it peeved her. He barely spoke as he readied himself to leave for the office.

Smarting pride from his turning away from her last night made her as taciturn as he. He didn't even come into the home office that morning. Once he was gone, she dressed to go to the school, left Asa with Hannah, and dropped Kamaria off before heading south.

There was so much work to do that she managed to forget the problem with Geoff, and was quite caught up in the work until the telephone rang.

"Sara?" a vaguely familiar male voice said, "it's Henry Morgan."

"Oh," she responded. The embarrassing scene at the housewarming drifted into her mind, and she felt a bit sheepish as well as wary. She also thought of the fight she'd had with Geoff afterward. Taking a deep breath, she decided to put a good face on things. "Yes, Henry. How are you?"

"Fine, my dear, and I've been thinking of you."

"Good thoughts, I hope," she said, aiming to behave as if the scene between them never occurred.

"Always, Sara. My thoughts about you are always very good," he said.

It wasn't what he'd said, but she did wonder about his manner. Yet, there was little she could say without sounding presumptuous. She took a deep breath and decided to wade in and get to the point of why he'd called.

"What can I do for you?"

"You're a fundraiser at that little school of yours, aren't you?"

"Yes." She tried to sound bright.

My company usually makes heavy donations to worthy charities, every year." Then, sounding as if he'd had an afterthought he added, "for tax purposes, you understand."

"Yes, I certainly do." She wondered if this would lead to the school getting some money, and tapped her pencil impatiently on the papers in front of her.

"Anyway, after our little talk, I said to myself, 'Henry, why not make a donation to little Sara's organization.' "

She didn't miss the "little Sara" bit, but his words made her sit up and put the pencil down. "That's wonderful, Henry. I'm so glad you thought of us."

"Yes, I've always thought that it sounded like a worthy organization. However, I think we should meet and discuss it."

"Of course. When would be convenient for you?"

"Why not today?" he said quickly.

"Today?" she said, looking askance at the desk calendar in front of her. Remembering the scene last night made her hesitate, but only briefly. She knew she would agree. The school needed all the money it could beg, borrow, or steal. "That would be just fine. What time shall we make it?"

When she hung up, Sara leaned back and thought. It seemed a little odd for Henry to call, but what did it matter? She also wondered if Henry would attempt to obtain sexual favors, but despite Geoff's behavior she wasn't worried about that. She didn't doubt for a moment that she could handle Henry.

Two hours later, Henry smiled broadly as he waved her to precede him. There was no kidding about it, Henry was a big flirt, but he also appeared a lot more harmless than she'd thought. And she had to admit that he certainly knew how to treat a woman—probably part of his charm. Some perversity made Sara wish that Geoff could see her being fawned over by pretentious waiters as she dined on filet mignon with a well-known man. But as lunch progressed and they spoke of the donation, Geoff grew further and further from her mind. She was enjoying herself, and Henry was good company, regaling her with stories about his trips overseas.

They were on the verge of ordering their coffee when a waiter came bearing a telephone. "You have a call, Mr. Morgan."

Henry looked a little peeved until he spoke but then his expression changed and he sat up quickly, saying, "Senator, so good of you to call. But do you mind if I call you back?"

After hanging up, he said, "Sorry about that, Sara, but I need to return this call."

"Oh, I understand. Perhaps I can call you later about the donation?" she asked.

"No, no," he said. "Why don't you come upstairs with me and we'll have coffee there by room service. As soon as I've finished speaking with the senator, we'll discuss the donation to your school."

She hesitated, but only for a moment. Some niggling doubt made her question whether this was some sort of ploy of Henry's, but she said, "Okay," and collected her purse.

As it turned out Henry was a pussycat, and a generous one, too. In no time, she was out of his hotel room with a quite sizeable check. Plus, he hadn't even made a hint of a pass. She wondered if his reputation as a ladies' man was inflated. Or, she realized, it could just be that she wasn't his type.

Sara was still in a great mood when she got home and went into the bedroom, where she switched on a few CDs and started on the paperwork she had to submit with Henry's donation.

Only half her mind was on the papers because her thoughts kept straying to Geoff. She wanted to make up with him. Their argument, which was silly to begin with, had already gone on much too long. She missed the love-making they hadn't had last night.

Suddenly, a noise made her look up. Geoff stood there in the doorway, watching her.

His sudden appearance startled her. "You scared me. I didn't hear you come in."

"I called the foundation and they said you'd gone to lunch with Henry at his hotel."

"What's wrong with that?"

"Then I called the hotel and they said you were dining in his suite."

"We didn't dine in his suite. We only took our coffee there. Henry was expecting an important call and he wanted to be where he could speak with comfort."

"I'll bet he did want to be comfortable, very comfortable. *You* can be very comforting, Sara."

Her heart fell as she realized that any attempt to make up would be useless now. She drew herself up, her voice hardening to disguise her disappointment. "Geoff, I don't like the way this conversation is going."

"Why didn't you tell me this morning that you had a luncheon appointment with him?"

"I didn't have an appointment this morning. He called and requested one after I arrived at the school. Why are you checking up on me?"

"Why are you asking? Have you got something to hide?"

"No, I don't, and what makes you feel you need to speak with me like this?"

"Because you're my wife, and this is Henry Morgan, remember? The man whose arms you fell into only a short time ago. A man who spends most of his leisure time in bed with the wives of his friends and business associates?"

"Henry's sex life has nothing to do with me. You're the one trying to make me guilty."

"You don't think it's enough to worry me when my wife decides to have secret lunches in his hotel room?"

"There was nothing secret about it."

"I don't want you going to his hotel room."

"I told you how that happened."

"Maybe that's what *you* think, but I know him. He probably set the whole thing up. You threw yourself at him, and he's assuming that you're up for grabs. You're too attractive a woman for Henry to restrain himself."

"I really resent your talking to me like this, Geoff."

"Resent it all you like but, if something like this ever happens again, I expect you to inform me before you do it."

His remarks made her furious but she didn't say anything more. She couldn't help remembering that he went with women clients all the time, and she'd never asked him to inform her.

A week later, the day of Lizzibit's birthday party, Geoff hadn't come home yet. She was annoyed because it had been difficult to get him to attend this party, as it was for all his parents' events, and she worried that despite his promise he would renege at the last moment.

Added to this was the fact that there was still a bit of ice in the air between them over Henry. She felt insulted by his doubts and restrictions. To keep her mind off this, she'd started to work on the project she'd taken over for the Ferguson School. She felt pressured, trying to get as much accomplished as possible before she had to get dressed.

Pouring over the lists of donations made to the school, she sighed at how short it was. They definitely needed more money. She tried to consider a projection for next term's donations, only to make the third error since she'd sat there. She threw the pen down, knowing that she was too distracted to focus on the task at hand. Her thoughts

kept straying to the party tonight. It was the third in such
a short time, and she was tired.

She absolutely dreaded going, and if it hadn't been
Lizzibit's birthday she'd have claimed to be ill. After the
last party and the incident with Henry, the mere idea made
her sick. This was what had become of her whole life, one
party after another, and she was sick to death of them. Yet,
after making an issue of it with Geoff and insisting that
this time he had to attend, she couldn't back out.

She was grateful that it would be primarily family. She
remembered the McMillan parties from her childhood.
Back in the days when the band was still working, her own
parents used to attend, also. It seemed so strange. She
couldn't imagine her parents attending one of the McMillan's parties now. It showed how much things had changed.

Unfortunately, gatherings held by Geoff's family were
frequently as full of subterfuge as an event given by the
ancient Zulus. And now there was Paula, who had taken
to attending these little get-togethers. Geoff never understood her discomfort. Despite his unwillingness to attend,
once there he somehow managed to move into them without a qualm.

She glanced down at the papers before her, thinking
that it wasn't working. She remembered how the school
board had eagerly asked for Geoff's help, but oh, no, she
thought, not Mr. Geoff Stone-McMillan. He never had
time for anything like helping out in something so small
potatoes. He only dealt with the movers and pushers.

Angrily gathering the documents together, she decided
to leave any further calculations until later. Her indignation rose as she thought of how his family was even taking
over her private time.

Once the children were dressed she left them with Hannah and went upstairs to take a long, relaxing bath before
getting dressed. As she lay there in a softly scented bubble
bath, she wished that she were free to lead her own life.
The thought, coming as it seemed from nowhere, startled
her, and made her feel disloyal. She was Geoff's wife,

and there was no way she wanted to change that. But resentment filled her again. Even as his wife she deserved a life of her own, and she didn't want to spend it all as his appendage. She didn't want to be his accessory, to be taken out and polished up whenever he needed her. She wanted her own life—she wanted to teach, not to live through him. She loved Geoff, but she didn't love the life that he lived—the life he seemed determined to make her live, also.

While she was in the tub Geoffrey came in. He glanced at her and hesitated, muttering some greeting. But he didn't come over as he usually did. Things had been a bit sticky between them since the incident with Henry. Part of her regretted it, but she also felt justified. There was no reason for him to have been jealous that night, and she had refused to reassure him. She was unwilling to be the one who made up this time. Instead, she grunted something and sank down into the water and closed her eyes.

She heard him start to shave at one of the double sinks. They continued dressing together. Once, when she stopped, becoming engrossed in her own thoughts, he zipped up the back of her dress, saying, "Times a-passing."

It was the least argumentive thing they'd said in days, but she was still annoyed. She pulled herself together, and soon they were on their way with the children in the back-seat. This time the party was at Hugo and Nora's apartment. Never again would she allow herself to be roped into one of her mother-in-law's little Machiavellian schemes.

When they arrived at the apartment on Manhattan's Upper West Side, Sara was glad that for once it was a small family affair, as Nora had promised. As soon as they arrived, Paula pounced on Geoff, taking him away to monopolize his time.

Chapter Fourteen

At sight of Paula hanging on to Geoff for dear life Sara began to fume, but she refused to allow anyone to see how angry she was. Lizzibit jumped all over her like a puppy. The girl was genuinely glad to see Asa, and spent quite a while playing with him. It gave Sara a break.

Nora took Kamaria over, as usual. While Geoff's mother often appeared to find Asa tiresome, she truly adored Kamaria. However, Nora didn't particularly like her name, preferring to call her granddaughter Maria.

Alexis came later, and Sara thought the girl looked even more pasty than she had at the housewarming. Guilt assailed her, thinking that she'd been too busy with her own problems to help her sisters-in-law. Without a doubt, Alexis had lost pounds, which she couldn't afford to shed. Was she anorexic, Sara wondered, or was it something worse?

Today, Alexis was accompanied by a tall, gaunt young man who looked equally ill. It was this which convinced Sara that she had to do something about her recent suspicions. Alexis was wound tighter than a spring, and Sara had smelt alcohol when the girl came over to kiss her.

Although the two girls obviously adored him, Geoffrey somehow, never seemed to notice his young sisters. He was inclined to ruffle Lizzibit's hair or pinch Alexis's cheek. Sara wondered if he even saw that they were no longer little girls, for he treated them as if they were ten rather than near adults.

Despite everything, now that she was there Sara was determined to enjoy herself. Looking at Lizzibit's face, Sara knew that for the girl's sake she was glad to be there.

Although this was supposedly her own birthday celebration too, her parents hadn't come. They rarely got to the city, and the plan was that she would go to Middletown when Kamaria had time off from school. Sara was looking forward to the visit.

One tradition of the McMillan family which Sara loved was that all the children received gifts whether it was their birthday or not. Kamaria's was an expensive gold locket on a chain. Sara thought briefly that Nora spoiled the girl, but didn't say anything. Asa got an intricately modeled car to add to his set, while Alexis's gift was a lovely silk blouse.

Sara was both pleased and surprised with her own gift. It was a slim, beautifully bound volume of poems, published during the thirties by African-American poets, including Countee Cullen and Langston Hughes. It seemed that Nora had actually taken time to find something that she would enjoy rather than simply picking up something expensive but not particularly appropriate. It was such a surprising, thoughtful gift that Sara spontaneously embraced Nora. She thought the older woman appeared slightly taken aback at the gesture. From Geoff, she received a lovely tennis bracelet, set with a row of exquisitely perfect diamonds.

What she was not pleased about was that during most of the day Geoff's private tête-à-tête with Paula continued. Sara told herself that Geoffrey only did this to avoid Hugo. She watched them when no one was looking and found herself fuming increasingly more. Once, Paula caught her glance and sent her a flashing, smug smile. It gave Sara a headache.

As the time passed Asa grew tired and cranky with all the excitement, and she took him to sit on her lap, which didn't seem to help much. He grew more irritable. Geoff, observing this, finally came and took him to nap in Lizzibit's bedroom. The intercom was open and they would hear if he woke.

The moment came for Lizzibit, the birthday girl, to open all her gaily wrapped presents, but she wanted to wait until Geoff returned.

The young girl glowed with happiness, and had already gone through several of the gifts when she came to one small packet of two boxes. She tore excitedly into it, pulling off the ribbon and shredding the colorful paper before coming to the first package. It was a small plastic disk of tiny pills.

Ominous dread rose like a lump in Sara's throat. They were birth control pills. It was just as she'd feared, remembering Alexis's birthday two years before. Nora, Hugo, and Paula chuckled as they watched Lizzibit, waiting for her reaction.

It took a few moments before comprehension dawned, but Lizzibit also remembered her older sister's birthday. The accompanying box, slightly larger than the first, held condoms. They looked incongruous in the girl's small, pudgy hands.

Lizzibit's rose-tipped skin reddened as she glanced, bewildered, from her mother to her father.

"Darling, don't you know what this means?" Nora said.

"What am I supposed to do with them?" Lizzibit asked.

"You're sixteen—a big girl, now." Hugo beamed.

Lizzibit dropped the packages, saying, "But . . . but . . . I don't want them." She started to cry and her voice rose. "I don't need them!"

"Lizzibit, of course you need them," Nora said, annoyed.

"What's wrong with that girl?" Hugo queried.

"It's a horrible, stupid gift," Lizzibit said beginning to cry harder.

"You silly, ungrateful little . . ." Nora said as she stooped to pick up the packages. She attempted to press them on Lizzibit.

"Hold on a minute!" Geoff said, stepping in front of Nora and taking the gift.

Once Geoff had become involved, Sara felt she had to back him up. Besides, she was so put out that she couldn't help saying, "This has to be one of the stupidest things the two of you have ever done."

Nora, preferring to have it out with her to confronting her son, demanded of Sara, "What do you mean? We're thinking about her health. What's stupid about that?"

"Did it ever occur to you to ask her? Not every sixteen year old is sexually active," Sara answered.

"Of course they are—" Nora started.

Lizzibit took that moment to turn to Geoff. She buried her head on his shoulder. When Nora would have stopped the girl, Geoff said, "Leave her alone. Can't you see this was a mistake?"

Suddenly, Alexis stood up, overturning her chair. Everyone went silent as all eyes turned to the thin girl. The McMillans had a habit of sudden disruptive behavior, but Sara couldn't get used to it. She stopped breathing and stared at the trembling girl, whose black dress seemed to cover almost bones.

Suddenly, Sara realized that the strange innocence that had been maintained around Nora's daughters was irreparably damaged. She turned to gaze at her own daughter. Kamaria, in the midst of the chaos, had also sought out the arms of her father. Sara realized, not for the first time, that she had to do something about her children being observers at these scenes.

"All of you think more about Lizzibit than you do about me! No one cared when the same thing happened to me. But for Lizzibit, you're all bent out of shape." Alexis' voice was slurred.

"That isn't true, Alexis. You were happy when we gave you the same present," Nora said.

"Because I didn't know what else to say, that's why." With this, she glared at Sara.

Sara felt her heart constrict. She knew she'd made a terrible mistake two years ago. By not voicing her opinion, she'd appeared to agree with Hugo and Nora. Suddenly, she felt totally in sympathy with Alexis, and Lizzibit, too. What would she have done if her own parents had given her such gifts? She realized that she'd have been as bewildered at these girls were tonight.

"What's the problem here?" Hugo muttered drunkenly from his chair as he topped his drink.

Sara stood and attempted to put her arms around the raging girl, but Alexis pushed her away. "You jumped in to save poor, precious, little Lizzibit. Lizzibit's as pure as the driven snow, but I'm just dirt. Right? Well, I don't need your pity, now!"

Alexis walked to the birthday cake and pushed it off the table, where it was crushed on the rug.

"Look at what you've done!" Nora's voice rose. "You've ruined the rug."

Lizzibit took that chance to squirm away from Geoff and run, crying from the room. Geoff stood, also, looking bemused as to which of his sisters he should attempt to comfort.

Nora called "Lizzibit!" and started to follow. But Geoffrey motioned for her to stop, while he followed his sister.

Stupidly, Sara stared at the cake. It reminded her of Geoff's behavior during the early days of their relationship. Before Sara could do anything else Alexis stormed out, running from the apartment.

Hugo drank from his glass and stared off into space, his mouth moving wordlessly.

A few minutes later Geoff returned with Asa in his arms and Kamaria at his heels. He looked both angry and puzzled. "Where's Alexis?"

"She's gone," Sara answered.

"For Pete's sake," he muttered, handing Asa into her arms. When Kamaria held on to her father, trying to follow him, he also handed her over to Sara. Then he approached Alexis's friend. The young man—a boy, in truth—looked so out of it that he seemed to have missed most of what had just happened. Geoff glanced at the boyfriend, saying, "Where's she gone?"

The young man shrugged. "I don't know." His eyes looked out of focus.

Geoff took two steps and pulled the young man up on his feet. "Well, you're going to help me find her."

"Okay, man, don't get so excited," the boy muttered.

"I'm coming, too," Paula said, throwing on a light jacket and following the two men out the door.

Sara watched Paula follow Geoff, feeling frustrated and helpless. Suddenly, she felt totally alienated and perplexed as she stood in the middle of the floor, clutching her sleepy, bewildered offspring. She could hear Lizzibit crying in her room.

Why, she wondered, hadn't she followed Geoff's suggestion and stayed away today? Why hadn't she refused to be exposed to Hugo and Nora's disruptive influence? She knew why—she'd been taught that family was important. She wondered if Geoff was right. Maybe it was time to set limits on their involvement with the older McMillans.

It was several hours later when Geoff and Paula returned with an angry, resentful Alexis in tow. The girl stormed into her room, refusing to talk with anyone. As soon as they could dress the children, Geoff and Sara left for their own home.

After Geoff and Sara were gone, Nora paced up and down the living room. She was absolutely furious with Sara's calling Lizzibits present stupid, but had been careful not to show it until after everyone was gone. Fortunately, both Alexis and Lizzibit had gone to bed. She didn't think she could take another moment with either of her daughters. And as for Sara, *she was livid with the little chit*. Then, what could you expect with a mother like Edna?

"You got to admit she's a spunky li'l thing," Hugo muttered, "Time to accept that she's your daughter-in-law."

He'd been dozing in the chair as usual, but it surprised her to realize that he'd been alert. It was rare to get any sense from Hugo lately.

Whenever she thought of Sara, Edna's daughter, as her daughter-in-law, it made her see red. Geoff had always been so beautiful, more beautiful than her or Hugo. He'd also been brilliant. "Whatever possessed Geoff, when he could have had any woman he wanted, to marry that little mouse?"

She hadn't realized that she'd spoken aloud until Hugo answered from behind her, "She ain't such a little mouse." Nora swung around to find her husband taking another slug from his everpresent bottle. "She's sure a match for you," he added.

"She's so *bourgeois*," Nora answered. "A damn schoolteacher, for Pete's sake. Could he have sunk any lower?"

"What's wrong with her being a teacher?"

"Isn't a man supposed to marry a woman like his mother? Does she resemble me in any way? It's like a slap in the face!"

"Give it up. Admit you're wrong. You've been bested," Hugo said.

"That's what you think. I'll never give up. And I'll win, too," Nora said angrily.

"You should admire her, old girl. You're no flyweight as an opponent."

Curiously enough, he was right, Nora thought. She had come to respect her daughter-in-law, if nothing else, but there was no way she was giving up now.

"Who'd have thought Geoff would have picked her to settle down with? Well, I'm not finished yet. You just watch."

"If you haven't broken them up in eleven years what makes you think you can do it now?"

"Because she's beginning to crack. What do you know? You're sloshed all the time."

"I can see it. No one knows you like me. You've always played Miss Anne, stepping down to take care of crude, low-life Hugo, but I know how much you loved it. And now, with all your messing around you still ain't managed to separate Geoff from his Sara. So, she ain't such a waste after all."

"Go to hell, Hugo," Nora snapped between her teeth.

"Baby," he said, slurring more suddenly as he waved the bottle, "ain't that what I've been doing all these years?"

It was a momentary glimpse of the old Hugo. Times when he was even partially clear were becoming increasingly more rare. She chuckled and he joined her when she plopped down on the couch and crossed her leg before lighting up a cigarette. She watched him quietly for a while.

He *was* getting worse, she thought in a short-lived spurt of panic. She hadn't told anyone about his being diagnosed over a year ago as having Alzheimer's, but she suspected that most people already knew. He was becoming more absentminded.

"You know, sometimes I get real sick of you and this Alzheimer's thing." She wasn't sure why she said it. Just because Hugo sounded like himself didn't mean that he understood anything.

He looked at the bottle and said, "Me, too." Then his eyes came to hers and he added, "Life's a bitch, you know . . ."

"Sure, sure," she answered, and left it at that. Still, she enjoyed that rare moment of his being lucid and allowed herself to hope. No one could ever imagine how much she missed the old Hugo.

On their way home Sara and Geoff got into their own fight regarding the scene at his parents' house.

"Geoff, I've been looking at Alexis, and I'm worried."

He ran his hand over his forehead, saying, "I know, but

what can you do? You know how my family is." He sounded exasperated. "They meant well, I hope. They just didn't take the time to think about it—"

"Listen, that was bad enough, but that's not what I'm alarmed about," Sara said, cutting him off.

"For Pete's sake, don't blow this up any more than it already is. You were the one always swearing that Hugo and Nora loved their children."

Geoff was right. She had always defended his parents. She tried to explain. "I meant that their trying to give their children everything wasn't a crime. But sometimes they're too indulgent, and that's not only an error, it's dangerous."

"Are we going to hear your usual lecture about how the Turners, due to Daddy who speaks with God, are morally superior to the rest of us dogs?"

She bit back the retort that came to her mouth, forcing herself to remember that he was tired, having just spent several hours looking for Alexis. She controlled the impulse to retaliate. "I never said anything like that."

"But you think it. Anyone can see you look down on the rest of us when you get on your self-righteousness kick. Right? My clients aren't right, the stock market is another name for Babylon—"

"You can't read my mind, and maybe it's your own guilty conscience talking."

"Why would my conscience be bothering me? What did I do this time?"

"Maybe you should tell me."

It wasn't what she'd meant to say. A quick image of Paula's smug smile stole into her thoughts.

"What's that supposed to mean? I've done right by you. You shouldn't complain, not with your portfolio."

"Geoff, this isn't about money."

"Sure, you can say that because I look after you."

"At what cost?"

"Meaning?"

By this time, they were in the house. Trying to pass by him, she said, "You just want to fight."

"That's funny. I thought that was *your* modus operandi."

Suddenly, she realized how far afield they'd gone. They were both tired and the argument was taking off in every direction. She wanted to get back to her original intent. Before he could interrupt her again, she said, "Alexis is drinking too much."

Her words stopped Geoffrey in his tracks. "You know Nora serves wine with meals. What's the big deal?"

"This wasn't a small drink at home with her family, which is legal even for a seventeen year old. Alexis had already tanked up before she arrived. She's too young for that. And what about the boyfriend? What was he on?"

"So, he was a little scuzzy. That's not Alexis. She isn't like you and Judith were, squeaky clean all the time. What do you know about kids like her?"

"I've taught school, for one thing. I know more about this than I want to."

"Grade school kids?"

"You forget I worked at the Student Center. She's hanging around with a doper, and all you can say is that he's a little scuzzy?" When he didn't answer she continued, "She doesn't look well, and she's too thin."

"That doesn't mean anything. Lots of girls her age are skinny."

Sara was exasperated. She sensed his denial was an attempt to hide from a truth he didn't want to admit. "I didn't say she was an addict, but these things are better caught early."

"I still don't believe it," he denied for the second time.

She put her hand over her eyes in sudden frustration, and sought to defuse the moment. "We're both tired. Maybe we should talk about this in the morning."

Geoff followed as she went into Asa's room, saying, "Alexis is a smart kid. She knows better. She can see what its done to Hugo."

"What's wrong with Grandpa Hugo?" Asa asked innocently.

It brought their attention to their listening children. "Nothing," Geoff answered and took the boy's hand, leading him into his bedroom, where he helped the child get ready for sleep.

Their conversation was on hold. She had known that expressing her fears about Alexis would shock him. It would be hard for him to face the truth. It forced him to admit that the girls were growing up, and probably brought back the nightmares of his own adolescence. But she was angrier than she realized, with his blindness and refusal to listen. It had been a difficult week between them, and tonight's discussion hadn't helped.

By the time she went to bed, he was already there, waiting. When she lay down, he moved closer and reached out to her. Suddenly, after the tension that had been between them and watching Paula chat him up all night, she was livid. All her attempts to remain calm evaporated.

"No!" she said, erupting out of bed to glare down at him.

"What the hell's wrong with you?" He jumped up to face her across the bed.

"You think you can just start making love after rejecting everything that I say and rebuffing me for over a week?"

"*I* rebuffed *you*? All week you've been as cold as an icicle—"

"And spending the whole day with Paula?"

"Paula?"

"That's right, Paula! I'm sick of her hanging on to you like a leech."

"Give me a break. Would you stop with this crap?" he said. She was so angry that she jammed her arms into her robe and pulled her pillow off the bed. Then, without another word, she walked to the door. "Where the hell are you going?" he demanded.

"To the guest room. I'm not sleeping here tonight."

He opened his mouth and she expected him to protest,

but he said nothing, only moved into bed, punched his pillow, and turned his back to her.

Sara lay awake a long time in the guest room, but it wasn't Paula she thought of. Unable to get Alexis and the scene at the party off her mind, she wondered what she could do. It wasn't that she thought the girl was in any real trouble yet, but knew she would have to do something. Worse, she couldn't help thinking of her own children in this mess. While she seriously disapproved of Geoff's attitude toward his parents, she knew it was time for a change, and she wondered what would it entail.

The next morning, Geoff left before she could speak with him. His giving her the cold shoulder only made her angrier.

Noticing the light flickering on the answering machine, she listened to the messages there. One was from her mother, who wished her a happy birthday and rambled on about some dream she'd had. Edna sounded worried, and insisted Sara call back.

It made Sara remember the crazy dream *she'd* had after the housewarming party. She shook her head. *Seems everyone's having troublesome dreams.* However, she knew that Edna took hers a lot more seriously than most people.

Still upset, she felt alienated and out of touch. Suddenly, she wanted to hear her mother's voice. It was strange but Edna, who had once predicted the worst of her marrying Geoff, was now one of his biggest fans.

Calling her parents was always difficult. There were so many old hurts that seemed to take forever to heal. Sometimes she wondered if things would ever be what they had. That was just another change that Geoff had brought into her life. No, that wasn't fair. Geoff wasn't responsible for this. Marrying him had been her own eagerly made decision. She dialed and waited for her mother to pick up.

"Hello, Mom?"

"Sara? That's you?" her mother said unnecessarily. "Oh, thank God. I've been so worried. I had a terrible dream last night. Don't tell me you and the children aren't coming. Your father will be disappointed."

"No, he won't," Sara contradicted.

"He still cares about you, Sara. No matter how it may appear. It's just that you were his pride and joy for so long. Give him time."

Sara didn't want to have this conversation, so she changed the subject. "We're driving up on Thursday."

She thought of what had happened at Lizzibit's birthday, and wondered if they'd be able to make it. She was determined to confront Geoff's parents about Alexis.

Geoff already knew of her plans to visit her parents, but she wondered if she dared leave before they'd done something about Alexis. They had planned for Geoff to drive them up. She would stay with the children for a day or so, while he'd return to work. She preferred him to drive, as it was difficult to take Asa on long trips. Her son easily became restless and often wanted to sit in her lap.

"Okay, see you then," Edna said.

Sara placed the phone on the hook, thinking that while she had managed to stop her mother's chatter now, it wouldn't be so easy later, when she would be a captive audience. Yet, she wanted to see her family. It had been a long time and she missed them. And with the things that had been going on recently, she felt the need to be grounded.

Chapter Fifteen

If she had been a little concerned about calling her family, she positively dreaded the call that she had to make to Nora. After repeated aborted starts, she finally reached to pick up the phone. They made plans for her to go there in two days.

On the morning she'd planned to talk with Nora, she left Asa in Hannah's care. She sighed, knowing that it was going to be a hard conversation, but it had to be done—for Alexis' sake. Geoff's behavior hadn't changed since the night of the party, but she couldn't wait for him any longer. With a frustrated grimace, she went to get dressed and take Kamaria to school.

Several hours later, after closing the books at the school, she realized that she was still haunted by Geoff's refusal to listen to her fears. Although she remained angry, she knew they needed to talk. She was tempted to approach him by telephone, but it seemed such a cowardly way to handle it.

Then, remembering the upcoming meeting with Geoff's parents, she took a deep breath to relieve the tension and prayed for courage. She drove west at One Hundred

Twenty-Fifth Street and went south on the West Side Highway.

"You're a liar!" Nora shrilled about thirty minutes later. "Of course, she hoists a few now and then. All kids do that."

The three of them were in the living room of Hugo and Nora's Upper West Side apartment. Hugo sat in his chair with a bottle of Scotch close at hand. Sara had glanced fleetingly toward him once, and realized that he was totally in his own world.

He had not joined in the conversation, and appeared not to have heard when Sara spoke about Alexis. Sara suspected that Hugo's mental status was deteriorating, but that was a subject she had no intention of approaching. Trying to help Alexis was as much as she could do.

"Not all kids," Sara answered Nora, but she sympathized with her mother-in-law, understanding how painful this conversation had to be. "I know it's hard to believe, but I think she's calling for help in her own way."

"What the hell would you know about that? If it were true, I'd be the one to know."

"Parents are often the last to see—"

"How dare you!" Nora's voice rose. "You'd be glad if something like that happened to me. You're trying to get back at me for Paula."

"What are you saying?"

"You're afraid Geoff's attracted to her. That's why you're doing this, and you know it, too. You're terrified, and you're attacking me through my children."

"That isn't true," Sara snapped back. Cold fear swept over her at Nora's words. While she'd confronted Geoff over Paula, she didn't truly believe there was anything to it. True, she suspected that Paula would be willing, but surely not Geoff. Nora's accusation cast terror into her bones. Then, forcing herself to speak calmly, she made herself stick to the subject, "This isn't about you. It's about Alexis."

"How could you say those things about my baby!"

"Nora, I love Alexis, and I want to help. I want us all to help her."

"Get out of here!"

"At least you need to look at this. You can help her now, but if you wait . . ."

"I'm calling Geoffrey. He'll make you stop these lies."

Nora dialed the phone with trembling hands. Sara wished that this visit hadn't been necessary as she waited for the older woman to make contact with Geoff's office. Her own hands shook, and another headache threatened.

Nora talked with Geoff briefly, telling about their conversation and then shoved the telephone at her. Sara looked into the woman's tear-ravaged face where mascara made dark streaks down her cheeks, and her heart constricted. She put the handset to her ear.

"Sara," Geoffrey said coldly, "why the hell did you go there without me?"

Without him, she thought. He never wanted to go to his parents'. But she didn't point that out. What she said was, "You refused to listen."

"Okay, stop this. I'll take over from here."

"Geoff, this is important . . ."

"I said I'd take over."

Sara was so upset that she could barely talk. Did he think she'd deliberately come to upset Nora? She slammed the phone down and picked up her purse to leave. It was the first time in all their years together that he'd sided with Nora against her.

As she drove back to Scarsdale, her eyes filled with tears. Despite Nora's accusations about Paula, it wasn't that which Sara thought of. Rather, it was her frustration with Geoff and his mother. She was more hurt than she'd have thought possible by their reactions. That he'd take Nora's side against her was a total shock. She'd worked so hard to become a part of their family, and now she felt an

intruder. About halfway to Scarsdale, she swung off the
highway, too shaken to drive in her present state of nerves.

When Sara slammed the phone down, Geoff had the
urge to throw something. Living with her had become like
trying to balance on quicksand. As he remembered her
jumping out of bed last night as if she'd been scalded, the
pencil he'd been holding snapped. He threw it down on
the desk and bolted upright to walk around the office.
Paula had been going through files on the coffee-table
and glanced up momentarily at his sudden action. Having
overheard his side of the conversation, she looked so sym-
pathetic.

It brought back Sara's accusations. She'd managed to
twist everything around so that it made *him* sound guilty.
He found himself looking at Paula with new eyes. He'd
noticed her before, but not truly put any energy into it.
Sudden resentment rose and he was reminded of how
young he'd been when they'd married, of how he'd given
up women to be with Sara. Of how he'd have given up
anything to be with her, yet nothing he did was good
enough for her anymore.

He suddenly realized how long it had been since they'd
made love. He could have used her touch just at that
moment. Remembering idly that as a younger man he'd
had the ability to make women respond whenever he'd
looked interested, he felt his curiosity rise, and he wondered if this would work now. Just before he could glance
away, Paula looked up again.

Upon seeing his expression, her face changed. Suddenly, she looked more aware, more knowing. He suspected she saw the question in his eyes.

Paula stood, walking toward him, and he waited. She
reached up to put her arms around him, and it was like a
movie playing in slow motion. Then it hit him, in a moment
of crystal clear insightfulness—*This is a mistake.*

Before he could put a stop to the whole scene, Sara spoke from behind him. "You bastard!."

He turned to see her standing in the doorway. She swirled around and disappeared. "Sara!" he called, and after a split second of shock, rushed after her, only to reach the elevator as the door slammed shut. She was gone. He slammed his hand against the button.

"Damn," he snapped. He was angry with himself. It was a stupid, asinine thing to do, letting himself get even remotely interested in Paula, and he knew it. He'd let his male ego get the upper hand. But he was also furious with Sara. After all these years, she trusted him so little that she never gave him a chance to say anything.

Paula had followed him through the door and placed her hand on his shoulder. "I'm sorry," she said, and seemed so soft and understanding.

"Forget it," he answered. "It wasn't your fault." It wasn't, he realized. He'd allowed the whole thing to develop, and he was the one responsible. He realized Paula still had her hand on his shoulder and he looked down at her feminine hand. *Why not? Sara has already accused me. What do I have to lose?*

Sara raced to Kamaria's school and picked up her daughter before going home. Once there, she packed quickly, determined to be gone by the time Geoff arrived. She was going to Middletown a few days earlier than planned and called to notify her parents. Her efforts to avoid him didn't work, for soon she heard him storm though the front door, calling loudly, "Sara!"

It reminded her of the day he'd come home early and they'd made love in the quiet house. That day seemed so far away now. She had to bite back tears.

He took the stairs two at a time and finally banged into their bedroom. "Where are you going?" he demanded, seeing her packing.

"To my parents," she said.

He moved into the room, looking jumpy, and walked

around, watching her. "Listen," he began, "It wasn't the way it looked—"

"No? How was it, then?" When he started to speak, she cut him off. "Don't bother. I don't want to hear it, especially after all your talk about Henry. Now, I can see that was just a red herring to keep me off your case."

"For Pete's sake, you can't possibly believe that."

"Oh, yes I can," she said as she swung the case off the bed and tried to carry it to the front door.

He took the suitcase from her. "Sara, we need to settle this before you go to Middletown . . ."

With arms akimbo, she said, "I'm going to Middletown today, and nothing you say will stop me."

She walked away, calling the children, and hustled them outside to her car. Geoff followed behind her with the baggage.

"I'll drive," he said, holding his palm up for the keys.

"I can manage," she said, but he waited with his hand extended toward her.

She threw them into his palm and went around to the passenger side. Both Kamaria and Asa were in the back-seat, and there wasn't much she could say in front of them. Aside from the children's chatter they were quiet. She seethed the entire ride, unable to rid herself of the image of Geoff in Paula's arms.

When they arrived at her parents' home, Kamaria and Asa ran in to see their grandparents. They were left to pick up the luggage.

"When are you coming home?" he asked when they were alone.

"Maybe never."

"What the hell does that mean?"

"It means I don't know yet." He put the baggage on the sidewalk and stopped. She realized he was not going in. "You're not coming in to say hello?" she challenged.

"It's getting late and I'm taking the train back. I need to leave early."

"Of course. You don't want to leave your lady love too long," she sneered.

You're going to take this to hell, aren't you?" he hissed.

"I'll take it as far as I want." She glanced at the front door, which was ajar, although no one had come to see what they were about. She didn't want anyone to overhear, but couldn't resist snapping, "No matter what happens to you and me, there's no reason for you to be rude to my parents. They're not used to your bad manners."

"Your father will be glad. He's still wishing you'd married that twerp, Chuck."

"Chuck, is it? I'm surprised you remember him—such ancient history. It's not Chuck that's our problem. It's your little cousin. But isn't it just like you to shove all responsibility off yourself?"

She turned abruptly, leaving him there and walking up the pathway to her parents' front door.

"You can be such a witch when you want," he said to her retreating back.

She stopped and without turning, said, "Witch? Is that all you're calling me?"

"Okay, how about you can be a bitch?" he snarled.

Despite her rage with him, the words hurt, and part of her wished that everything that had happened that day could be forgotten, but she knew that could never be. She proceeded toward the house. As she went, she looked around at the familiar old front yard. Usually, just being in Middletown would have been soothing, but not today. It made her think of how she once couldn't wait to leave this small city. Now it was like a haven, an oasis of peace.

It had only been a few days since Lizzibit's birthday, but seeing the simple life that her parents led made it seem light years away. She wished she could keep her children there forever. Maybe her family were inclined to be a little judgmental and smug. Still, the peace and calm were wonderful.

When they hadn't followed the children into the house,

Judith stepped out onto the porch just as Sara walked up the steps. Judith lived not too far from their parents now.

"I came over when I heard you were expected," Judith said. They hugged, briefly.

"When no one came out to see what was going on, I was beginning to think there was no one here," Sara said, forcing herself not to show her own anguish. It wasn't as hard as it could have been, because seeing her sister always lightened her mood, even on a day like this.

Judith, dressed in a business suit, looked wonderful, and Sara had a fleeting moment of sibling jealousy that evaporated with Judith's next words. "Everyone's inside. Surprised to see me, huh? Well, not only am I glad to see you, but coming here gave me the best excuse in the world to get away from Johnson."

Sara was aware that all was not well in Judith's marriage of three years to Johnson Devry. Today, with her own marriage reeling, that knowledge seemed more ominous. And knowing that many of her sister's problems were Judith's fault didn't make her feel any better. Her sister trusted less, especially men, and this attitude played havoc with her marriage. Sara also knew that much of this was the result of Judith's abortion eleven years ago. Bitter recriminations between Judith and her then boyfriend had followed the surgery. To make things worse, it had also caused physical damage. Judith had been unable to carry a baby to term since.

At a closer glance, her sister appeared brittle and tired. Sara was surprised to see her light a cigarette on their parent's porch. Judith threw a guilty glance over her shoulder before hastily taking a few puffs. Blowing smoke through her nose, she put out the cigarette. Then she asked, "What were you and Geoff arguing about? I could see you."

"We're having problems," Sara answered carefully, not able to talk about her recent troubles.

"That surprises me. You two always seem like a perfect

love match. But then I guess everyone has their fights,'' Judith said.

"How is Johnson?" Sara asked, wanting to avoid talking about herself for as long as she could.

"Well, I guess you could safely say that he's not a love match," Judith answered. Her hand shook when she smoothed back her hair. "At least not mine."

"What's going on?"

"We're getting divorced. He's found himself someone else—a pregnant someone else."

Sara gasped. It was a shock to hear Judith's problems so closely mirroring her own. "I'm so sorry," she said, and was glad to see that Judith was too absorbed in her own troubles to detect the pain in her voice.

"Well, I'm not!" Judith said, "I'm sick of the whole thing. I'm sick of the miscarriages. Even more important, I'm sick of him. This way, we'll all be happy."

Sara didn't know what to say. Judith had had two spontaneous miscarriages during her short marriage. She knew it had taken a toll on her sister. She put her arms around Judith, but the other woman seemed unwilling to be touched and moved away rather quickly. It pained Sara to see her sister suffer, and she followed when Judith went inside.

They both stopped in the kitchen. Sara embraced her mother, spending a few moments there before going to see her father. There she discovered that Geoff had come into the house. She had expected him to be gone already. A televised basketball game was in progress and both men sat with their eyes glued to the screen. She didn't hear a word pass between them.

She headed toward the downstairs bathroom to refresh herself after the drive, but before getting there she passed an old-fashioned, glassed-in cabinet in the hallway and noticed that the pepper mill that she'd bought her mother on her last visit was displayed there. Somehow, her gifts all seemed to wind up used for show purposes.

Once in the bathroom, she looked into the mirror and

suddenly had a disconcerting urge to cry. Quickly, she splashed cold water on her face and returned to join Martin and Geoff in the living room. She could hear Kamaria and Asa from the backyard.

Later, her mother sent a tray of snacks via Judith while the children ate in the kitchen.

"Where are the cookies?" Martin asked querulously.

Judith answered, "Mom says forget them and make yourself happy with what you have." Her father grumbled.

Sara nodded, tight-lipped, to Geoff when he passed the plate to her. She couldn't get the image of him and Paula out of her mind.

Later that evening after Geoff had left and her father had dozed off on the couch, Edna, Judith, and Sara were cleaning up in the kitchen. Sara was lost in her own thoughts, and was glad that somehow she had managed to appear composed in front of her family. No one had noticed how upset she was. All day her mind had been playing every little nuance of the scene she'd witnessed in Geoff's office—how Paula had reached to embrace him. How he'd gently caught the woman's hands in his own. Pain lanced through her with each viewing. It had been so intimate, so private. But curiously enough, it was Paula's action that made her want to scream. Initially, she had believed that Paula had seen her enter through the door and known that she was there. She sighed, and went back to stacking the dishwasher. Edna and Judith were talking behind her.

You know, it's funny but Geoff has changed. The light around him isn't perturbed anymore," Edna said.

Sara turned at Edna's statement but didn't answer immediately. Her thoughts were in such a turmoil. It wasn't new information that Edna had become one of Geoff's biggest admirers, but today it galled her. Also, the irony wasn't lost on her, either.

"You mean his aura's changed?" Judith asked.

"Did I say anything about auras?" Edna challenged angrily.

"Isn't that what you meant?" Judith responded.

"No! I just said light. He's changed, and it don't have nothing to do with anything like that."

Sara had been surprised by her mother's earlier statement, thinking it was more forthcoming than Edna usually allowed herself to be about her strange moments of prescience. But this later remark was much more in character. Any suggestion that Edna might be clairvoyant was anathema to her mother. Judith glanced knowingly at Sara.

"How's Hugo and . . . Nora?" Edna asked her.

Sara paused, suddenly remembering her suspicions about Alexis. She realized she'd totally forgotten everything except the scene she'd interrupted today. Finally, she answered, "They're all right."

"Lately, I've been getting such funny feelings about them two."

"This ain't their auras," Judith mumbled.

"Thank you for that, miss," Edna said.

"Anyway, you're always getting funny feelings about them," Judith said—not knowing when to let it go, Sara thought.

Sara wondered if Edna had guessed something was afoot about Alexis.

On the long ride home, Geoff found himself remembering a time during their first two years of marriage. It was summer, a time before the children and near the semester's end. Sara had come to pick him up at the university and they'd walked hand in hand across the campus toward the car. It had been a good day, and he was feeling on top of the world.

They had been quiet for the last few minutes, and he had just turned toward her when he'd become unable to take a deep breath. It burst upon his senses like a bolt out of nowhere. He realized what a lucky man he was. She was beautiful. He couldn't take his eyes off her.

"Look!" she said, pointing to something behind him. "Isn't it gorgeous?"

He swung around and there before them was the sun, setting with an incredible array of colors—reds, yellows, oranges, purples. He was distracted and glanced at Sara as much as the sunset, but she was right. It *was* breathtaking, and they stood there watching for long moments. He'd been too busy to notice things like the sun setting. He kissed her and she laughed and glanced around to see if anyone had observed them. Sara had always been rooted in the present, and it was one of the things that he had always admired about her. How could he have been so stupid? he wondered.

The next evening, Geoff called to tell her that his parents had taken Alexis and Lizzibit on a sudden trip to Florida. At least, Sara thought upon hearing this, there would be little opportunity for Alexis to get into trouble in a totally different state, if for no other reason than she didn't know anyone there. But she felt so lethargic and down that she didn't say much, not even to vent any more spleen.

It was quiet in Middletown during the next few days, so peaceful that Sara suddenly didn't want to return to Scarsdale. Geoff called every day but there didn't seem much for them to say. Each time he asked her to come home, but she refused.

The night that he called she'd been quiet most of the time, allowing him to speak. Neither of them had mentioned Paula's name.

"I spoke with Nora—" he said, "about Alexis." Sara perked up slightly. "Nora's going to get counseling for her."

"That's good," she answered lackadaisically, although she was glad that something had been done about her young sister-in-law.

When she didn't say more, he went on. "The principal

at your school asked me to help with the fundraising. I've promised to lend a hand."

Although she was surprised at this news and knew that it was a peace offering, it didn't lift her out of her doldrums. "I thought you didn't have the time," she answered.

"I decided that I did." When she didn't say more, he said, angrily, "When are you coming home?"

"I don't know."

"This isn't about Paula."

"What do you mean?" she snapped, finally coming alive.

"You were never jealous of her, despite all your complaining."

"If this is more of your ducking responsibility, it won't work."

"No, it's knowing that you've been soured on everything that's connected to me or to us."

"Oh Geoff, please. Did it ever occur to you that it also has to do with you, and the way we've been living?"

"Okay, so tell me what you're talking about. Be specific. Don't just throw down the gauntlet and then not follow through."

"Why? So you can pretend to listen to me for a change?" She thought of how frustrated she'd been, how much she'd wanted to teach again.

"Sara, we' need to talk," he said, sounding more concerned that she'd expected.

But it didn't deter her from saying, "I told you in the beginning that if you ever had another woman, we'd be through. I meant it then, and I still do."

"Are you talking divorce?" he demanded.

"What do you think?" she shot back.

She realized that despite her threat she was ambivalent, and still her mind played over the incident until she thought she'd scream. However, the word *divorce* made her realize that she had to do something about her situation.

Chapter Sixteen

Later, when the children were asleep and Martin dozed in front of the television, she went to find her mother, who was alone in the kitchen. "Would you mind if I stayed here for a while?" she said.

"What does Geoff say about that?" Edna asked, not appearing the least bit surprised.

Sara took a deep breath and plunged in. "Geoff and I are having difficulties, and we need time away from each other."

"Rubbish! Sounds like one of them foolish modern advice to the lovelorn. Husbands and wives should sleep in the same bed, and they should never let the sun go down on their anger. I knew you two were fighting. Anyone looking at you that first day couldn't miss it."

So much for trying to be discreet. "It's about Paula. I caught them together," she blurted out.

"What does 'caught them?' mean?"

"She had her arms around him," Sara said. Her mother didn't look too disturbed by that. "He knows that I'll never tolerate infidelity."

Edna said, "Go home to your husband. Successful men are always highly sexed, and you're his wife."

It was not something that Sara ever expected her mother to say, not that she'd ever considered her mother a prude. "Are you condoning his behavior?"

"No, but one woman's arms around a man don't mean cheating—not to me. You've got children, and you just can't throw your marriage away."

"How could you doubt when you know his history?" Sara demanded.

"The past doesn't always determine the future. Besides, I've seen that Paula, the little chippy, and I wouldn't give her the satisfaction, if I were you. You've got what she wants. If you leave, she'll grab him in a snap. I wouldn't let her have him. He's been faithful for all these years when no one believed it was possible, and I don't believe he isn't now."

"How do I know he's been faithful?"

"You know," Edna said, sounding incredibly sure.

Martin came into the room, arms stretched over his head. He looked a little fuzzy as he rubbed his stomach, but one glance at them and he was suspicious. "What are you two cooking up now?"

Sara didn't want her father to know, but Edna spoke out. "She wants to leave Geoffrey."

Martin frowned, looking askance. "Why?"

"She caught that Paula hugging up on him," Edna answered.

"What did Geoff say about it?" Martin asked.

"We haven't talked yet," Sara admitted.

"That's the first thing you got to do." He sat down and leaned back, shaking his head. "Now, you want to leave him? When your mother and I wanted you to do that, you were determined to stay."

"Dad, are you going to hold that over my head forever? So I made a mistake."

"No, you didn't make a mistake," her father said solemnly. "You two have been good together, and no, I don't

hold it against you. Maybe I was hurt about what happened
with both my girls, but that's over, now. Besides, marriage
is a sacred contract. You took vows." She thought about
her sister at that point, and wondered how they'd take it
that once again both their daughters were having troubles
at the same time. "You're always welcome here, Sara," her
father said, "but you need to go home and return your
children to their father. Maybe I didn't agree with this
marriage, but Geoff's been a good husband despite anything."

The next day, she thought about their talk as she drove
home, remembering that in her parents's day, especially
in the south, couples remained together through problems
that would rip them apart today. She wasn't willing to live
that way. She respected their opinions, but knew she could
never live with Geoff's being unfaithful. And she didn't
feel as sure as her mother did.

She also realized that she was proud of herself. The
worst thing that she could have imagined—Geoff with
another woman—had happened. Yet, she'd been pretty
calm, despite the fact that she thought about it almost
constantly. Although she'd wanted to remain with her parents, she had never despaired. She'd always believed she
couldn't survive such a situation.

Seeing Geoff with Paula had hurt—hurt a great deal—
but she was not shattered. She was stronger than she'd
ever thought. *Why am I not shattered? Has my love for Geoff
waned? Have I outgrown it?*

No, she answered her thoughts. She loved him, and
would all her life. It wasn't just sex, either, it was exactly
as her mother had implied years ago—he was her soul
mate. But she could never accept infidelity. Even once was
too much.

She went back to Scarsdale the day before the children's
schools opened. She was already in bed when Geoffrey

came home late that night. He looked exhausted, with fine lines around his eyes.

"So, you're back," was all he said, but she thought he looked relieved. He rubbed his forehead.

"How are you doing with the fundraising?" she asked.

"Good," he said, sounding up for the first time.

His sudden spurt of enthusiasm annoyed the hell out of her. *What's wrong with me? I should be glad.*

He was almost literally asleep when his head hit the pillow. There was no further talk and she was glad, because she wasn't certain what she wanted to say. She was too confused. Geoff's having said that Paula wasn't the issue didn't help, either, for she wasn't certain that he wasn't right.

When Geoff left that next morning, she pretended to be asleep. The usual rush of getting the children out took up most of her thoughts for the next hour, but her ambivalence continued.

Not long after she'd returned home, having dropped both children off, the phone rang. Picking it up immediately, she heard Nora's near hysterical voice.

"Geoff?" her mother-in-law said.

"He's not here," Sara said, not realizing that Nora was back in New York.

"Oh, Sara, I'm so glad you're back. Hugo's in North Central Hospital—in intensive care. He's in liver failure. He may not make it. Please tell Geoffrey."

Nora hung up and Sara tried to contact Geoff. He wasn't there, and she told a bored sounding Paula about Hugo. Next she called her parents.

"Hugo? Oh Lord," her mother answered. "Your Dad will be so upset. We'll be there as soon as we can."

For the rest of the day, Sara kept trying to call Geoff, but each time Paula answered, saying Geoff's cellular wasn't working. She was angry, wondering if Geoff was avoiding her call.

She couldn't get to the hospital until she'd picked up

the children and left them with Hannah. Her anxiety levels soared.

Finally, she was able to reach the hospital. Sara walked into the waiting room and glanced around, praying that Geoff had gotten her message and was there already, but there was no sign of him. Nora, Alexis, and Lizzibit, as well as her parents, were already in the waiting room, sitting on the hard plastic chairs.

After nodding to her parents, Sara went to Nora first. Both Alexis and Lizzibit were huddled on either side of their mother, giving Sara tearful nods. Sara noted with relief that Alexis looked better than she had in months.

Tears ran down Nora's face. The older woman was devastated, and grabbed Sara's hand. She sounded so pitiful when she asked, "Where's Geoff? Isn't he coming?"

Sara felt heartless having to say that she hadn't spoken to him but had left messages. Helplessly, she patted Nora's hand.

A glassed-in area showed part of the Intensive Care Unit but curtains were drawn around most of the beds, giving little access to what was happening. A nurse in green scrubs came out, giving Nora and the two girls permission to enter.

With Nora out of hearing, Sara spoke with her parents. "Have you heard anything from Geoff?" she said.

Edna's and Martin's glances met briefly. "Nora asked me to call him—" Martin said and stopped.

"He's not coming," Edna finished for him, shaking her head. "This is so terrible." Sara collected the purse that she'd placed on the seat nearby and stood up. "You can't leave, too," Edna whispered, shocked.

"I'll be back," Sara promised, and returned to the parking lot.

She sat there in the hot car for a few minutes, staring off into space. Then, taking a deep breath, she put the key in the ignition and turned it. On the way to Geoff's office, she drove the limit. Once there, she circled the block several times seeking a parking spot. Finding none, she took a chance and stopped in a forbidden zone. Her watch told her that she'd already wasted too much time. She glanced around, hoping that she'd be back before anyone ticketed her.

Upstairs, she found Paula in the outside office. "What are *you* doing here?" the woman asked.

"None of your business," Sara answered and headed for Geoff's door. Paula made a move to bar her entrance and Sara said, "Get out of my way." Paula stepped aside, her face tomato red.

Sara opened the door and Geoff looked up. His eyes widened at sight of her, and a hopeful expression flitted across his features. He looked more tired than he had last night, as well as slightly disheveled. A shadow on his chin showed he needed to shave.

"You should be at the hospital," she said without preliminary.

At her statement, he became tight-lipped and something told her he was disappointed. "Did you come all the way here to say that?"

"Your mother is devastated. It's the least you could do."

"I have no desire to visit that old reprobate."

"He's your father, and he could die there."

"What do you care? Doing one of your Turner good deeds? Or are you still trying to reconcile my family before you walk out? Why don't you leave it alone?"

She refused to let him antagonize her. "At least think about your sisters. They need you, too." He remained silent, but he glared at her. "I'm not leaving here without you."

He bolted upward and she expected real fireworks, but all he said was, "The noble Sara stoops to walk among the savages. All right! But I've got to wash up." He went to the bathroom and slammed the door.

"I'll wait for you downstairs,' " she called through the closed bathroom door.

Planning to go back to her illegally parked car, she stepped to the door and opened it, only to see Paula backing quickly away. "Eavesdropping?" Sara asked.

"No, I wasn't," Paula denied.

Instead of going downstairs, Sara wandered around the area. As usual, Paula was perfectly groomed, maybe a little too sexy for the office, but still quite attractive. She bustled around as if very busy, but Sara suspected it was all for show. Several times she tossed her long, lovely hair away from her face, and Sara wondered idly why she didn't simply pin it up.

Sara watched dispassionately for a few more moments and suddenly, as if a light had gone on, she realized why she hadn't fallen apart over the whole episode. In shock, she realized that she simply didn't really believe it.

Why should it surprise her that after eleven years of marriage she would believe Geoff over Paula? Of course she would. Her mother was right. She knew instinctively that Geoff had been faithful.

Thinking of that scene, it was quite possible to believe that Paula *had* seen her and had deliberately set out to provoke jealousy. *And Geoff had held Paula's hands—held them to keep her from embracing him.* He'd even stepped back before realizing that they'd been seen.

"Your listening doesn't matter, anyway," Sara assured her. Then she quickly said, "You're fired."

"What? You can't do that. Geoff's my boss."

"He's also my husband and that makes me the boss, too—of sorts. But I'll be generous. You can have eight weeks severance."

"But you're divorcing—" Paula spluttered.

"You wish. Take my advice and forget it."

"We've already been lovers," Paula taunted, looking defiant. "They always say the wife's the last to know—"

"Not this wife," Sara cut in. Then, smiling, she said, "By the way, I know you're lying."

"You're bluffing. I know you're jealous of me."

"Paula, I may envy things about you, but not any imaginary relationship you *think* you have with my husband."

"How can you be so sure? How do you know he wouldn't prefer me over you?"

"I know Geoff very well. If you think he'd choose you, you're dreaming." And as she said the words, she knew they were true. Why had she allowed herself to worry?

"You're only guessing," Paula hissed. "What about Nora? She won't let you do this to me."

"Paula," Sara answered, almost feeling sorry for the woman now, "surely you know that Nora was only having a little fun—cruel fun—but still only fun. She knows what side her bread is buttered on."

Finally, Paula was goaded into saying, "I could have had him any time that I wanted."

"Over my dead body," Sara said sweetly and then, as if thinking better of it, "or maybe ever *yours?*" Paula blanched and suddenly Sara discovered that she was enjoying herself. She had absolutely no intention of touching Paula, but for once in her life she was grateful for stereotyping.

"I want to hear it from Geoff," Paula said, and by her very admission Sara knew there had never been anything between her and Geoff. If there had, the woman would have been a lot more secure in her position.

"You've got five minutes to pack and get out," Sara answered and walked back into Geoff's office, softly closing the door behind her.

When Sara and Geoff came out some minutes later, there was no sign of the beautiful woman. "Where's Paula?" The freshly shaven, handsome Geoff glanced around and said.

"She had to leave, I guess," Sara answered, deliberately sounding offhanded, In feigned, wide-eyed innocence, she added, "Maybe you should lock up?"

Downstairs on the street, Sara's car had been ticketed. Geoff glanced at the fluttering paper tucked under her windshield wiper and remarked, "You're lucky they didn't tow it."

Once back at the hospital, Nora stood up and held her arms out to her only son when they walked through the door. Geoff took over consoling his mother. Sara breathed more easily.

It wasn't long before the chief surgeon came and told them that Hugo was bleeding and had to have immediate surgery. Nora was so distraught that they would not have been able to control her if Geoff had not been there.

Lizzibit cried inconsolably, saying, "Is it my fault, Sara? Did I hurt him when I didn't want the birth control?"

"No, Honey. Your daddy's been ill for a long time. He loves you as much as he can," Sara said, knowing it was true, as things went, also knowing it would do Lizzibit no good to denigrate her father now. "You know he always wanted his children to have everything they wanted. He wouldn't have been hurt that you didn't want something. Right?"

That seemed to be something for the girl to think of. She was still crying, but she didn't look as wretched as she had before.

Not only Lizzibit was having trouble. Alexis was also in obvious distress. The older girl sat clasping her hands in her lap. Sara sat and embraced her. This time she wouldn't make the same mistake. Because Alexis was more stoic, people often thought she was coping when she wasn't. At first Alexis was startled by Sara's gesture, but then she leaned her head on Sara's shoulder and started crying quietly.

The wait for news of Hugo's condition seemed interminable. They were all in little groups, with both Alexis and Lizzibit asleep. Geoff sat near Nora, with her parents on the other side of the room. Sara was suddenly restless, unable to remain still. She stood and walked the corridor several times before returning to sit alone.

Then a strange thing happened. Edna stood and silently approached to sit on the other side of Nora. She motioned for Geoff to leave them alone, and he relinquished his place, coming to join Sara.

Nora turned in shocked wonder when Edna put her arms around her. "No matter what happens," Edna said, "you were the best thing in Hugo's life."

"You don't blame me for what happened to him?" Nora said, tears in her eyes.

"No one blames you. You were only a girl. Everyone knew that. Hugo's problems began long before he met you."

"I loved him so. He was such a genius. I thought I could save him," Nora said, her voice barely audible.

"It was Hugo's talent, Nora. And it was *his* responsibility to use it in a way that it would do the best."

The two older women sat huddled together after that.

Sara watched them, and when she glanced at Geoff she realized that he was observing them, also. Something prompted her to put one hand on his arm. He glanced down at her fingers for a long time before looking up into her eyes. Trying to keep her voice down, she said, "Why do you hate him so much?" He tightened up and almost moved away, but she held on, saying, "You never told me why."

"It's hard to explain when I look at him now. All that's left is a fragile, foolish drunk, but back when I was a kid he was a madman. He broke everything that he could get his hands on. In the beginning, I think he even abused Nora, but miraculously she managed to stop that. I think the reason I truly hated him was because I feared I'd be just like him."

"Oh, Geoff, not you. You were never like Hugo."

He glanced at her before saying, "Maybe you're right, but I couldn't take a chance. When you've been sired by someone like him, you have to keep vigilant."

"Is that why you decided to come back to the States?"

"Your letter came at the same time. Maybe that's what woke me up."

"I suppose you thought that I could save you?"

"No, I knew that my love for you could save me. That it might be the only thing that could. It was one of the few things that I'd managed to hold on to."

She was touched by his obvious sincerity. She glanced away, unable to maintain eye contact with him, but she had to finish what she'd started. "You need to forgive him, you know—for your own sake as well as his."

The chief surgeon picked that moment to stride through the swinging doors and they all stood as if on cue. "Mr. McMillan's all right. The procedure stopped the bleeding, and he's resting comfortably." He spoke to Nora, then, saying, "Only you can see him now."

After Nora left, her face aglow, the doctor spoke with Geoff. "Your father's condition is chronic but he's stabilized, now. In the long run . . . well, no one can predict what the end results will be. He must stop drinking, however."

It was a tired but calm group that left the hospital building and headed toward the parking lot. Geoff was still inside, making certain that Nora, who was staying overnight, was settled before they left. Edna and Martin were driving back to Middletown in their own car. Sara came out with Alexis and Lizzibit. Geoff's sisters were going to stay with them for a few days, and as soon as they got into the car, both fell asleep in the backseat.

She sat on the passenger side, waiting for Geoff to join them. Within a few minutes he was there, buckling up. Before starting the car, he turned to her and said, "No matter what you decide, I want to thank you for coming to get me. And you're right, I do need to let go of this thing."

She nodded, remaining quiet for a few moments. "I've made up my mind what I'm going to do, too." He turned looking wary. She noted his hands gripped the steering wheel. "I'm going back for my master's," she said.

"That's good," he answered, still guarded.

"Yes, I thought you'd agree. That way, I'll be home for

the next few years with a little volunteering, of course. After that, well, we'll talk about it.''

His eyebrows shot up in surprise, and he turned to glance at her. He must have seen her heart in her eyes, for he leaned to take her into his arms. The kiss was awkward in the confines of the car, but it was long and passionate. Neither of them wanted it to end.

When she'd caught her breath he said, "What about Paula?"

"What about? Oh, you mean her kiddy crush?"

"That's my girl." He smiled. "Let's go home."

They were on the way to Scarsdale when she took a deep breath and said, "Of course, being as I fired her, I'll help out until you find a replacement."

Horns blared when the car swerved slightly. "You fired Paula?"

"I also threatened her with bodily harm." She smiled, feeling mischievous.

"You, the peacemaker, did that?" He laughed. "Did she believe you?"

"That woman's a smart cookie," she said.

"What does that mean?"

"It means she knew I had every intention of seeing the last of her in your office."

He smiled—with a hint of male pride, she thought. "You didn't have to go that far," he explained, "I'd already found another job offer for her. The whole damn thing was my fault. I'd totally discredited that she used—"

"Let's not worry about that," Sara cut in. "Oh, by the way, I promised her eight weeks severance pay."

He glanced her way. "Eight weeks? I don't know about that. It's only supposed to be six," he said.

"You can afford to be generous. After all, she's a cousin."

"A distant one."

"And don't forget that . . . kiddy thing," she said facetiously.

"Okay, if you insist. But you'll be the one to make it up." When she looked askance, he said, "Sure, I'll add it to the rent, and that way you can work it off in the usual way."

He pulled into their driveway and leaned over to kiss her again.

"Oh, naughty landlord," she purred.

Book Three

Chapter Seventeen

Early JUNE 2002, SCARSDALE

Geoff arrived sometime after midnight. She turned when he leaned over to kiss her, but his lips landed on her cheek. He undressed and climbed wearily under the covers, coming to lie spoon fashion at her back. His arm circled her waist and drew her near.

He'd taken the red-eye. Geoff had never been a good night flier. Luckily, it was only from Washington. Had it been farther away, he would have been jet-lagged and out of sorts for most of the day.

"How's the golf?" she asked sleepily.

"Perish the thought," he grumbled. She wanted to turn and embrace him, but she was exhausted herself.

It had been a difficult couple of weeks at the Maggie Ferguson School with her having sped around at breakneck speed, trying to tap new sources for funds. "You know what I'd like to do?" he asked, caressing her abdomen, but before he could finish she heard his breathing change, becoming slow and rhythmical.

She'd lay there seeking to go back to sleep, but it didn't

work. Naturally, she thought, now that Geoff was asleep, she was awake. With a sigh she climbed out of bed and went to make herself a glass of warm milk.

The man's luck was phenomenal. Like magic, it seemed as if everything he touched flourished. Thirteen years ago he'd done some fundraising as a favor to the Ferguson School, and it had led to a new career. He'd been so successful in his efforts that he'd been offered a position with the New York City Mayor's Office, as a financial adviser. After divesting himself of the investment group, he was off and running.

Sometimes she felt a little guilty about his leaving the group, because she knew he'd done it to please her. She'd been so unhappy during those trading years. But still, he was a busy man. Within a short time he'd gone from local government to national, now working for Senator Robert Doddsworth in the same capacity.

The microwave pinged and she took her milk into the dining room. Actually, other things had changed in that time, too. Eight years ago, Hugo had died after a period of declining health, leaving Nora resigned if grief-stricken.

She had accomplished a lot in the last thirteen years, too, she thought not without some pride. She had earned both her master's and doctorate, as well as worked her way up the ladder, becoming principal. She had taken over the Ferguson School four years ago and instituted changes that preceded a wonderful increase in the scholastic average. She believed the latter was due to her changes.

With both of them having demanding positions and Geoffrey spending so much time in Washington, D.C., it often meant they had a long distance marriage.

Thoughts of the school brought a sigh. As usual, it was in straitened financial circumstances. For many years, the New York City Department of Education had been considering ways to assist such facilities, but so far no action had been taken. Various bills had been debated ad nauseam, and she wondered if anything would ever come of them. Several years before, things had looked close, but recently they had regressed and now the school desperately needed help.

There was also a federal bill under consideration, and she was more hopeful about this legislation. If it did not come, she feared they'd have to close their doors forever. Already, she was plowing much of her own salary back into the school.

Education was having a hard time nationally and, as had been true for decades, national test scores were down. She feared this was to be expected in a country that placed so little value on the education of its children. She turned over, thinking these were certainly not new thoughts.

Geoff's new political associates were certainly no improvement over the old Wall Street investors. There were as many social get-togethers as ever, only these weren't like Nora's old parties. These were political things, which meant they were a lot more serious. Then there were the perennial fundraiser events. True, it wasn't an election year—that was two years away—but the pace was hectic. She still did as much entertaining as she'd ever done, but now she rarely seemed to resent it. Perhaps that was because she had her own work.

Suddenly, she was too tired to keep her mind on these thoughts, and pushed them away. It wasn't long before she felt her eyelids grow heavy again and returned to bed.

The next time she awoke it was later that morning, when Geoff quietly slipped out of bed and went into the bathroom. She turned over and stretched, but didn't rise immediately. It was terribly cozy, lying there listening to her husband in the bathroom. She heard the water running. The door was open as usual, and she finally rose. In the bathroom, she could see the outline of his body against the opaque glass doors of the shower stall. The room was steamy.

With very little hesitation, she decided to join him. She let her silk nightgown drop, and pulled back the door. Geoff turned his head to look at her as the water sluiced down his strong, hard body. His eyes shifted down over her unclothed frame.

She moved in and took the soap to wash his back. She put her arms around him and started soaping down his hairy chest to the thick thatch of hair below. He kissed her over his shoulder then positioned himself to face her. He began smoothing soap over her, too.

"You do know that I've got to meet Robert?" he said, closing his eyes as she touched him.

"Do you?" She continued to caress. "Well, Robert Doddsworth is the distinguished Senator from New York. Surely learning a little patience would do him well."

"You're a cruel woman, Dr. Turner-McMillan, and I think you're turning into a delightfully dirty old lady."

"Watch that *old*. And how can you say such a thing? I'm just trying to be your personal body servant, which I signed on to do almost twenty-five years ago."

"Just what I always wanted—a personal body serv—"

The phone rang, the sound carrying minimally into the bathroom and barely heard over the water.

Geoff raised his head. "Telephone?"

"I can't hear a thing," she lied. He kissed her again but the phone kept ringing. She felt his withdrawal and groaned. "Let it ring," she said.

"You know I can't." Geoff stepped out of the shower and tied a towel around his middle.

She watched him, thinking that he was still one of the best looking men she'd ever seen, looking especially good for forty-eight. He was slim and flat bellied, with a full head of hair that was now turning silver at the temples.

She smiled. If she hadn't ruthlessly squashed her jealousy of women who came on to him, she'd probably be living in a padded cell by now. She kept gazing at him until he had gone into the bedroom and was no longer visible. Then she quickly showered herself, rushing to finish and catch him before he dressed.

Lord, look at what I've become—I have to waylay my husband to get myself laid. In a way it was funny, but it was also true.

She was suffering from sexual deprivation. It seemed as if
Geoff hardly ever got home in the past year. Their sex life
had always been healthy except for those few months years
ago, and indeed, she *did* feel deprived—very much so—
though she knew it was no one's fault. Then she changed
her mind. *It's Geoff's fault,* she thought with a smug smile.
He'd taught her too well, creating in her a woman who
expected to be satisfied.

Generally, he worked with Robert Doddsworth, but since
the beginning of the year he'd been on loan to the State
Department, dealing with several countries in South
America.

Hurriedly, she stepped from the stall and threw a toweling robe over her still wet body. As she passed the partially
steamed mirror, she opened the robe again and inspected
herself. She looked pretty good too, she thought, for a
woman nearing fifty. It was curious but she often felt that
woman of her own generation, The Baby Boomers, seemed
to age slower than she remembered older generations
aging. Then she remembered having heard that, according
to the experts, hers was the first generation that thought
it never had to die.

Suddenly, an old thought seeped into her mind. Friends
often remarked how Geoff had everything—looks, money,
brains. But she'd always wished that he was older than she.
Strange silly thought. A year wasn't something to worry
about. She closed the robe.

As she entered the bedroom, she heard Geoff speaking.
" . . . yes, I'll be there in an hour."

Ah, well, she thought. *I won't get laid this morning.* She
was disappointed, but she knew they'd get together later.

She went to him and placed both hands on his shoulders.
He turned, still speaking on the phone and parted her
robe. With raised eyebrows and a wolfish grin of apprecia-
tion, he walked backward, pulling her with him until they
both tumbled backward. They landed amid the fluffy
feather pillows, with her on top.

He reached into her robe, caressing her breasts as he

hung up the phone. She kissed him hungrily, needing a reaffirmation of their love. He responded immediately, his proud male flesh stirring and jolting against her stomach. As he kissed her, he slowly pulled the robe from her body, already baring one shoulder.

She sighed ruefully. "Didn't I hear you say you were going to be somewhere in an hour?"

"Did I say that? I don't remember a thing," he said huskily, nibbling her ear.

"By the time you get dressed and drive there—I don't think you have time for this."

"I'll be quick," he said, kissing her neck.

She laughed. "Hah! Not with me, you won't."

He groaned, stopping with his forehead pressed to the spot where her throat met her shoulder. He took her hand and pressed it on his manhood. "Look at what you've done to me. You're always making . . . things hard for me."

"Oh, I need much more than an hour of your time, Mr. McMillan. You'll have to get back with me, later—when you have plenty of time." She laughed again as she squirmed from atop him.

"You're such a tormentor," he said sulkily.

"Me? Little ole' me? Anyway, you should be glad you have a wife like me. I keep you on your toes."

"That you do. I'm taking you up on that 'later.' Headaches don't count."

"When's the last time I had a headache?"

Geoff stood up and his towel stuck out at a right angle straight in front of him, extended by his rock-hard erection. He looked at it ruefully and asked, "Now how am I supposed to concentrate on Doddsworth? All my brains will have herniated into my—towel."

"Save it for me."

"Have no fear. I intend to do exactly that."

Sara glanced quickly at her watch, remembering that she, too, had an appointment for that morning. She went to her closet and began shifting hangers, deciding which outfit to wear.

As she rushed to dress, she thought of an old adage that claimed that no matter how much things changed they remained the same. She was proud of Geoffrey, inordinately so. And there was no denying that, although he was now in a totally different type of work, he remained the same.

Geoff had already donned his underwear and was pulling up his pants when he said, "Well, at least now that the school term is nearly over you can come to Washington. I'm truly sick of this long distance, commuter marriage."

She paused, one hand holding up an outfit from the closet. "Washington? I thought you were going to be here for the summer?"

He put on his shirt and answered without missing a beat as he buttoned it down the front. "I have to be at that committee hearing."

"During the summer?" She was so disappointed that she rushed on without listening to any answer that he might have had. "What committee? They're never in session during the summer."

"This is a special situation. They'll break briefly, but they're not going to stop until they iron out more of the issues."

"But what's that got to do with you? I thought you were on loan to the State Department for this year. You're not a part of Congress."

"The Senator's asked me to stay until the final vote." Then he paused. "There's also a delegation that will be going to South America in September. The State Department wants me to accompany them."

"I thought you'd be based in New York at the United Nations, starting this month. Now you tell me that you'll be back in D.C. for most of the summer, and you'll also be out of the country? What about the beach house that I've rented?"

"So, we're going to be a little delayed in our plans, but at least you're free for these summer months."

"You expect me to spend them in D.C.?"

Annoyance made her turn away. He was doing exactly what he always did. He thought of his own work first. Months ago, they'd made plans to spend a long leisurely four weeks together. After years of non-stop work, they both deserved it, and Geoff had been as eager as she. Now, after she'd rented a house at the shore, he might not be able to go. Not only would she be disappointed, but Kamaria and Asa were going to be there, also, as well as her parents and Nora. The only thing that kept her from voicing her anger was that she hadn't seen him all week and it seemed such a poor way for them to start.

"I'd like to see more of you, Sara, he answered. "Is that asking too much?"

"No," she said and thought he wasn't asking too much. It was a good point. They needed to spend more time with each other. "You're right," she said, coming to touch him. "Anyway, maybe we'll be lucky and you'll be back in time for us to get some time at the beach."

He smiled. "That's my girl."

She was glad that she'd refrained from arguing when he kissed her at the door. "Say hello to Beverly for me," she said, remembering Robert Doddsworth's wife.

"It's never ceased to amaze me how you two took to each other. But of course, I guess I should have expected it. You're quite good at charming all the correct beasts."

"I must remember to tell her that one," she answered.

She straightened his already perfectly knotted tie and flicked an invisible speck of lint from his impeccable suit, knowing it was only an excuse to touch him.

"Maybe, everything will turn out for the better," she said. "You'll be there for the MacKarren Bill, and that will surely be a good thing. Things are so bad that we can't afford several of our traditional activities next year. And as for our adult classes, forget most of them. Lord, will I be glad when that bill is passed, and we can borrow on the promise of the money."

Suddenly he stiffened and moved back. Then, quickly

turning away from her, he said, "Well, I've got to get out of here."

Some premonition made her feel that he wanted to say more. Despite her disappointment she waved to him, already lonely for his return.

Afterward, she hurried around the house, trying to finish dressing and make her own appointment. Hearing that their summer plans would be severely curtailed still stuck in her craw. Opportunities for such a leisurely family summer were rapidly fading into the realm of the impossible.

Kamaria was twenty-two, and Asa nineteen—both young adults. Their daughter lived on campus and they only saw her during holidays. Already, she had a job offer that would mean her relocating to the San Francisco area.

As for Asa, he attended a local community college but he was so involved with his own life that they never saw much of him, either. He, too, was rapidly moving away from them, and soon would be gone. She missed her children already. She missed Geoff, too. Lately, they'd had so little time together. Although the commute wasn't a long one, flying back and forth, sometimes several times a week, had been daunting for both of them. Most of the time it was Geoff who did the traveling, but often in an attempt to help, she'd done it. At best, it was an exhausting experience.

Sara managed to overcome her annoyance about their delayed vacation plans and tried to make the best of things. After all, Geoff had helped her with the school many times in the past. She could accept the change with some good grace. She had done all the commuting during those warm days when he was delayed.

On one of those visits to Washington, she'd run into Beverly, Senator Doddsworth's wife. Although Beverly had a sharp tongue and was quite capable of saying what she wanted, she was also charming and generous.

They met for lunch one late spring afternoon in one of D.C.'s rather posh restaurants. Up until the coffee, the talk had been on various topics.

However, with the coffee, Beverly leaned toward her and said, "What about Geoff's past? Has he ever had affairs?"

The sudden, blunt question flustered Sara. "What?" she started, and then took a deep breath. "Why do you ask that?"

"Geoff's power base is expanding here in the capitol. He's coming under the media spotlight, and we need to know where he's coning from," Beverly said and then added, "do you have something to hide?"

"No, but I do know we're entitled to our privacy," Sara bounced back.

"Once you're a public person, you lose a great deal of that, but don't get upset. This isn't an inquisition. I'm not attacking you. That's why it's *me* asking the questions. This isn't official, but it could cut straight to the core. You can stop this right now by simply admitting that either you or Geoffrey have something in your life that would damage you if it were discovered."

"Would you mind breaking that down?"

"Do either of you have anything you don't want people to know?

"Doesn't everyone?"

"Yes, but I'm talking about things that would truly damage."

"Like what?"

"Affairs, financial irregularities, alcohol, drugs? Have you ever had an extramarital affair?"

"Of course not," Sara said, more puzzled than ever by where this was all leading.

"What about Geoffrey?"

Sara didn't answer as quickly. There was a beat of hesitation before she said, "No."

"What about Paula Stone-Weills?"

"No!" *How did Beverly know that?*

"How do you know he didn't?" Beverly probed.

"He told me."

"And you believe him?"

"Yes, I do," she answered, firmly this time.

"Well, I guess that should be good enough for me," Beverly finished. It had been a harrowing minute and Sara was glad to see the conversation move on, but she couldn't help asking, "Is Robert always made vulnerable by the people he associates with?"

Sara thought that Beverly's explanation wasn't terribly enlightening, but she let it go and they finished their lunch.

Weeks later, Sara was seriously trying to put a good face on the time she spent in Washington. Even when Geoff made plans without conferring with her to entertain the Pessachs over the weekend, she had jumped in with as much good grace as she could.

She'd spent the whole day with Myra Pessach, touring interesting spots in the District of Columbia. But unlike in those past days of nonstop entertaining Geoff's old trading customers, this time she thoroughly enjoyed herself. Besides being an old friend, Myra was a woman that Sara both liked and respected.

Although she had made the tour of the nation's capitol before, Myra hadn't. They'd elected to spend the morning at several different areas, and reserved the afternoon for the Viet Nam Memorial.

Upon first glimpse of the site, both women stopped and stared, silent for long moments. Then they slowly continued walking toward the black marble, boomerang-shaped monolith sunk into the ground. It was both awesome and moving.

"It gives me such an eerie feeling," Myra voiced.

"Me too," Sara admitted.

"Did you lose anyone there?"

"No," Sara said, but she hesitated.

"Thank God Saul was deferred. I protested the war back then."

"Yes, I was against it too," Sara said.

But not for the first time, she'd wondered about the veterans who'd returned and been denigrated by Americans who'd protested that war. It must have been agonizing for those young men who often received only derision for having risked their lives. Her eyes followed the incredibly long list of names of the men and women who'd paid the ultimate sacrifice for their country—knowing that a disproportionate number of them had been African-Americans.

"Thank God Geoffrey came home unharmed," the other woman said.

"Yes." Sara pulled her attention back to her friend.

However, Myra's words sent her imagination reeling off on further memories. Did Geoff come back unharmed? It was a strange thought. To all appearances, Geoff had not only survived but he'd thrived. Suddenly she remembered the intent, edgy young man who'd come to her home almost twenty-five years ago. She remembered the scary, restless energy that had seemed to vibrate around him. Somehow he'd moved back into the fabric of a normal life, but had he been unharmed?

"He was lucky," Myra said, as if on some sort of telepathic link with Sara.

"Lucky or blessed," Sara said automatically.

"I do want to thank you for letting Saul and me have the beach house for those two weeks," Myra said.

"No problem," Sara said. "I'm just glad you were able to take it—not just for the expense, but because it would have been stupid to let it to go to waste." She thought of how disappointed she was that it wouldn't be her and Geoff at the house or those two weeks of much needed rest. As it was, by the time they went the whole family would be there, making it crowded, to say the least.

"I know these are difficult times with you two, but you've been handling it very weld, considering how dedicated you are to your school," Myra said.

"Yes," Sara answered automatically. She waited, expecting Myra to elaborate, but after seeming on the verge of speaking, Myra sighed and remained silent. Several times that day, Sara had sensed that Myra had something on her mind. "You were going to say?"

"Nothing," Myra answered, "just that I admire your restraint."

"Restraint?"

"Forget it," Myra said.

It was so unlike Myra not to speak her mind that Sara still expected her friend to continue, but when the other woman didn't pursue it, she allowed the conversation to stop there. *It will come out later,* Sara thought.

Three weeks later, to Sara's relief, they did make it to the shore for the last two weeks of the vacation. Saul and Myra had taken the first two weeks, as they'd planned.

She lay protected from the late August heat by the shade of a huge, colorful, beach umbrella. Geoff sat near, engrossed in the papers that he'd brought down to the beach. He had also brought a cellular phone, and a small portable fax machine, and was totally engrossed in the laptop computer that sat on his knees. His phone rang and he picked it up. She glanced at her watch.

The house had been more expensive than she'd anticipated, yet they were lucky to have gotten it. Summer rentals could be costly. It was everything the owners had promised, a huge, rambling, old frame structure, with rooms and alcoves everywhere. This was fortunate because there were so many people, and even more were expected.

With both their parents visiting, things were a bit crowded. Judith would be there any day, now. It was even possible that Alexis, with her family, and Lizzibit would come. She smiled, remembering that her younger sister-in-law no longer answered to the name Lizzibit. Now, she was Liza.

Time passed and things did change, Sara thought. Alexis and Lizzibit were thirty-one and twenty-nine, respectively— both grown, the difficulties of their adolescent years long behind them. Alexis had been clean since Hugo's death, and was now married with a small son. Lizzibit, surprisingly enough, had opted for a career and cohabitation with her longterm lover. She didn't seem interested in marrying any time soon.

Sara sighed, her thoughts returning to their original bent. This was not the vacation she'd expected. For one thing, it had been difficult to get Geoff to take the time. And the atmosphere palled. The children were grown and were busy with their own plans.

As for Kamaria, she'd been aloof and indifferent to most of the activities that Sara had suggested, studying as if she had not graduated already. All of her interest was on the job that awaited her in San Francisco. The girl had left her things already packed at home. She was completely ready to leave at the end of the month. When she did have time she spent it with Geoffrey, talking about Washington. It was enough to try Sara's patience.

Asa was just as bad. He worked during the day and rehearsed long hours with the small band he'd assembled during the last year. They were pretty good, she thought. He returned late most nights only to fall into bed. Most of his energies went into his music.

But there was more. Simmering just below the surface brewed the threat of confrontation between Geoff and Asa. It stemmed from Asa's barely passing last semester. It was only a matter of time before it boiled over.

She must have dozed off, for she came to herself abruptly when a slight breeze picked up and deposited a sprinkle of sand on her. Her eyes felt gritty when she awoke and saw the sun glare, reflected from the water. Despite the very light wind, it was still beautiful. Sitting up and grabbing for the straw hat that she'd brought with her, she gazed around.

Geoff glanced up when she moved and said, "I'm glad you're awake. I'm going to be returning into the city this evening. I have a meeting early tomorrow morning, and I don't want to be on the road with the morning traffic rush."

She couldn't help the immediate anger that swept over her at these words. "Why?" she insisted.

"It can't be helped. You know the trip to Ecuador is coming up, and there are a lot of loose ends for me to tie up."

"But you said that we'd have these two weeks, and after all this trouble we're not going to have even that?"

"I'll be back before you know it." Refusing to listen to another word, she stood up, grabbing her towel and carry-all and started walking toward the house. "Where the hell are you going?" he demanded.

"I'm not listening to any more excuses, Geoff. I don't care why you're breaking your promise. Go if you like. Why bother to tell me?"

She continued toward the house, annoyed—all the effort she'd gone through to make this trip happen, and here he was totally involved in his work. She'd left all her work at home, determined to make these weeks good, while he couldn't be bothered to spend any real time with his family.

Chapter Eighteen

Later, after Geoff had left for Scarsdale, Sara was sitting on the porch with Edna and Nora, drinking Edna's famous lemonade. She couldn't forget the fight she'd had with Geoff, but was determined to make the best of this trip. She had planned to spend it having quality time with her family, and whatever Geoff did, that was exactly what she would have.

They had pulled out a television set, which was connected by a long extension cord that everyone had to step over. Some Olympic tryout competition was in progress. She found listening to the talk of the two older women and the vague sound from the television comforting.

Sara wasn't watching, as she'd closed her eyes, savoring the occasional slight breeze that gently ruffled the wind chimes. And much as she resented it, her mind was on when Geoff would return.

Actually television watching was at a minimum, as the two older women were more interested in the rare neighbor or the cars going by than by anything on the tube.

"Now that's what I call real designer genes," Edna said,

her attention on the television as she pointed to a young black athlete.

"Please, none of your racist remarks," Nora said.

"What's racist about what I said?" Edna spoke querulously. Her mother tried to lure her into the discussion. "Sara did you think there was anything offensive about it?"

Sara responded with a vague, "I didn't hear it."

Since Hugo's death the two women had become close, and it was best not to get caught in any of their little squabbles. While they'd once been arch rivals and perhaps even enemies, now they were bonded together in a strong friendship. Their bonding was so powerful that neither claimed to remember a time when they hadn't been friends.

"Why ask Sara?" Nora snapped, taking up the gauntlet. "You know she won't take sides."

At this, both older women united against her. They gave her annoyed glances before humphing and turning away. Sara took a sip of her lemonade and closed her eyes again.

Some moments later, Edna said, breaking the quiet of the moment, "You know what's missing? Some of my cold mushroom soup."

At her mother's words, Sara's memory suddenly took flight back to her childhood, when Edna used to prepare that particular recipe. Suddenly, she longed for a taste of the remembered dish. But she hadn't invited her mother to the seaside to cook. "Oh, Mom, don't start. This is supposed to be a relaxed time."

"Amen," Nora piped in, "Anyway, who wants to stand over a hot stove?"

"I'm always relaxed when I'm cooking," Edna said tartly with a sharp glance at Nora. "As soon as Judith comes, I want you girls to go out to that farm where you can pick your own vegetables."

Sara said, "You know I hate picking mushrooms."

Edna answered, "It can't be avoided. The only ones I

trust are the ones that have been picked fresh. There's no telling what those supermarkets will sell you."

Sara sighed. It was a lost cause. Once Edna got onto an idea, wild horses couldn't make her change her mind.

They all looked up as a very low-slung, red car, an old Triumph, pulled to a stop. A tall, brown-skinned young man unfolded himself and stood up, gazing toward them on the porch. He appeared to be in his mid to late twenties. Sara at first wondered if he was a friend of Asa's, but somehow he didn't have the look of Asa's musician friends. He was too clean-cut with his khakis and oxford shirt. Soft moccasins covered his bare feet.

"Wonder who this is?" Edna mumbled, voicing what was on the rest of their minds.

The young man was rambling along the sandy path, nearing them, when Nora spoke *sotto voce.* "Who cares? He's a hunk."

It sounded like the old Nora, and Sara smiled and wondered if he had heard the remark.

"Good morning, ladies," the stranger said, looking up at them as he came to the bottom of the steps. I'm John Rivers, here to see Kamaria. She's expecting me."

Nora launched into some aimless chatter to engage his attention while Edna called out, "Kamaria!"

Sara stood, holding her hand toward him, saying, "I'm Sara, Kamaria's mother." She then introduced the two wary grandmothers.

"Come up and have a seat, John," Nora said in her sweetest voice.

Kamaria chose that moment to walk through the front door, wearing a pair of faded jeans and loose cotton top. Her bare feet were clad in leather slides. Suddenly, Sara was caught by the sheer beauty of her young daughter. Kamaria's shoulder length, crinkly-curly hair was caught up in a barrette at the back of her head, and she smiled briefly at John. "Hi. Nice of you to come," she said, sounding noncommittal.

"Why don't you two sit down? I'll bring more lemonade," Edna said, standing also.

"Oh, we're going into town," Kamaria answered quickly.

"Have a seat," Edna insisted. Then she muttered as she left the porch, "How important can it be that he can't have a glass of lemonade? It don't take that long."

Both Kamaria and John Rivers sat—probably not wanting to annoy Edna any further, Sara thought. She wanted to laugh because the whole scene reminded her of her own youth. Yet she was glad that Edna had taken over because she, too, was curious about this handsome young man who'd come to visit her daughter.

Many young men had come to their house over the last few years, but Kamaria always found fault with them. Of course, it was foolish to worry about this now. Her daughter was only twenty-two. There was plenty of time for that later.

Yet, sometimes she was concerned that the girl's close attachment to Geoff would give Kamaria problems. It wasn't uncommon for a daughter who loved her father too much to have difficulties settling for a husband. Girls saw their fathers as gods, and judged men of their own generation as too small in comparison. Sara worried that no man would be able to live up to that competition.

It was these thoughts that made Sara agree to go pick mushrooms with Kamaria that next morning. What with the house jammed with family, there hadn't been much opportunity for her to have any private time with her daughter.

The next morning, Sara and Kamaria drove south to a local farm for Edna's mushrooms.

"Have you and John been seeing much of each other?" she asked Kamaria when they were looking through trays of vegetables.

"No," her daughter answered bluntly. When she said nothing else, Sara wondered how to approach the subject again without offending the sometimes prickly Kamaria. Just before Sara could say anything, the girl spoke, "Why do you ask?"

"Just curious. He seems nice."

"Oh, Mother, you're so transparent."

"Okay," Sara said, placating. "So maybe he just has nice manners?"

Another long pause and Sara wanted to sigh. Kamaria was long past the sulky teenager phase—thank God—but sometimes she could be exasperating.

"He *is* nice," Kamaria admitted, sounding reluctant. "But just don't go making a big deal out of it."

"Lord." Sara walked away, throwing up her hands. "And I thought we'd both outgrown those years when everything I said was wrong. I can see we haven't."

A few minutes later, Kamaria came up behind her. The girl put her arms around her neck in a quick hug, saying, "It's just that I know you so well. Next thing it'll be a big palaver between the grandmothers, Aunt Judith, and you."

"Oh, it will not," Sara denied hotly and suddenly had a moment of *déjà vu*.

The whole conversation reminded her of talks she'd had with Edna as a young woman—before the coming of Geoff. When had the shift occurred, she wondered. When had she become the older mother figure to her own grown daughter? In truth, there were times now when she was a mother figure, of sorts, for Edna too.

By the time they got back to the house, Judith had arrived. Sara had barely gotten to the house before Edna said, "Good. Glad you're back. Now, you can go dig up some mussels. It'll be good for all of you, give you some togetherness."

"Mom, I just got back from the mushrooms," Sara protested as she flopped down.

"These are good activities for two sisters who don't see much of each other."

"In case you didn't know, there's very little chance we'll see any, and besides, mussels are an endangered species."

"Always some excuse," Edna complained.

Judith glanced at Sara, and said with a conspiratorial

shrug, "All right, Mom, but give me a little time to settle in. We need to do that later in the evening, anyway."

The older woman's efforts to get Kamaria involved petered out when John Rivers showed up the second day in a row. The young couple drove away, again.

Later, Sara was sitting on the porch with Edna, looking through the mushrooms that they'd picked. Martin was down on the beach, while Nora napped in an upstairs bedroom. The house was quiet.

"Do you think Geoff ever suffered from that syndrome that sons of famous fathers get? You know—where they feel the need to prove themselves? Maybe that's why he's so singleminded," Edna said.

"I don't know—maybe," Sara answered after contemplating Edna's question. "But he's already accomplished more than Hugo ever did. Besides, they went into drastically different fields."

"True." Edna nodded at that.

Suddenly, Asa drove up, parked, and walked toward them. Sometimes, Sara was amazed at how much like the young Geoff, Asa appeared. His hair was braided in a mass of short spikes, and he wore a single, small earring. He was incredibly handsome. He stood there chatting with them for a short time before entering the house.

Once Asa had gone, both Sara and Edna looked at each other. "What about Asa?" Edna said. "Maybe *he* suffers from that old syndrome."

"Of course not," Sara snapped. "Asa has his own interests. He has no problems standing in his father's shadow."

"You don't think he's spending too much time with that little group that he's put together, and not studying enough? It worries me."

It wasn't something that Sara wanted to hear voiced. In truth, she was more worried than she ever wanted to admit. It was funny the way she felt about Asa. With Kamaria it had been different. Her daughter was not as vulnerable as her son. She trusted Kamaria to make wise decisions.

Kamaria's fault was that she was inclined to be too self-absorbed, rather than anything else.

"What do you think about this one?" Edna handed Sara a mushroom, effectively bringing her back to the present.

"Oh, Mother, you know I hate doing this."

"You shouldn't. It's important to know how to pick them."

"Lord, I'd rather cook without them. Anyway, I think that's a good one," Sara answered.

"You're right," Edna agreed. Then looking around suspiciously, she said, "Where did Judith get off to?"

Probably ducking this chore, Sara thought, but she said, "I think she went walking on the beach with Dad."

"Humph," Edna grunted. "Never could figure how that girl always managed to avoid any work."

Sara's thoughts were still with Asa. She could hear him walking about upstairs. She knew that in a short time he'd close his bedroom door. Soon, just as she expected, she heard the sound of his guitar strumming. Mellow notes drifted from the windows overhead.

"That boy plays just like Martin used to," Edna said.

"Really?" Sara asked.

"Or maybe . . ." Edna stopped to stare off dreamily into her own space. "Maybe it's more like Hugo. The old Hugo, before his vices caught up with him."

Sara's glance traveled up to the window, listening to the soft, lovely, guitar sounds. She had often wondered herself at Asa's obvious talent. Geoff played, but he'd never had the expertise that Asa seemed to have been born with.

Edna's glance came to rest on Sara. "Hugo had such a touch, you know. Truly. You could get lost in his music."

"Yes, I've often listened to "Somewhere In Time," Sara said.

The older woman shook her head and went back to the mushrooms. They listened in silence. Some time later, after they'd finished and Sara was preparing to go upstairs, Edna said, "There's something that I want to say."

"Yes?"

First Edna stared off into space, looking out toward the roadway. Then she seemed to shake herself and said, "I have this strange feeling about Geoff. I can't explain it."

"Oh, Mother, please. Not more of your hovering dark cloud."

Edna's chest rose and fell. "I know you don't want to hear it, and I can see that the two of you are at each other's throats like cats and dogs, but take my advice, don't fight so much right now. There's something afoot, some turbulence."

At Edna's use of that word, Sara was reminded of Edna's earlier hostility toward Geoff. "Mother, what are you talking about?"

"Something's about to happen. It's hard to say."

Sara didn't answer. Although it had been a long time since Edna had predicted anything of this sort, Sara found she couldn't take her mother seriously. Edna had too often said things like that, and she was truly fed up with them. Besides, her mind was too much on the problems they were now having. What worse could the future offer?

That next day, Labor Day, Alexis and Lizzibit came. Alexis with husband and son; Lizzibit with her boyfriend each bringing their families for a visit. Geoff was there, also, but his plans were to fly to Washington the next morning. From there, he would soon be on his way to South America.

He'd driven up with Dave, Judith's lover. And shock of all shocks, John Rivers was in attendance, too. Usually Kamaria didn't have this much patience with her admirers.

Everyone came prepared with a dish to eat. Sara and Judith had spent most of the day cooking, while Edna proudly served her cold mushroom soup. When the combined families sat down for dinner, Sara was aware of the joy she felt at their all being together again. It was wonderful. Why, she thought, couldn't Geoff see that this was more important than anything in their professional lives?

Later, Martin and Nora became nostalgic with talk about
Hugo and the old band days. Even Geoff seemed to enjoy
the talk. The only thing that worried her was that Asa
wasn't there. She kept glancing at the clock, and once
during such an act, she glanced up to see Geoff watching
her.

Fortunately, Asa did arrive before Alexis and Lizzibit
left. As her son ate a plate in the kitchen, all three of his
aunts kept him company, teasing and fussing over him.
She could see, however, that Geoff was angered by their
son's late arrival.

The women and men had separated after dinner, the
women into the kitchen to clean up and collect their various dishes while the men sat in the den telling tall tales.
Sara took coffee for the men, which they carried with them
for a walk on the beach.

By the time she got back to the women, they had gone
to sit in the living room. She had just entered the room
when she heard her mother hiss at everyone to be quiet.
All talk suddenly stopped and everyone sat there, watching
her. Nora and Edna sat together on the loveseat, looking
rather guilty. Aside from the mothers, Judith, Alexis, and
Lizzibit all sat very close to the older women. Sara looked
around at the guilty faces and wondered.

Now that she thought of it, she realized the two families
had obviously been up to something for most of the day,
not to mention that both Edna and Nora had been in
cahoots during the whole week. She'd been too upset with
Geoff's behavior to pay attention to anything else.

"What's going on?" she asked.

They all looked at each other, but it was Edna who
answered. "Going on?" Edna glanced around at the others
as if seeking an answer to Sara's question. She appeared
all puzzled innocence.

"Don't try to hide it," Sara said. "All of you have been
as thick as thieves."

"Really, big sister. Aren't you getting a little paranoid?"
Judith answered.

"Never mind," Sara said, realizing that she didn't have time to get to the bottom of this now. It would have to wait until later.

It wasn't until Alexis and Lizzibit had both left that the pending eruption between Geoff and Asa finally occurred. Suddenly, Sara remembered Edna's premonition.

"Where were you tonight?" Geoff demanded, speaking to Asa.

"I forgot," Asa said, and added, "I had rehearsals."

"Why are you spending all your time goofing off with those friends of yours?" Geoff said. "A little bit of this, I could understand. But you're at this several times a week. When you're not with them, you're holed up in your room playing guitar."

"I didn't know that was a crime," Asa answered.

"You should be using some of that time to study."

"School's out, or haven't you noticed? I guess you're away so much you missed it."

Sara knew the boy's attitude was annoying Geoff, but somehow her husband managed to maintain his temper.

"Think you're going to be a kid all your life?"

"Do I look like a kid?" Asa shot back.

Sara's heart thudded against her ribs and she was suddenly frozen with apprehension. Asa was as tall as his dad and they faced each other off in the middle of the floor, looking nearly combative.

"You act like one." Geoff's voice intensified.

"Cause I'm not doing what *you* want?"

"Because you're not preparing yourself to be self-sufficient. You didn't apply yourself last semester, and you should be in summer school. Your marks need all the help they can get."

"Why not tell me what you really think?"

"What's that mean?"

"That I'm a disappointment. That you were finished by my age? Things like that?"

"Let me tell you what I really mean—so you don't need

to guess. Being as you opted not to go to summer school,
I expect to see you spend some time with your books.''

"You want to give me an assignment, too?''

"That's not such a bad idea, mister. But as you're no
kid, you can do that all by yourself. And if I don't see
you're making an effort, I'll want an in-depth explanation.
You understand that?''

"You made yourself clear,'' a sulky Asa answered, suddenly looking more the boy than usual.

"Good,'' Geoff said. When Asa remained there, looking
furious, Geoff added, "I say this conversation is over. What
do you say?''

Sara's stomach clenched and her heart stopped. She
was always uncomfortable when Geoff and Asa had words.
Somehow, she knew that both of them were vulnerable
when they clashed, and always feared one of them would
create an irreparable breach.

Asa's mouth tightened but he didn't speak again and
he left the room, taking the stairs two at a time. Sara
exhaled in relief, she'd been holding her breath.

When she heard her son's door close, she turned to
Geoff. "You didn't need to be so harsh.''

"Sara, you let him get away with too much.''

"Me? How dare you? You're away most of the time, and
you're blaming me?''

"Okay, maybe you've got a point, but I meant what I
said. His marks had better pick up or he'll answer to me.''

"What would you do? He's nineteen.''

"I don't give a damn how old he is,'' Geoff said, seemingly more angry with her than he'd been with Asa. "As
long as he's in my house, he follows my rules. You know
how much trouble I went through to get him transferred
out of that community college for next semester?''

"He wants to be a musician.''

"What?''

"He wants to take his group on tour.''

"No way! He's going to school.''

"He's already in school, but he doesn't want to go to Harvard—"

"Do you know how many strings I had to pull to get him accepted? His marks simply aren't that good."

"Asa's marks aren't exceptional because he's more interested in his music than school.

"Look! He wants to play music? Okay. He can play for a hobby."

"That's what it is to *you.* "

"So what?"

"Music made a great hobby for you. But Asa wants to make it his career."

"Is that so? Maybe he wants to starve? Or maybe he thinks I'm going to support him? Well, he's wrong." He paced angrily up and down the room. "That boy's been spoiled and coddled all his life. You hear me?"

"Geoff, he's no worse than you were."

"What do you mean?"

"You were an oddball, too." That made him stop, and when he didn't answer she said, "You were just as focused on what you wanted. Just as determined to go your own way. Just as secretive. Just as isolated—just as self-centered."

"I was never self-centered. My world always evolved 'round you and the kids."

"Your world evolved around whatever your current obsessions were. We never got more than a few crumbs."

"That isn't true."

"Now we're getting less than ever, because you're never here. You spend most of your time in Washington or some far off place."

"If you're talking about this Ecuador project, you know how important it is."

"All your projects are important."

"Wasn't it you who wanted me to leave Wall Street and get into this? Wasn't this what we planned?"

"I don't know what we planned, Geoff. All I know is that we're going in opposite directions. Our children are grown and it seems we have nothing to keep us together."

"Nothing to keep us together? Spare me this, will you?" He backed away, holding both hands up in front of him. "I've got too damn much paperwork to fight with you tonight."

When Geoff stormed out she stood there with an urge to follow and pursue the conversation, but didn't. Besides, although she was annoyed with Geoff for several things, she had to admit that she agreed in many ways with his statements to Asa. But she also knew that their son was in a difficult period of his life, and it took careful handling to keep things from deteriorating.

After one quick glance upstairs, she went up and tapped at Asa's door. He didn't answer and she opened the door, glancing in. He was lying on his bed, his arms folded across his eyes. He looked up when she entered and moved to sit at the side of his bed. The room was dim and music played softly.

"Your father's right about one thing, Asa," she said. "You need to finish school and prepare yourself with something to fall back on."

He stood up away from the bed. "You're saying I'm going to fail, too?"

"No. Neither of us means that."

"He's saying it."

"Your father loves you, no matter what you may think."

"Sure, as long as I'm not making any waves."

"The entertainment world is hard. It's not that you'll fail, but it could take longer than you expect—years."

"Who says I'll have to wait that long? Besides, others have done it."

"What would be wrong with being self-supporting?"

"You sound just like Dad," he said. "I don't have to finish school for that."

"But it would make it easier on you. It's only two more years. Please consider that it takes money to survive in this world."

"Thanks," Asa said, standing there as if he owned the world. "That never occurred to me, for some reason."

Sarcasm scored his speech. "Do you mind if we finish this some other time?"

He wanted her to leave. "All right," she said, feeling let down and realizing that she couldn't think of anything more to say. It seemed to be a time when both her children wanted her to keep out of their lives. She stood, turned, and left him there.

She met Judith on the stairs. "Come on, we can dig for those mussels," her sister said.

"This late? You're not tired?" Sara responded.

"I've got two weeks vacation, and I'm going to enjoy every moment of it. Anyway, we need to stretch our legs and talk."

That idea was so tempting that Sara went and grabbed some small trowels and pails. She followed her sister for some distance away from the house.

"Wouldn't you think," Judith said, "that our mother would be willing to accept the fact that we're grown up by now and stop assigning us tasks like this?" Judith asked.

"Not likely," Sara said.

"Well, if we're still stupid enough to let her railroad us into this, I guess we have nothing to say. Has she done any of her fortune-telling bit this trip?"

"Not much, considering." Then Sara remembered. "She did mention something. Said she was worried about Geoff."

"Oh, for heaven's sake!" Judith exclaimed. "I thought she'd given up on that. And you believe her?"

"No, and to tell you the truth I didn't want to hear about it, either."

"Good for you. Speaking of Geoff, honey, he really laced into Asa, didn't he?"

"They're becoming like two bulls in the same china shop."

"Don't worry. Geoff's just being a concerned parent, and Asa's a great kid. He'll be all right."

"Wish I had your faith," Sara said.

"You're standing too close. You can't see things like I can."

"And speaking of seeing things—what's with all the subterfuge?" Sara changed the subject.

Judith looked away hastily. "Gee, this looks like a perfect spot," her sister said, pointing to an area in the sand at her feet. "Maybe I should start digging right here?"

"Out with it," Sara said.

"Well, if you must know, it was about your anniversary coming up in a few months. They're excited, and both Nora and Mother want to give you a big bash for your Silver Wedding Anniversary."

Chapter Nineteen

Yes, of course, Sara thought, she should have guessed.
The Silver Anniversary. Suddenly, she was more depressed
than ever. How the years had passed. Yet in her heart, it
seemed only a short time since she'd looked up one day
and seen Geoff. He'd been standing there looking like a
thunder cloud because he'd caught her kissing Chuck
Grant. She couldn't even remember what Chuck looked
like now.

However, that didn't matter. What was important was
that she didn't feel she could stand another big anniversary
celebration despite its being months away, not in the mood
she was in now.

"No big event this year," she said. I don't think I could
handle it."

"Neither Edna nor Nora will let you get away with that,"
Judith said. "This is a milestone. You'll simply have to
suffer through another of your hated parties."

"I don't hate parties," she answered absently.

"That's not what you usually claim. But a woman who
married a politician has to accept them."

"Geoff's not a politician."

"Call it what you like. But you know what they always say—'birds of a feather'? He's flying with a helluva lot of politicians."

"Listen, forget that. You have to stop this from getting out of hand. If they truly want to celebrate, then make it small, and just family—like what we did today. That would be good enough. But no big bash."

"No way. Nora's got all flags flying, and our mother has jumped right on the bandwagon. Besides, you should be proud and pleased that they want to do it."

"Well I'm not," Sara said.

Suddenly, Judith looked around and said, "Listen, I need to talk to you."

"Talk," Sara said.

"Not here. What say, we escape and go out for coffee at some diner? Besides, you know there're no mussels here."

"This late?" Sara said, feeling dubious.

"There's bound to be someplace still open in that tourist trap."

Sara drove them to a nice restaurant close to town, located on the main pier.

They had sat down and picked up menus when Judith said, "I've always envied you, you know."

"It's called sibling rivalry," Sara said, opening her menu.

"Haven't you ever felt that way about me?"

"Of course. You know it," Sara said.

"What do you envy about me?"

"Looking for compliments, sister dear?" she said. "Okay, I admire your toughness."

"Not just my feet, I hope?" Judith cut in, smiling.

Sara held up a hand to stop the levity before continuing, "I admire that you never allow people to railroad you into anything you don't want. That you're free to pick your own path."

"I guess by 'free' you mean that I'm single and don't have any children?"

"Well . . . in a way, that's part of it," Sara answered.

"Have you ever wondered what I envy about you?"

"Yes, tell me."

"That *you're* tough." When Sara looked askance, Judith insisted, "Yes, you are. You manage to accomplish what you set out for with a minimum of fuss, and that's tough. I also hate you for being married, especially to Geoffrey. It's a good thing we're sisters or I'd have given you some real competition. And I envy that you *do* have children." They both laughed.

"People are never satisfied with their lives," Sara said when they'd gotten serious again.

Judith went silent at this. She stared down at her hands laying on the table. Sara knew something was coming and waited. Finally, Judith took a deep breath and said quietly, "I'd be very satisfied if I could have this baby."

"Baby?"

"I'm pregnant again, and this time it's already gone into four months. The other times I never got past the first trimester. I'm forty-five, and if it's ever going to happen . . . well, let it be now."

Sara glanced at Judith's stomach and then into her eyes. She took Judith's hand across the table. "I'm so glad. What does Dave say?"

"Hah. He's happy as a hog in slops."

"But you still don't want to get married?"

"If I can carry this baby to term, then we'll get married. Otherwise . . ." She spread her hands. "What do you think Mom and Dad will say?"

"They'll be glad for you—once they've gotten over the shock, of course," Sara said, and they laughed again.

"Do you think Dad has ever forgiven me? For . . . you know?"

"Of course he did. That was a hard year for him, with both of us going off the deep end together like that. Mom twisted his arm until he was glad to let us off the hook."

"You don't think I'm too old?"

"No way."

"I only hope Dave and I have as wonderful a marriage as you and Geoff."

Sara's first impulse was denial, and the instinctive response caused a moment of truth. She suddenly had to acknowledge that her marriage wasn't looking particularly great, despite Judith's admission of envy and implying that Sara had made the better choice. There had been trouble in their marriage. No one's marriage was without problems, but she'd never felt so frustrated or disappointed in Geoff before.

"And," Judith added, "the way you've taken the loss of funds to the school is truly remarkable. You're not even worried. I can't help but marvel."

It was a few moments before Sara was able to focus on these last words. "What loss of funds?" she asked, her eyes on the large menu she'd grabbed in an effort to distract herself from thoughts of her marriage.

"You know, the MacKarren Bill," Judith answered, leaning over the table. "How they're going to table it in the compromise for that other bill . . . you know the one."

A cold chill went up the back of Sara's neck. She looked up, staring straight into Judith's eyes. Her breath caught in her throat, but she schooled her face to show nothing. Then, forcing her mouth to smile, Sara asked, "Where did you hear that?"

"Dave mentioned it. He knows everything happening in Washington," Judith finished, a note of pride in her voice.

Sara's face felt like dry, old paper that broke apart when she tried to smile. "Oh, that. Well, I'd rather not talk about it now."

"No, of course not. I understand. You've been very loyal to Geoff, and I want you to know how much I admire you for it."

Judith's use of the same word that Myra had favored didn't go unnoticed by Sara. *Loyalty,* she thought, *more like stupidity.* Suddenly, she felt like a fool. Everyone knew but her. Why hadn't Geoff told her? Why had she let him get away with it? She was furious.

Judith happened to look up at that moment. One glance

and comprehension dawned on Judith's face. "You didn't know?"

Out of that same hated loyalty, Sara wanted to deny it, to lie and say that Geoff had warned her. But this was Judith, her sister. Suddenly, she felt her cheerful mask crumble and she closed her eyes, the whole scene too painful. "No," she choked out.

"Oh, Sara. Me and my big mouth." Judith moved around the table to comfort her.

After a few minutes Sara said through stiff lips, "It's okay."

Then, looking down at the menu, she realized that she couldn't even see the words any longer. She put it down, knowing she wasn't interested in anything to eat or drink. When the waitress came, Judith suggested coffee and Sara agreed, surprised that her voice sounded calm.

The minute she arrived back at the house, she stormed into their bedroom, finding Geoff sitting at the desk with a stack of books and sheaths of papers laying in front of him.

"When were you going to tell me?" she said, forcing the words between her teeth.

He turned around and removed the reading glasses that he'd taken to wearing during the past few years. Without asking what she meant, he answered, "Keep your voice down. I was going to tell you tomorrow, before I left for Washington."

"I don't believe you. How could you do this?"

"Sara, I haven't done anything. It wasn't in my power to get that bill passed, and you know it."

"People would have listened to you. You could have spoken up." She remembered the conversation with Beverly Doddsworth. People respected his opinions. Geoff had a lot more influence than he liked to admit.

But it was his attitude that hurt. It was his willingness to allow it to happen that galled her to the bone. It was his attempting to explain it all away that made her know that this was one betrayal she wouldn't tolerate.

"At times I've wondered how you can face yourself in the mirror. And I've also wondered how I could live with a man as selfish as you. You've always sacrificed me and whatever was important to me for your own needs. But this time I won't stand for it."

"Damn it!, will you stop!" Geoff yelled at her as he jumped up. Books and papers tumbled everywhere, scattering across the floor. "Sara, I'm sick of your complaining. You're never satisfied. First you complained about the investment group and Wall Street. Now it's Washington. Give me a break."

"You knew better than anyone how important it was to the school, and yet you sat back and allowed it to be pushed behind because of some horrid, back room deal making."

"Of course, *you'd* see it that way. Are you menopausal, by any chance?"

Her anger rose. "What is that supposed to mean? Is that supposed to be a crime?"

"No. But it would be a lot better than what your real problem is—that you're a prissy, fault finding bitch . . ." She gasped. It was the second time in all their years that he'd called her that. It was like a slap in the face. "What do you want from me? I'm only human."

"Go to hell, Geoffrey."

"What? Not asking for a divorce because you can't get your way? Don't be bashful. This time you can have it."

Although they slept in the same bed that night, they remained at opposite sides.

That next morning he left for Washington. He would leave from there with the fact-finding group for South America on the next day. It would be at least two weeks before she would see him again, and, thinking of the words they'd said to each other she wondered if it might prove to be longer.

She didn't get out of bed to say good-bye, although she heard voices when he went downstairs to say good-bye to the others. She put her arm over her eyes, then later turned over and coiled into a fetal position.

She thought of how easily he'd moved from the Wall Street days into being a consultant for Robert Doddsworth. Trust Geoff to make everything work out for himself, while the rest of the world had to take pot luck with destiny. Thirteen years ago, he had helped her with the school funding, and afterward his star had risen faster than a helium-filled balloon. The irony wasn't lost on her that the fight last night was also over school funding.

Was she jealous? While she might have overcome her fears of other women, was there any envy of his success in his career? She exhaled on a long, extended breath. Well, maybe just a little. She rolled over and turned on the bedside light and sat up in bed. No sense trying to sleep— it was a hopeless cause.

He'd never mentioned divorce to her before. It had been she who toyed with the idea, and that was years before. And his calling her hurtful names had been shocking. Had he grown tired of her? Was her mother's prediction that he'd outgrow her coming true after all these years?

She moved to get up from bed and pulled on her peignoir. Feeling the silken fabric against her made her examine it in the mirror. When had she taken to wearing things like that, she wondered, staring at the suddenly strange woman looking back at her from the mirror.

She remembered racing barefoot through the grass, in the years before Geoffrey. How often did she do such things now? Heck, when was the last time she'd done anything like that? She sank into the chair. He used to call her the wild girl, and she had been just that. When had she changed? Or was it so long ago that she would never truly remember the moment? Why had she allowed it to happen? Why was her life and career subordinated to Geoff's?

Geoff was in the plane's bathroom shaving when he suddenly watched as a narrow red ribbon snaked down his cheek. It was his first realization that he'd cut himself. He threw the razor down on the sink, wanting to hit something.

Instead he took a small cauterizing pencil and stopped the bleeding.

God, he was sick of the whole thing. He was fed up with trying to appease a woman who could not be pleased. This whole mess was Sara's idea. He'd have been just as happy rushing around in his car with a quotrex in his hand or puzzling over graphs. It had been she who'd wanted him to do something meaningful.

Meaningful? What a joke. What the heck was meaningful about living hip-to-hip with a bunch of greedy men, many of whom took on the job of public office to control other people's money? What was wonderful about the misappropriation of funds or the purchases of three hundred dollar toilet seats?

And to make matters worse, there was always Sara goading him to do something more wonderful. He was sick of it. If she wanted a divorce, she could damn well have it, and good riddance.

Suddenly, there was a lurch and he grabbed the sink to keep from falling. He heard screams outside. Something was wrong. The plane was losing altitude. He slid away from the sink and had to move hand over hand to open the door.

Two days after Geoff had flown to Washington, the beautiful early September weather had gone from balmy that morning to threatening storm clouds by that afternoon. Everyone was still at the beach house, where they'd remained to say their good-byes to Geoff. Now, the atmosphere seemed anticlimactic. They were all packing in preparation for their trips home back to their everyday lives. Judith had stayed to drive their parents home, while Nora would accompany Sara.

Kamaria's flight to San Francisco was scheduled for the weekend. Asa grudgingly prepared to return to Scarsdale and school.

Sara, however, was still furious from the fight with Geoff.

The longer the time passed, the angrier she became. Geoffrey's mentioning divorce had left her truly spoiling for a real showdown. *How dare he?* Did he think that the word would intimidate her? That it would make her acquiesce to his perfidy? Well, he was sadly mistaken. *If he wants a divorce, so be it.* She'd show him that two could play that game.

She'd kept to her own room for as long as she could, and when she'd come downstairs she heard everyone in the kitchen talking. Sara walked into the sitting room determined that she'd make arrangements to return to Scarsdale. But before she could pick up the phone it rang. She fumbled in her anger before finally putting the receiver to her ear. And in that instant, before whoever was on the other line spoke, the small hairs on her arms suddenly rose.

"This is Michael Todd, from the State Department. I have bad news." The State Department. That could only mean Geoffrey. Her heart seemed to slam into her throat. "I'm sorry to say," the man's voice went on, "that your husband Geoff McMillan's plane is missing and has been forced to land . . . didn't want you to hear it first from the media. We are inviting the families to come to Washington while we find out what has happened."

She barely heard what the man said, her mind becoming a jumble of frightening, fragmented thoughts once she'd heard that Geoffrey's plane was missing. In the end, she wasn't even certain of what she'd said, but dropped the phone from nerveless fingers and clutched the side of the desk in an attempt not to fall. Then she raced outside to the porch and turned on the television.

"We interrupt this program to inform you," a male reporter announced, "that the plane carrying a government fact-finding committee on a visit to South America has been reported missing."

Sara went into the kitchen and everyone glanced up at her entrance. One look at her and their faces flashed from smiles of greetings to alarm. Everyone who saw her knew something dreadful had happened. Fear clutched her throat, making it almost impossible to utter a word.

"What is it?" Martin and Edna said together, as if they spoke from one spirit.

Nora went deathly pale and slowly placed her spoon down on the table. Sara went to her mother-in-law, wringing her icy hands. "Tell me," Nora insisted.

Sara forced the words out, "I have to go to Washington . . . it's Geoff. His plane's missing."

"Oh, no!" Edna exclaimed. Standing, she clutched her hands together over her bosom.

"God have mercy," Martin said.

Nora bowed her head and said something so quietly that Sara could barely hear it. "Not my beautiful boy," the older woman murmured in a broken voice. She sounded as if all strength had left her. Suddenly, Nora seemed to have aged greatly.

Sara bit her lip and swallowed back tears, trying to be strong for Nora.

"Help me to my room," Nora said, and Sara supported the older woman to stand. Nora then held a hand to Edna, who came quickly.

Slowly, they helped Nora into bed and sat there in her room until she dozed off. "I'll take care of her," Edna said. "You go on."

As Sara threw clothes into a carry-on everyone, including Judith, wanted to go with her, but she managed to convince them to wait.

"You need someone to be with you," Judith said, coming to help her get packed.

"Please," Sara said, "I'd feel better if I knew you were here with Mom, Dad, and Nora."

"I guess you're right," Judith acquiesced, "Thank God I still have a week of vacation. But at least take Asa. I'll call the rental agency and see if we can stay here for a few more days. It might be better for us to be together until we learn what's happened. Pray this house is insulated in case it gets chilly."

"Yes," Sara said, glad that her sister was there and could even think of such mundane matters. Her own brain seemed frozen on one thought—where was Geoff?

Kamaria came back an hour later, accompanied by John Rivers. The girl was stunned when she heard the news. She collapsed on the loveseat and putting her head into her hands, cried, desperately. Sara sat with her, holding her daughter. John joined them there, putting his arm around Kamaria's shoulders. At first the girl remained stiff and unyielding, but soon she seemed to relent and leaned against him, finally putting her head on his shoulder.

Even in her present condition, Sara could recognize the intimacy between the young couple.

Later, as she raced out of the house to Judith's car, her sister and Asa were waiting to drive to the local airport. She wondered when her icy calm would break. She had somehow managed to contain her own feelings of bewildering fear by focusing upon other members of the family. But how long could she stave off the fears that she knew waited just under the surface?

Edna and Martin watched them pull out from the driveway. When they were out of sight, Martin said, "What's happening to him, Edna?"

"What are you asking?"

"You know what I mean. You can see things. Will he be all right?"

"You're asking *me*, Martin? You're asking me to predict Geoffrey's future?"

"Edna, just tell me! Is he still alive?"

"You don't understand. I've never been able to see Geoffrey's fate. He always made his own."

In Washington, Sara and Asa spent hours at the White House being briefed, attending press conferences with the families of the other members of the committee. Most of her energy went into containing her fears in what was the most horrible situation she'd ever known.

The tension created an almost palpable pall in the room. A White House press aide was in the process of briefing the press. Later, the President would be there to inform the group of the current situation and answer questions. There was a lot of talk among the families. A hushed fear came over them when someone spoke of another tragic crash some years before, carrying the then Secretary of Commerce, Ron Brown.

Sara talked with many of them, including one man, Irving Jenkins, whose daughter had also been on the plane. He was determined to go to Ecuador, explaining that he'd been there before and knew quite a bit about the country. Asa latched onto every word, expressing a desire to go, also. Despite the official statement from the government discouraging this, Sara's sympathy was with Jenkins, and she suddenly had an overwhelming desire to accompany him, as well. But she squashed that thought. It was too insane. Besides, what could she do?

Then, in the midst of all this, another press aide walked quickly into the room and whispered something into the speaker's ear.

"Ladies and gentlemen, there's been further communication from South America. The plane carrying the committee has been captured by terrorists who threaten to execute them unless their demands are met."

Chaos hit the room as aides tried to comfort the various families and newspaper men started leaving quickly. However, just as spirits soared because at least there was hope, worse news followed. The President spoke, saying there were reports that the passengers had been found dead. Stunned shock brought the room to total silence before the families erupted in horror. It was the conflicting stories that brought mass confusion. No one knew what to believe.

The ambassador was there and spoke about recent unrest. Sara felt insulated in cotton. Somehow, she couldn't accept any of it. She couldn't believe it. Her mind rejected the words, the very possibility of Geoff being dead. If it was true, she would have felt some premonition, some feeling—something. And that had not happened. Now, it seemed obvious that the disconcerted relatives no longer needed to visit the country. However, there were still a few who wanted to go and claim the bodies of their loved ones.

She glanced at Asa, who was still talking with Irving Jenkins and made her way to her son. "I want to leave," she said.

Her son was reluctant but he came and tried to comfort her. His ability to rise above his own concern didn't escape her notice. They left for their hotel rooms.

On the way, they didn't talk. Asa glanced at her several times. She suspected he was trying to gauge her condition. She tried to be strong, for she could see that he, too, was badly shaken.

For herself, she felt frozen in a foggy land of numbness. But she wasn't fooled. She knew her own time of horrendous grief would come, and wondered if she would be able to stand up under it.

Her head felt as if it would split. A pounding had started behind her temples. She rubbed cold fingers against one side of her forehead. She couldn't believe that Geoff was gone. He had always landed on his feet. Part of her mind tried to convince her that everyone failed at some time. But she fought against these thoughts. *Not Geoff.*

"What are you going to do?" Asa asked. "Are you going back to the shore?"

"Not right away. I thought I'd stay for a few more days. It's just that I couldn't stay in there another moment, today."

Asa said, "Jenkins is planning to leave within the next two days, and I want to go with him."

Sara stared at her young son. She was proud of him, realizing that he'd risen to the challenge as well as anyone could have expected. He obviously had more emotional reserves than she'd given him credit for. Asa had been more helpful than she'd thought possible. It was a curious feeling to realize that somewhere within the last day or so, he'd crossed over the line into manhood. However, the thought of his leaving at that time was too much for her to accept.

"We need you here. I was going to ask you to return to the shore."

"I can't stay here without knowing what's happening with . . . Dad," he said quietly. "I'm sorry."

She took a deep breath, saying, "It's all right." Somehow, it seemed too much to absorb. She'd just lost her husband, and here she was saying okay to her son moving into the same danger. But she could see from Asa's face that he wouldn't let her stop him. "I'll only be here for a few more days and then I'll return to the shore."

Sara called the beach house, telling them about the new information. She felt at a loss that she couldn't be there to help, but Martin, Edna, Judith, and—not too surprisingly—John Rivers, were holding things together quite well. She didn't mention Asa's decision. Best to tell that when she was there.

"Should we tell Nora?" Judith asked.

"Do we have a choice? We will have to tell the truth— that we don't know. Maybe we should get a doctor to see her. And what about Dad?"

"We have to tell both of them, I suppose. There's no way we can hide it." Judith shared her chagrin over the conflicting information. "You should come home."

"I won't be here long, but I can't leave without getting some sort of truth here."

Once Asa was gone, she feared her own sorrow could easily take over. She wondered if it would matter. While the numbness protected her from the pain, it also made her ability to function at an all time low.

The next morning, having been unable to sleep, she sat on her bed looking down at herself. Asa had gone to see Jenkins yesterday. He'd called to say they were preparing for the trip, and she knew he wouldn't be back.

Now, she'd just spent the last two hours trying to get

dressed. She'd fumbled through her clothes, barely able to remember how to perform the simple tasks. She'd managed her underwear after a few stops and starts, and her dress had gone on too, although she'd been too tired to actually pull up the back zipper. If Geoff had been here, he would have done that for her. Geoff would have found her shoes and even put them on her feet. She could have leaned on him or even left everything up to him if she'd wanted. These thoughts weaved themselves into her mind. For one split second tears threatened, but she forced herself away from them.

Her chest hurt with her efforts not to cry. She feared that once she started she'd be unable to stop, and she had to take hold. She had to pull herself together. She couldn't give way until she knew what had happened to Geoff. One glance at the clock made her realize how quickly the time was passing. If she didn't finish dressing, she wouldn't make the press conference. She didn't think that would be any great loss, for the information was a jumbled mess.

Her determination to know everything that she could was what forced her to finish.

Chapter Twenty

Thinking that she needed to be on her own, she'd rented a car, not realizing until she had gone several miles that she should have taken a taxi. Her mind was not up to driving in the D.C. traffic. The green light in front of her suddenly turned amber and she slammed on the brakes. That move brought blaring horns from behind her.

She glanced through the rearview mirror only to see the driver behind her lift his hand and give her a single finger signal. She could hear others behind her yelling. It made her jumpy and she wondered if her numbness was waning. She wished she could let herself weep—even rend her clothing. More blasting car horns brought her back and she stepped on the gas, jerking the car forward on the green light.

When she finally pulled into the South Lawn area, bright rays of sunlight beaming on the structure created a halo-like effect. Suddenly she thought the scene would be perfect for a Viking's funeral. A chill went down her back.

Not Geoff! her thoughts screamed. She put her head on the steering wheel and took several deep breaths, dragging air into her lungs.

She didn't know how long she sat there in that manner. When one of the aides came to the window she rapidly exited the car.

Inside the White House, conditions had not changed. She glanced around for Asa or Jenkins, only to find them missing. The other families were in various states of mourning—from numbness to anger to resignation. She felt like a zombie, realizing that coming had been a mistake. There was nothing new, and the not knowing caused wild speculations.

Hours later, she returned to her hotel room, knowing no more than she'd known before. Her mind went on many things. She thought of her expectations that Geoff should have been able to pass the MacKarren Bill almost all by himself. Why had she allowed her anxieties over the school to cloud her judgement in that way? Was she more jealous of Geoff's success than she had wanted to admit, she wondered, realizing that she'd asked herself that same question not too long ago. Today when she thought of this, she realized there was no sense lying to herself. She had been jealous, and perhaps that was why she'd overreacted.

Already the days seemed to have gotten shorter. Night came, and she stood at the windows of her hotel room looking through the drapes. A pale, tepid moonlight filtered through the glass curtains, hanging under the drapes, and she found herself resenting that the world still carried on. How could it? Without Geoff, how could the sun shine or the rain remember to fall? How could the stars come out?

At the thought of stars, she remembered the night Geoffrey had returned from Asia, twenty-five years ago, and she felt as if she'd fallen into the deepest pit of hell. Tears tore through her raw throat. Several hours later she was exhausted, and knew she had to pull herself together.

She tried to think of things her father had taught her about grief—that she would see Geoff again. That he was in a far better existence, that he was happier than he'd ever been. But none of those thoughts helped—maybe later, but not tonight. Tonight she was far too selfish and she wanted him there at home, with her and their children, with Nora and her parents. There was still so much for him to do. Maybe later, she could accept his loss. Now, all she wished was that they'd made up before he'd left, not daring to approach the possibility that they might have never made up. She finally fell asleep, exhausted, with those thoughts.

A wrenching sob tore from her as her eyes flew open and she bolted upward in bed. She was drenched in perspiration, her hair plastered to her forehead. She gasped, her chest heaving as she sought to pull air into her lungs.

It was only a dream, though it had frightened her so much that she could barely breathe. But as scary as it had been, it had also carried some comfort, for while Geoff had been in terrible danger, he had also been alive. To wake and realize that he wasn't beside her was like being scalded. She fell backward upon the pillows, her breath labored as if she'd been in some great race.

She couldn't remain still, for the more she lay there, the more she felt his spirit. How could she feel this if he were dead? One glance at the clock showed that she'd only dozed for an hour. She got out of bed, shoving her arms into her robe.

How could he have done this? she wondered and abruptly realized that she was blaming Geoff for his own death. It was so insane that it stopped her for a few moments. Yet, upon examining her feelings, she remembered that grief always worked itself into our lives in a very specific pathway. First, numbness, and then, anger. She tried to keep that in mind as she went to get a drink of water.

It didn't help. The anger continued. Several hours later, she was standing, staring out the window at the dark empty street, wishing that she smoked. It would have given her something to do with her hands. Maybe a cigarette would have kept her mind from traveling over the same road. How could Geoff be dead? It simply did not seem possible.

Suddenly, she realized that she couldn't believe Geoff was dead. A strange thought insinuated itself into her mind. Suppose he wasn't? Suppose he was alive?

It was such a crazy idea that she feared she'd become unhinged in her grief. The President had said there were no survivors. Surely, his sources were impeccable. What made her believe that an airplane could crash and Geoff could come out alive?

She realized that no matter how deranged it seemed, she wanted to go and see for herself. Without another thought, she walked quickly to her bed and picked up her purse. Her hands shook as she rummaged through it. In the end frustration made her dump the contents onto the spread. She searched until she found a small white card. She reached for the phone, feeling more at peace than she'd felt since the first call from the State Department.

"Hello, Mr. Jenkins?" she said when a vaguely familiar male voice answered, "This is Sara McMillan calling. Yes, Asa's mother. I'm going to Ecuador with you." She listened to his adamant refusal for a few seconds before cutting in. "Mr. Jenkins, if I don't go, nobody else will." It was blackmail, pure and simple, but she was willing to bluff her way into this.

Ten days later, determined not to fall behind the small expedition that was hiking across the Ecuadoren Andes, Sara focused all her attention upon placing one foot in front of the other. The group of six people, including herself, had left the small mountain hut, or fugio as it was called, shortly after midnight and now five hours later, dawn was approaching with a barely pink tinged sky. Ahead she could see Asa walking beside Jenkins. Her feet were sore and blistered inside her boots and already she was exhausted, but she wouldn't allow it to show. It didn't help that she'd been sleeping poorly, too. Every time she closed her eyes, dreams of Geoff, alive and healthy, engulfed her.

When they stopped for a few minutes, she looked

around. The mountain air was pristine clear and with the
rising sun, the view was bathed with a beautiful luminosity.

The time since Geoff's plane had been reported missing
seemed an eternity. To keep herself from thinking of him,
she went over all that had happened since they'd landed
in Ecuador as she trudged along trying to keep on her feet.
It had been an incredible adventure and they'd covered a
lot of ground.

Only the day before, they'd been in the small town of
Columbe for the feast of the Black Madonna or Mama
Negron. Had Geoff been there at her side or had the
journey been for any other reason, she'd have loved every
moment of it. Instead she'd resented the unavoidable side
trip, feeling that it took too much of their precious time.

Sara had almost stepped on the heels of the man in front
of her before she realized that the hikers had stopped.
Glancing up, she got her first glance at the morena people
before them. Morena was the name used for people of
African descent. It was an unusual group, being the only
mountainous community that was not Indians.

She stepped toward the front where Jenkins and Asa
stood and suddenly, she glimpsed a man among the tribes-
men ahead wearing khaki clothing. It was his tall statue
that made him stand out but it was his rare wondrous grace
that caught her attention.

Somehow at the same moment, the man appeared to
have caught sight of her and he, too, started walking toward
them. Her heart pumped erratically. She feared her eyes
were playing tricks upon her. Her knees threatened to give
way and she heard Asa gasp.

It was Geoff! She started moving toward the apparition,
at first stumbling and then with increasing speed. All
thought of fatigue or sore feet vanished. She raced toward
him. When Irving Jenkins tried to stop her from crossing
the invisible line that separated the two groups, she tore
from his grasp. Geoff met her there and she flung herself
into his arms, weeping tears of joy as she buried her face
in his chest.

Sara?" he said, sounding stunned.

"I knew it wasn't true. I knew nothing bad could ever happen to you."

He held her so tight that she could barely breathe and still she wanted to be closer. He set her on her feet but they didn't release each other. His mouth met hers in an over powering kiss. Their tears mingled as they clung together as if for bare life, as if to absorb each other. She would have climbed under his skin if it had been possible. Long moments they remained there.

"Ah, Sara, has a man ever been so lucky? Rescued by my very own wild girl?" Then, he spied their son standing behind her and added in shock, "Asa?"

However, it was Asa's response that truly moved her. He was visibly shakened and when father and son embraced there were tears in both their eyes. Later, Geoff leaned over and said, "Next time Asa's band is scheduled to play, I think we should go and show our support."

She smiled. "He's decided to finish school before touring," she told Geoff.

"Good. I knew he'd make the right decision."

"Edna says he plays like Hugo."

Geoff pondered that before answering, "She ought to know. I always respected your mother's opinions." Then he seemed to bring himself under control. It was funny, she thought, that they talked about such mundane things at a time such as this. Later, Geoff placed an arm around her shoulder and with a smile, said, "Surely you've come a long way just to—have the last word? But you were right. You and our family are the most important things in my life.

It was supposed to be a jest, she suspected, but it didn't work. She'd been under too much stress to take the words lightly. It effectively cut off a great deal of her happiness at seeing her husband when she'd thought him dead. However, trying to respond in the spirit it was said, she smiled back.

* * *

It was late October and Sara was home in Scarsdale. Geoff was in Washington as part of his extended debriefing. After making new reservations, Kamaria was finally ready to leave for San Francisco. Her new employers had been very understanding in extending the girl's starting date. Sara had spent the morning helping and found herself already missing her daughter, despite knowing that this was a time that had to come. They had talked about various things, with Sara scrupulously not mentioning John Rivers. It was Kamaria who brought up the young man's name.

"Now that I'll be in San Francisco, John and I won't be seeing much of each other. But we plan to write and call each other—things like that. Maybe even visit a couple of times a year," Kamaria finished airily.

"Oh, that's nice, honey," Sara said, determined not to pry.

"I sort of like him," Kamaria said shyly.

"Really?" Sara said, shocked to hear Kamaria admit this.

"But we're not engaged, Mom," the girl said, sounding more like her old self.

Sara wanted to smile when she said, "I know that. Anyway, you're too young to get engaged. Your Dad would have conniptions." They both laughed.

"John reminds me of Dad," Kamaria said, quietly.

Although Kamaria's statement made her stop, she was relieved, for she knew that she didn't need to worry about Kamaria any more. She knew that her daughter would eventually make the change from being her daddy's girl to the lover of some deserving man, and that she would do it with her customary grace.

She also had to agree that John *was* like Geoff—as Geoff had become. But it was Asa who resembled the youthful Geoff—the wild boy that she'd married.

Then Kamaria was off on another subject. "You know what Grandma Edna said to me? She swears that Dad did something that he'd wanted to do when he was a child—

he united both black and white into a family." That caught
Sara's attention, and she suddenly straightened up to gaze
at her daughter. Kamaria went on in explanation, "—our
family. You know, the way he did with Grandma Nora and
Grandma Edna?"

"Yes, I understand what you're saying," Sara said, realizing that in a way, it was true. Geoff had done just that. It
hadn't been an earth-shattering event, but maybe that's
what life was about—the small things that you did in your
own family. Maybe that was the way we saved the world,
by saving our own small worlds.

There had been little time while they were leaving South
America for them to talk. Besides, Geoff had been too
exhausted. And as soon as they arrived in the States Geoff,
along with all the other members of the group, had been
debriefed by the State Department and others. Initially,
they'd insisted upon her telling her story as well, but for
some reason—she suspected because she'd been an
embarrassment—she'd been allowed to return home
rather quickly.

News of Geoff's courage during his time in Ecuador was
in the newspaper, the story of how he'd worked to keep
morale high and how he had protected the group from
capture by terrorists.

Due to the school, she'd had to remain in New York
while Geoff was still in Washington. Aside from Geoff coming home, something else good had come from her traveling to South America. She'd gotten her name in the papers
and quite a bit of publicity. The publicity had brought the
school's plight into the public eye, and donations had been
pouring into the school's coffers with incredible regularity.
It began to look as if they were going to make it.

One morning, Beverly Doddsworth called and invited
her to a luncheon given by a powerful woman's political
club. Sara, remembering their last conversation, was not
particularly enthusiastic.

"Do come," Beverly said, "I know that many of the women are dying to meet you. They're quite impressed with your decision to rescue your husband. You know that took quite a bit of courage."

"Well, I didn't rescue him."

"Maybe not, but still it was brave of you to go. Shows a good image for women. Besides, chances are you could do a bit of fundraising."

That, naturally made her take notice. Also, she knew that she owed it to Beverly, who had been good to her in many ways. Beverly was a woman that Sara admired immensely.

"All right," Sara responded. "I'm honored by your asking."

On the day of Beverly's luncheon Sara felt a little trepidation, but once there began to relax. Beverly, Sara could see, was quite busy, but somehow managed to introduce her to many of the other women there. Sara watched the older woman, thinking that she always seemed to have inroads into closed circles.

Sara was encouraged and after taking a deep breath, she waded in and began to mingle. The members were of all races and colors, and were quite excited to hear her story. Many of them actually wrote checks and pledged their help with even more.

The speeches at the women's club were fortunately brief, and after lunch Beverly Doddsworth leaned over, saying, "Come to the ladies' room with me."

"All right." Taking her purse, she followed the older woman.

In the ladies' room, there was one other occupant. Both Sara and Beverly chatted briefly until the woman left.

When they were alone, Beverly freshened her lipstick before closing the small tube and dropping it into her bag. She looked at Sara sharply and said, "I've heard more good things about that husband of yours, aside from the heroic things he did while in South America. No one will ever forget that. But other things. With this incredible feat that he's managed there's no telling how far he could go. There are a lot of very grateful people. To America, he's a hero of the first magnitude."

"Thank you,' Sara said, feeling flushed with pride and gratitude.

"In another few years, it could take him as high as a cabinet appointment. Of course, he wouldn't be the first black man to reach that level, but it would be a wonderful opportunity." Sara must have looked doubting, for Beverly went on. "This is true. Some are even saying it could take him straight to the White House."

"What?" Sara had thought at first it was the upcoming State dinner of which Beverly spoke. There had been rumors of such an event. But she could see by the woman's glittering eyes that she meant something more than that.

"We have Colin Powell to thank for it, of course. With him, people became acclimated to the idea. Don't overlook the possibility of the vice-presidency in a few years. But who knows, there are other groups who might go first. Maybe even a woman." Sara became more bemused as the woman continued.

"The vice-presidency?" Sara said. Just about the only thing she'd understood.

"Of course."

"Geoffrey?"

"People are talking. Most of our top people have law backgrounds, but many have economic, too."

"But Geoff's no politician."

"I have a feeling your Geoff could be anything he wanted." Sara certainly agreed with that. "Anyway, remember who told you."

"Yes," Sara said.

The two women left and were soon swept up in more mingling. Several times, Sara's glance was drawn to Beverly during the networking that followed.

Geoffrey, the cabinet? The vice-presidency? What else?

Dare she even think it? And why not? Beverly was right. Men like Ron Brown and Colin Powell had made anything possible.

Still flushed with pride by the time she arrived home, she found an envelope in the mailbox. The White House address was displayed in the upper left corner, and it was written on fine parchment paper. Despite her personal feelings she opened the envelope carefully and found an invitation, reading, "You are cordially invited to a State dinner at the White House." Further down it read, "Black tie optional."

Excitement raced through her as she propped the card up on the table in the foyer before going upstairs. She wanted it to be the first thing that Geoff saw when he came home. He probably already knew that it was here. By the time she reached her bedroom and started removing her clothing, she was already planning what she'd wear and seriously considering a shopping trip as soon as she could arrange it.

By the time Geoff came home, she was eager to find out what had happened, and fill him in on all that had occurred to her. But first, realizing how tired he was, she decided to make him comfortable and give him time to rest. Her little questions seemed unimportant against all of these things.

Despite his fatigue, they made love that night. Nothing had been settled between them, but when he reached for her, she went eagerly. And while it was wonderful, she knew only too well that they had things to discuss. For one, they had to talk about their last argument. But the time was wrong, and after the passion they both fell asleep.

Later, she awoke and found that he wasn't beside her in the bed. Arising, she went downstairs looking for him and found him in the living room with a fire going.

He watched her come down the stairs and said, "Couldn't sleep," when she came toward him.

"Want some coffee?" she asked.

"Sounds good," he answered, his gaze upon the flames in the hearth.

While in the kitchen, she knew that the time had come for their talk. Geoff, like most men, did not go in for a great deal of self-analysis, but there was no escape.

She carried the tray back into the living room and after a quick hesitation went to sit next to him. He put his arm around her shoulders and said before she could ask, "I'm sorry about that last night before I left."

"It was my fault," she surprised herself by admitting.

"No," he put a finger to stop her talk. "It's been my fault. You were right. While on that mountain, I could see that as clear as crystal."

She wanted to accept this, but knew that they had to go further. "What about the divorce?" she said.

"Baby, you know that much as I hate to admit this, there are times when I can be a complete fool."

"Meaning?" she persisted.

"What can I say? That I was afraid that you'd blame me when the MacKarren Bill fell through? That sometimes you seemed so involved with your own work that I felt you didn't need me?"

"Oh, Geoff, that could never be true."

"I sure as hell hope so," he said, leaning closer and kissing her. "What made me say it?" he repeated her question. "Fatigue, maybe? Frustration? Or maybe I was scared by your getting restless again. It reminded me of when you left me before. You're still the only woman for me. All I have to do is look at you across a room and I want you.

"I know what you mean. When you were missing, I suddenly realized how stupid all my anger was. Still, you're a lucky man to be alive."

"Don't I know it?" he said.

"I'm not talking about anything like simple plane crashes or terrorists, but your threatening me with divorce and calling me menopausal, for heaven's sake. That had to be the living end."

"You?" He reared back to assess her. "Nothing so provincial as menopause or divorce would keep you down."

"You don't understand anything. No woman wants to see herself get older and unattractive."

"Sara, you'll never be unattractive, and you're the only woman for me, no matter how many years pass."

"You're still lucky. It's a wonder I didn't shoot you, or something worse."

He laughed. "Well, baby, I learned that from you. You were never one to mince words."

They laughed and were quiet for long moments before she said, "I think the worst part was that we'd parted in such anger, yelling at each other worse than we'd done even in the early years. Do you remember when you came back from Asia?"

"How could I ever forget?"

"I always wanted to ask you why you came back."

"You *have* asked me—*many times.*"

"Not really. Nor have you truly given me an answer."

"I loved you, Sara. I've always loved you."

"Yes. I know that. You loved me like a friend, even like a brother. But that's not the way you came to me then. Suddenly you'd gone from a childhood friend, a little boy that I remembered, to a lover. And you were so sure that it was right. How did you know? I never understood why you came when you did."

"Because you wrote me."

"I know . . . and maybe I *was* calling you, but why did you come?"

He didn't answer for long moments. Then he said, "I've come to believe that we're soul mates. Isn't that what your mother used to imply?"

"She doesn't even imply it any longer, she just comes right out and says it. Now that my father's no longer in charge of the church, she admits that she always had some strange beliefs or half-beliefs, whatever they are. How could you have loved me in the way that you said?"

"My heart knew, and I simply did," he answered.

"My mother used to predict that something dire would happen to you."

"And despite this you joined your destiny to mine? You're a brave woman, Sara mine. But your mother was right," he said after a few moments of silence. "I was doomed until you came back into my life." She came into his arms and they sat there quietly until he spoke again. "You brought the stars and flowers, and made me into a new man," he said in a deeply sincere voice as he turned to gaze into her eyes.

"That's a nice thing to say, Geoff," she said, awed by the words.

"It's true. You know, in the Orient, I heard a wise man say that men were created to serve women. I think he was right."

"Well, speaking of serving," she reached over and touched his nose, "I have something to tell you. I spoke with Beverly and she seemed to think that you were being considered for a cabinet position or maybe in a few years . . . the vice presidency?" Her voice rose, excitedly, on that last.

"Oh, yes?" he answered, but he didn't look surprised.

"Someone's mentioned this before?"

"Yes, a couple of people spoke about it," he admitted.

"But that's wonderful!"

"You wouldn't mind?"

"Geoff," she started, "I know I've been difficult about your work these last few months, but if you want any of these positions, it's okay. Anyway, I have plans for you, and the vice presidency. I'll always support you in whatever you do."

"I know. You've always been there, and when I'm not being a fool, I know that." Later, he said, "You think I should grow my braid again? It's more in style now than it was back then."

"Whatever made you think of that?"

"What with all the talk of a cabinet position, I was thinking I could use a little style."

She looked at his head, as if seriously considering his question. "Well, don't blame me, but I doubt Robert Doddsworth would approve, not to mention the future president of these United States."

He kissed her, saying, "Who cares about them? It's you I'd rather please."

"I've always been pleased and proud of you."

"Even when I wasn't much help with the school funding?"

"Well, you're not perfect. You've had a moment or two over the last twenty-five years."

"Twenty-five years, Sara? How can that be? You're as beautiful as you ever were. And you're certainly still my barefoot girl."

"Flattery will get you everywhere."

They kissed long and hungrily. He slipped his hand beneath her robe. "Think it can get me where I'd love to be?"

"Not out here, it won't." She covered his hand with her own. "Much as I hate to stop this, Asa could walk in on us at any minute."

"Ah, well," he said, sitting back. Then he went on in a different voice, "You know, you're right. Asa is like me. Fortunately, he had you to raise him. And fortunately for me, I had you to marry me. You think he'll find someone like you to keep him on the right track?"

"I don't think he'll need it, just as you never did. You did what you wanted. That's why you were always successful."

"Your life has been successful, too, whether you appreciate that or not," he said.

"Yes, I know and I do appreciate it."

"You did quite a feat with Jenkins, making him take you."

She smiled smugly. "Yeah, I thought so, too. So did the women at Beverly's club. Seems I'm a natural diplomat."

"Everyone always knew that," he said.

"How do you think I'd do using that talent for the country?"

"Hey, you know I'm your biggest fan. I think the country would be lucky to get you."

"Smart answer. But there's one thing I'd like to remind you," she said, playfully.

"Like?" he said, not opening his eyes.

"That vice-presidency thing? Well, it would definitely mean more golf."

He groaned.

Layle Giusto danced professionally in Modern and African folk dance before she left the theater to marry and raise a family. She then got a degree in nursing and now works in a drug/alcohol rehabilitation center. She enjoys writing, sailing, swimming and travel.

ed Kate Coady died of pneumonia, leaving Matthew and Ann-
marie. Mike makes sense of this through her letters and
their family stories. John Sandiego, meanwhile, sent three
boys to Vietnam and lost two. Matthew serves. She raised
another, left a sizeable fortune.

BOOK YOUR PLACE ON OUR WEBSITE AND MAKE THE ARABESQUE ROMANCE CONNECTION!

We've created a customized website just for our very special Arabesque readers, where you can get the inside scoop on everything that's going on with Arabesque romance novels.

When you come online, you'll have the exciting opportunity to:

- View covers of upcoming books
- Read sample chapters
- Learn about our future publishing schedule (listed by publication month *and author*)
- Find out when your favorite authors will be visiting a city near you
- Search for and order backlist books from our online catalog
- Check out author bios and background information
- Send e-mail to your favorite authors
- Meet the Kensington staff online
- Join us in weekly chats with authors, readers and other guests
- Get writing guidelines
- AND MUCH MORE!

**Visit our website at
http://www.arabesquebooks.com**